CHALLENGE FOR
MARSHAL RAMSEY

There were two of them, dressed in dark, dirty clothes. Their faces were mean, hard-bitten, and scarred. One held Abel Jackson's shotgun on the small crowd that was bunched up along the right-hand wall. The bar owner himself lay on the floor, blood seeping from a long gash in his forehead.

The other gunman had Ada Belle pinned up against the bar. Paddy Sullivan was crumpled in a heap not far from Jackson. Though the bar owner appeared to be breathing, the photographer was lying in a thick puddle of blood. He seemed dead.

"Just throw her skirts up and have at her, Cully," the man with Jackson's shotgun said, laughing raucously.

"I aim to take my time and have some fun here, Honus," the other said.

Ramsey took a deep breath as he slid the LeMat out and cocked it. He shoved through the door, taking aim at Honus's head. "You set that scattergun down nice and easy, Honus."

Honus started to turn toward the door.

"Stop there and set that scattergun down or, by God, if you got any brains at all, I'll blow 'em all over the wall. Do it. Now!"

RAMSEY'S BADGE

WILL McLENNAN

JOVE BOOKS, NEW YORK

RAMSEY'S BADGE

A Jove Book/published by arrangement with
the author

PRINTING HISTORY
Jove edition / July 1990

ISBN: 0–515–10350–0

For Scott Siegel,
without whom
this would never
have taken place.
Thanks.

CHAPTER

★ 1 ★

Kyle Ramsey stopped for a moment with his only hand on the door latch of Webb's Mercantile Store. He cocked his head, listening intently. He knew he had heard a rumbling noise from off in the distance. But it was gone now, masked by the sounds of the small, bustling town of Plentiful.

He had thought at first that it was thunder, but there was not a single dark cloud marring the perfect azure of the sky. Ramsey listened for a moment longer, but all he heard were the comforting sounds of Plentiful: children's excited yells, the rattling passage of wagons and carriages, snorting horses, braying mules, and barking dogs; the sounds of life's normal flow.

Ramsey shrugged. *Most likely just my imagination*, he thought. He entered the dim interior of the general store, appreciating the slightly cooler air. Ramsey was not the sort of man given to the overworkings of imagination. But he had heard something—of that he was sure. The sound had drifted to him in one of those rare moments when all the noise of the town had halted as if by design, for just a fraction of a second. It was a sound that tantalized him with familiarity, though he could not place it for certain.

"Damn," Ramsey muttered, wishing he could put his finger on what the noise was. But it only tugged at the edges of his consciousness. He knew it probably represented danger of some kind. But of that he was not afraid. Far from it. Kyle Ramsey and his year-younger brother, Matt, had gone through the Civil War together, loyal sons of Texas fighting in a war in whose causes they did not believe. But they had seen it as their duty to defend their sovereign state, and so they had enlisted, spirited and fresh members of the Second Texas.

Kyle had paid the price, losing his left arm in the horrendous fighting that raged for some weeks around Vicksburg. Then Captain Kyle Ramsey and his brother Corporal Matt Ramsey had been captured. For months they languished as prisoners of war in Vicksburg before finally winning their parole as the war ground to an end.

After the war, Kyle found life in Fannin County, Texas, not like he had left it. Not with all the carpetbaggers and Yankees flooding into the state, running things, treating decent Texans like dirt. So Kyle had left the family homestead, looking to make his fortunes in the gold fields of Colorado. That had been three years or so after his parole, nearly six years ago now. He had not struck the mother lode, though he had at least stopped running from himself and the disability with which he had to live.

"Mornin', Mr. Ramsey," Tice Webb, who owned the general store with his wife, Abby, said.

Ramsey shook his head to clear away the fog of his reminiscences. "Mornin', Tice." He tipped his hat to a young woman at the counter who had turned at his entrance. "Mornin', Miss Tucker," he said affably.

"Mr. Ramsey," Sally Tucker said politely, but with a distinct chill in her voice.

Ramsey held back the grin he felt forming. Sally Tucker was, without a doubt, the best-looking woman in Plentiful—perhaps in Colorado Territory. She was rather tall for a woman and slim. Her finely tailored clothes, of satin and lace, set off her trim figure. She was widowed more than a year, and she knew that any man in the town, or the county, would want her. She did not have to be anything more than correctly civil to a man like Kyle Ramsey.

Tucker and two young boys, perhaps nine or ten years old, were the only other customers in the store. And Webb was having a devil of a time trying to wait on Tucker while still keeping an eye on the two rambunctious youngsters.

While Webb took care of Tucker, Ramsey waited patiently,

keeping a loose eye on the boys, who seemed somewhat cowed by the Texan. Ramsey was fairly tall—about six feet—and stocky, with a weather-etched face. He was dressed roughly, in denim trousers and off-white cotton muslin shirt, both stained from his job at Dodge Carver's gunsmith shop. From under his spotted gray Stetson poked a thatch of sandy-colored hair, and below that, cool blue eyes caught every movement.

His look was enough to restrain the boys, but his weaponry added to the effect. Kyle Ramsey carried a LeMat pistol, bought from another Texas veteran of the Civil War. Ramsey had used such a pistol during some of the fighting, and he liked it. And he found after he had lost his arm that it was a good weapon for a one-armed man. It was an odd-looking weapon, though it was deadly in the hands of a man who knew how to use it. One of its two barrels was loaded with a dose of buckshot; the other was used for the nine-shot .40-caliber revolver. He wore it on his left hip, the butt facing inward toward his right hand. Near the pistol was a Bowie knife with a twelve-inch, razor-sharp blade.

The two boys were not sure if this tall, hard-looking man might suddenly pull one of those two weapons and start raising havoc. It served to calm the boys down some.

Ramsey became aware again of a sound—the same one that he had heard before but much louder. He recognized it now as coming from a bunch of hard-riding men.

Several gunshots split the air outside. Tucker looked up, surprised and worried. The two boys stopped playing altogether and looked toward the windows with wide eyes. Tucker headed for the door, but Ramsey stepped into her path, blocking her way.

"Please move," Tucker said, fright making her usually bright, pleasant voice quaver.

"You'll be safer in here, ma'am," Ramsey said politely but firmly.

More gunfire erupted, closer now, and the pounding of horses' hooves grew louder and more urgent. People outside in the street and on the wooden sidewalks of Plentiful screamed and ran for cover.

"I want to get home," Tucker pleaded, her face pale.

"You'll not make it ten feet past the door," Ramsey said harshly. "Now just move on back toward the counter, away from the door and windows."

Biting her lush lower lip, Tucker backed up, all the while keeping fearful eyes on Kyle Ramsey. The Texan moved with her, making sure the woman did not stop until her back was pressed against the counter, next to a large barrel of flour and another of pickles.

Ramsey spun when the door burst open. Almost in the same movement, he shoved the two frightened boys behind him, where they cowered, clutching to Tucker's skirts. Tucker gasped in fright.

Three rough-looking men stumbled in, guns drawn but not cocked. They were arrogant, certain of themselves and the fear they aroused in people.

As Ramsey yanked out his LeMat with practiced ease, he noticed with his peripheral vision that Tice Webb had grabbed out his 10-gauge double-barreled shotgun from under the counter.

"Best back on out, boys," Ramsey said in a low voice.

The three gunmen, still unconcerned, turned as one toward the voice, not taking much notice of Webb. All three were of medium height and slim build. All wore blue denim pants and had stubble covering their faces. Each wore a cotton shirt, the one nearest Ramsey in flat blue, the middle one dull brown, and the farthest one in a shirt that had at one time been white. Stetsons of various hues and quality shaded their eyes.

"Who the hell are you?" the one in blue snarled.

"The man that's goin' to plant your ass in a pine box if you don't get it out of here right quick," Ramsey snapped.

"The hell you say," the man said, chuckling at his wit and showing several gaps in his foul teeth.

Without hesitation, Ramsey thumbed back the hammer of the LeMat and let the ill-smelling fellow have a blast of buckshot.

The outlaw caught the charge in the chest and was snapped backward, smashing into the companion wearing the brown shirt. "Damn!" brown shirt snarled, shoving his bleeding compatriot away. He turned his Colt on Ramsey, as did the third outlaw.

As Ramsey snicked the small lever on the hammer of the LeMat so he could use the revolver, he heard the thundering twin blasts of Webb's scattergun.

Brown shirt was knocked out through the door with a crash and onto the sidewalk. The other was spun by the impact of the gunshots, smashing one of the large windows. A bullet from Ramsey spun him again, and he fell back into the store and lay twitching among the broken glass and blood.

There was still plenty of noise from outside as the other outlaws continued their raid. But the silence inside the musty store seemed complete.

"Stay low," Ramsey ordered Tucker and the two boys. As the three crowded behind the two barrels near the counter, Ramsey stepped up to the one unbroken window. He heard Webb reload his shotgun.

Ramsey saw only one townsman—dead, by the looks of him—on the street. He could not tell how many outlaws there were, since all but three of them who sat on their horses in the middle of the street, were running into and out of buildings with whatever loot they could carry. The dead outlaw on the sidewalk outside the battered door of Webb's Mercantile had not been seen by his companions. The outlaws outside were too busy enjoying themselves, and the dead men's horses were still tied to the hitching rail right in front of the store, blocking the view.

Ramsey looked down at the two inside. Brown shirt was dead, most of his face blown away by shotgun pellets, and he had several bullet holes in his chest. Ramsey did not know whether he or Webb had killed the man, but it did not matter. White shirt was still alive, but not by much. He would be dead in seconds, perhaps minutes.

Suddenly the outlaws were racing out of town, heading southward, the direction from which they had ridden into town. They were either unaware or unconcerned that three of their number had been left behind.

"Stay where you are," Ramsey ordered Tucker, who had risen and started moving stiffly toward the door. There was no reason, Ramsey thought, that she—or the boys, for that matter—should have to see the damage of the three dead outlaws lying in her path.

Ramsey slid the LeMat into its holster. "Stay there till I tell you different, ma'am," he said, not harshly, but with undeniable firmness. "You too, boys."

He stepped outside and grabbed the dead outlaw by the shirt, then dragged him from the sidewalk out into the middle of the street. He went back into the store and did the same with brown shirt, then white shirt, dropping each body next to the first.

He went back into the store again. "Y'all can leave now," he said quietly. "But mind you watch where you put your feet. There's more'n a little blood and such about."

Tucker, her face drained of all color, hurried out, trying hard not to notice the gore while at the same time trying not to step in it. The two boys, trying to put on a brave front for each other, left more slowly, chuckling worriedly as they stomped through the blood and shards of glass. Still, they were every bit as pale as Tucker.

"You need any help cleanin' up this mess, Tice?" Ramsey asked.

"Nope. I'll get Josh to handle it directly. He's always willin' to make some extra cash." He shook his head. "I'll tell you, Mr. Ramsey, I never seen a darky work so hard as Josh Cord does." Joshua Cord, the town's only black man, was something of a jack-of-all-trades, taking on almost any job no one else wanted, as long as it was legal.

Ramsey was a bit annoyed by the reference to Cord as a darky, but he held his tongue. "You certain, Tice? I helped make it."

"I'm certain. Thanks for your help."

"My pleasure," Ramsey said a little sourly. He was used to such things, but he never did enjoy it. He looked over the elderly store owner. Webb was in his sixties, though his back was as straight as ever. His snow-white hair was thick and full, and he usually had a ready smile for folks. The only signs of his age were the white hair, a bit of slowness in his movements, and the brass-rimmed glasses he wore. Webb seemed unconcerned by all that had just occurred.

"This kind of thing happen often around here?" Ramsey asked.

"More'n I'd like to see. Cotton Roberts's bunch has rode through here like this several times before. The last time wasn't long before you came to town. Midwinter it was too, by Christ. Damnedest thing."

"You watch your foul tongue, Tice Webb," Abigail Webb said, stepping out from the backroom, where she had been all along. "I'm sure I don't know where he's learned such speech, Mr. Ramsey," she said with a sigh. "But I'll get after him about it, don't you think not."

Webb grinned sheepishly at Ramsey, who smiled back. "Reckon we'll see 'em again?" Ramsey asked.

"Yes, sir," Webb said with conviction. "Especially when they realize three of 'em's not comin' back." He chuckled. "God damn, it feels good to pay them bastards back."

"Tice Webb," Abby scolded, wagging a finger at her husband.

She was a portly, once-pretty woman, with gray hair and full, flushed features. She was a formidable woman, but one whose bark was usually far worse than her bite.

Webb shrugged. Ramsey shook his head, not pleased with the thought of a rematch with this band of outlaws. He had liked Plentiful from the beginning. It had seemed such a nice place. Now this. He sighed.

"What was it you came in here for, Mr. Ramsey?" Webb asked.

"Some shavin' soap," Ramsey said, almost surprised by such mundane talk after what had gone on. "And a couple bandannas."

Webb got him the items, and Ramsey paid. "Be seein' you, Tice," he said, leaving.

"Thanks again, Kyle," Webb called after him.

Outside a crowd had gathered around the three bodies in street. Arguments were heating up as the town marshal, Royal Burch, tried to calm everyone down. With a sinking feeling at what the future might bring, Ramsey headed toward Parker's, the boardinghouse in which he was living.

CHAPTER

★ 2 ★

Center Street, the main thoroughfare of Plentiful, Colorado Territory, was pretty well back to normal the next morning as Kyle Ramsey moseyed down it from Parker's Rooming House toward his job at the other end of town. All the trade places were at the south end of town, below South Street: Carver's gunsmith shop; George Port's livery and blacksmith shop, abutting his brother Sam's wagon shop; Lopez's saddlemaking and tack shop; Sawyer's tannery; and Vessig's sawmill.

Ramsey breathed deeply of the sweet, pine-scented spring air. It was a fine day, he thought, much too nice to be spent cooped up in the foul-smelling gunsmith's shop, which reeked of oil, gunpowder, and dust. Not to mention the emanations from Carver's corpulent, sweaty body.

He stopped for a moment outside Webb's Mercantile. Its shattered front was the only remaining testimony to the action that had taken place the day before. That and the two funerals going on at the same time at the white clapboard church up at the far north end of town. Even the blood in the street, where Ramsey had dropped the three bodies, had disappeared.

Ramsey shrugged. It was no more of his affair, he thought.

He found out differently that night. After a dinner of steak, boiled potatoes, deep-dish apple pie, and hot black coffee at Cordelle's Restaurant, Ramsey drifted toward the Lone Star Saloon.

The Lone Star was one of half a dozen saloons in town, and the one Ramsey had found out quickly that he preferred. The owner and usual bartender was Abel Jackson, an old-time Texan who had fought with Sam Houston at San Jacinto. Jackson was old now, but the years had done little to salve his itchy feet. Which is why he was in Plentiful.

"Y'all done good, boy, yesterday," Jackson said to Ramsey after slapping a mug of cold beer down on the bar in front of Kyle.

"At what?" Ramsey asked, somewhat surprised. Being co[...] up inside all day and doing close work always made hi[...] mind for a spell.

"Takin' care of those God damn gun punks like y'all [...] terday over to Tice's store."

"Wasn't nothin'."

"That ain't what some folks is sayin'."

"And what are some folks sayin'?"

"I'll tell you when I'm damned good and ready," Jackson growled good-naturedly. He headed off to wait on another customer.

Ramsey took the time to look around the room. It was about half full, with maybe thirty men drinking and a half-dozen of the girls from Miss Maggie's run-down bordello next door. Not a one of them was fit to work at the high-class cathouse run by Miss Prudence Applegate. The Lone Star Saloon was not a fancy place by any means, which was another reason Ramsey liked it. It was small, with a cheap wooden bar along one wall. A painting of a buxom nude woman lounging on a couch hung behind the bar, but it was of poor quality, the paint flecked and peeling. The only gambling was the poker games the men got up on their own. Jackson would supply a dealer—male or female, at the players' convenience—if the card players asked. What tables and chairs that were in the place were nicked and scratched and had had chunks torn out in the numerous fistfights—and gunfights—that broke out with depressing frequency.

A busty but otherwise thin strumpet named Ada Belle sashayed up to Ramsey. "Buy a girl a drink, sweetheart?"

"A drink's all you're gonna get from me tonight, Ada," Ramsey said with a grin. "Old Carver ain't paid me in a spell, and

I'm nearabout down to usin' old Confederate bills for my spendin' cash.''

Ada Belle chuckled. She must have been pretty once, Ramsey thought. But though she was barely past twenty-five, she was worn and haggard, with a hard, unforgiving edge to her thin, pinched face. Ramsey had availed himself before of Ada Belle's services and had found that on those rare occasions when she could relax, she was quite pleasant to be with. But that did not happen frequently enough.

"Well, damn, it's better'n nothin'," she said, still chuckling, but without much real humor.

"_____ure," Ramsey said, masking his surprise. He realized that _____n't just want a drink—she seemed to need it.

_____ Jackson returned, Ramsey ordered a drink for Ada and _____ beer for himself. The drinks were served and Ada raised her shot glass in a mock toast to Ramsey, then drifted off.

"She's been in this business too long, Abel," Ramsey said sadly, watching the girl over his shoulder.

Jackson shrugged and poured himself a shot of red eye.

"All right," Ramsey said firmly, facing Jackson squarely, "what's all this cowshit that people are sayin' about me?"

"You know who it was y'all killed yesterday, don't you?" Jackson asked, squinting in that way he had at Ramsey.

"Just a couple gun punks is all I know. Tice Webb told me they belonged to a gang run by some fellow named Cotton Roberts. And it ain't the first time Roberts and the others have run through here. That's about all I know."

"Well, the three you put up in boot hill weren't nobody special. Just some of the rummies that run with Roberts. I believe they were Curly Wade, Otto Bruckner, and Carney Philbin. I reckon that together you might get yourself a reward of maybe a hundred dollars for the three of 'em. If Marshal Burch gives you the money, that is."

Ramsey shrugged and sipped some beer. "Don't make me much nevermind, Abel. I can always use the cash, but . . ." The sentence trailed off as Ramsey drained his beer.

Jackson refilled the mug and set it before Ramsey, "It don't make Roberts no nevermind either, Kyle. Don't matter to him if it was Simon Waddey—Roberts' right-hand man—or some useless, half-drunk pistoleer like Otto Bruckner. What does matter to that son of a bitch is that three of his men are dead, gunned down by some defiant bastard in a town he's run roughshod over for as long as he's felt like it.''

"So?" Ramsey sighed. He knew what was coming. "I reckon you're gonna tell me now that he'll be back, lookin' for revenge.''

"I expect so. Roberts ain't a man to take such things lightly. Anyway, that's what folks are sayin'.''

"Why haven't folks got up a posse and gone out there and took care of this before?''

"Shee-it," Jackson snorted. "These chickenshits?" He waved a hand around the saloon. "Put 'em all together and they ain't got the balls of a prairie dog. Every time somethin' like this happens, Marshal Burch and John Starkey—he's the sheriff of Sagauche County and has his office here—try to get up a posse. They ain't had a one volunteer.''

"Never?" Ramsey asked in disbelief.

"Never.''

"Christ!''

Jackson hustled off to take care of some customers. Ramsey stood up for a moment, not believing what he had heard. He picked up his beer and shuffled off across the room. He chatted with a person here or one there, flirting occasionally with Ada Belle or Sad-Eyed Sally or Big Knickers Mabel or one of the other prostitutes trying to make a living on the sometimes skimpy pickings of the Lone Star Saloon's clientele.

But mostly what Ramsey did was to listen in to other folks' conversations. And he got an earful. Finally he sat in on a poker game with four other men: Colby Grimes, the town baker; a man known only as Alabama, who had no job but always had a few dollars in his pockets to try his luck at poker; Adolph Bock, who owned the feed and grain store down the street; and Paddy Sullivan, who ran a photographic studio next door to the Lone Star.

Ramsey said little, as did Alabama. Ramsey suspected Alabama was a cardsharp, but he could not catch him cheating. Especially when his attention was focused on what the other men were saying.

"What do you think of all that's been going on, Mr. Ramsey?" Sullivan asked, the words rolling around his brogue. "I mean, you were in the thick of things yesterday. Don't you think Marshal Burch and Sheriff Starkey ought to take care of setting it to rights?''

Ramsey shrugged, annoyed at having been put on the spot.

"Well, I do," Sullivan continued, not waiting for an answer from the Texan.

"Got damn, me too," Bock retorted, carefully checking his hole cards as Alabama tossed him another card face up.

"It's sinful, absolutely sinful," Grimes said, folding his hand. He sat back, hands across his ample stomach. Being a baker, he often sampled his wares more than he should, hence the sizable midsection that stretched his white shirt and the waistband of his flour-speckled work trousers.

"Good God," Grimes continued, "this is the fourth time in the past year those outlaws have terrorized Plentiful. You would think that with two lawmen here something would have been done long before this."

"Neither Sheriff Starkey or Marshal Burch has the courage to do vhat's needed, is vhat the problem is," Bock said in his thick German accent. "They must get up a posse; take the initiative; and put the owlhoots out of business for goot. Ya, dot is vhat is needed."

"You ever think of joinin' in when they try to get a posse up, Adolph?" a disgusted Ramsey said, tossing in his hand.

"Vot?" Bock asked, truly surprised. "I am a seller of seeds and grains and such. I am no gunman."

"I reckon the rest of you have excuses too, eh?" Ramsey said, as Alabama began dealing again. Despite his anger, Ramsey was paying closer attention to the dealer now.

"Well, I . . ." Sullivan started.

"None of us is used to handling a gun, Mr. Ramsey," Grimes said in a whiny voice. "It is not our job. That is why we pay taxes to the town—to support a marshal who should be able to take care of these things."

"You expect that old man to stand up to, what, maybe a dozen gunslingers by himself? You expect . . ." He fixed a piercing stare on Alabama. "If you pull that ace off the bottom of the deck for yourself, boy, instead of that top card, I'm gonna chop off your hand."

Ramsey slid out the heavy Bowie knife and placed it next to his cards, never taking his eyes off Alabama's.

The dealer was sweating, but he smiled. It was a grim smile, but it grew in brilliance as he worked up his courage. "That's a mighty strong accusation, Mr. Ramsey," he said in an offended tone.

"What really matters here, Alabama—if that's your real

name—is the truth of it. Now, suppose you set that deck down nice and neat in front of Mr. Grimes next to you.''

The dealer, his face hard but worried, did as he was told.

"Ah-ah," Ramsey said harshly as Alabama's right hand started to leave the table, "you just leave both your hands where I can see 'em. Flat on the table!" There was no mistaking the menace in Ramsey's words.

Alabama snarled but lay his hands flat, palms down, on the scarred wooden table.

"Now, Mr. Grimes, if you would be so kind as to give Mr. Alabama the top card, face up."

Ashen faced, Grimes lifted the top card on the deck and dropped it face up. The seven of clubs fell next to the two aces already there.

"Thank you. Now, carefully lift the entire deck up and turn it over so the bottom card is face up on top."

Bock and Sullivan watched as a nervous Grimes went through the motions.

"Well, lookee here. An ace, all set to pop up to give you three of a kind, Alabama. Ain't that somethin!" The words were lightly said, but a thick layer of irony gave them weight.

"Pure coincidence," Alabama said in a shaky voice. "Come on here, Adolph. Colby." He looked imploringly from one to the other. "Paddy. You boys've known me longer'n you've known this damned Texan."

"You'll not get another man to play cards with you in this saloon, Mr. Alabama," Sullivan said sharply. "And as soon as we can get the word out, you'll probably not get into a game anywhere else in Plentiful, either. I suggest you leave those winnings in front of you and get your ass out of here now!"

Alabama looked like he was set to argue, then thought better of it when he glanced over and saw Ramsey fingering the butt of the LeMat. He rose and hurried out the door.

"I don't know how to tank you, Mr. Ramsey," Bock said, "Ve neffer knew he vas cheatink."

Ramsey shrugged. He was disgusted with all of them at the moment: Alabama for cheating, the others for not having any courage. "Well, maybe y'all can help me out some time," he drawled. "You never know when someone with only one arm might need an extra hand."

He slipped the Bowie knife back into its sheath and stood up, picking up his hat at the same time. Ramsey swept up his few dollars and nodded to the other men. "Good night, gentlemen," he said, walking out.

Over the next several days, he would pay attention to what people around town were saying. The raid by Roberts' gang would still be the talk of the town. And almost uniformly, the townsfolk of Plentiful would blame most of the trouble on Burch and Starkey, as if the two men could withstand the army of outlaws by themselves.

Ramsey was nearabout ready to leave Plentiful. He wanted nothing to do with such people. But, still, the small comfortable town on the banks of Sagauche Creek in the La Garita Mountains was a nice place mostly. There were plenty of pines in the area, and cottonwoods. There was game in the woods and fish in the streams. It was a nice place to be.

It would be an even better place if this problem were resolved, he thought somewhat sourly.

CHAPTER
★ 3 ★

Ramsey was angry when he stomped out of the Lone Star Saloon, so angry that he was in no mood to go back to his room. He wandered across Center Street and then south, past the marshal's office, Scheibel's Restaurant, and the office of the *Plentiful Bugle*, heading for the Cloverleaf Saloon.

It was a warm, muggy night, but a light breeze helped keep things pleasant. Only an occasional puff of cloud blocked out the bright blazing carpet of stars. Ramsey stopped for a moment in front of the newspaper office, looking out into the dark street that was lighted only by lanterns, enjoying the evening and hoping his anger would dissipate some.

"Fine night, ain't it?" someone said behind him.

Ramsey turned slowly, forcing a smile onto his lips. It wasn't that he disliked Sagauche County Sheriff John Starkey. It was just that he was still angry and did not feel the want of company at the moment. And, he realized belatedly, he had let the other men's comments about the "lack" of law enforcement color his own judgment ever so slightly. "Yep," he muttered, not harshly, but letting it be known through his tone that he did not want company.

"Somethin' eatin' at you, Mr. Ramsey?" Starkey asked quietly. He had heard the rumors about this one-armed Texan. Most of those rumors had a decidedly deadly tinge to them, and the sheriff was sure that at least some had truth to them. It made him wary—though not afraid—around Ramsey.

Ramsey sighed a long, drawn-out sigh. He had no reason to be angry at Starkey, and he knew what the others had said was nonsense. "Ah, just some cowshit some folks over at the Lone Star were spoutin'."

"Such as?"

"Well, a heap of it concerns you, Sheriff," Ramsey said, not really embarrassed to say it but not fond of repeating such foolishness either.

"I see." Starkey chuckled. He shifted his weight and looped his thumbs in the wide black belt that held up the large, walnut-handled Colt Army pistol. Starkey was a big, barrel-chested, barrel-bellied bear of a man, a little shorter than Kyle but outweighing him by a good fifty pounds. He had sausagelike fingers and a ruddy face, with curving bushy eyebrows over green-tinted eyes and a fleshy nose. A trim mustache showed that he cared for himself, as did the clothes: a good wool shirt, clean and well pressed by Ling Su, the laundryman; a string tie; creased dark-wool trousers. A clean black Stetson with a high round crown topped his head.

"Let me guess," Starkey said after a moment's pause. "A bunch of folks—half of 'em likkered up, like as not—have been spoutin' off about how fat Sheriff John Starkey and creakin' old Marshal Royal Burch ain't worth the thirty or forty dollars a month they're gettin' paid. Not with the poor job they been doin'. And how the two useless old lawmen ain't got the balls to save poor Plentiful from those maraudin' bastards and how any lawman worth his salt would have taken care of things long ago and . . ."

Ramsey laughed, feeling a bit relieved, though much of the uneasiness remained. "You hit that one dead center, Sheriff," he said.

"Ain't the first time I've heard such talk," Starkey said with a low chuckle, but Ramsey could sense anger in the big man.

"Most likely won't be the last time you hear it either," Ramsey said quietly.

"I reckon." Starkey pulled a plug of tobacco from a shirt pocket and sliced off a chunk with a small penknife. He slipped the knife and plug away, then stuffed the tobacco in his cheek. He chewed a while, watching the people who moved along the dark street. Ramsey turned away from the lawman to also watch the street.

"You do know, don't you, Mr. Ramsey," Starkey said softly, "that me'n Marshal Burch ain't the only ones bein' talked about in such a poor fashion about this latest episode of adventurin'?" He spit some tobacco juice into the night.

"Oh?" Ramsey was only mildly interested.

"You been the subject of some of the town's anger yourself, Mr. Ramsey."

"What?" Ramsey asked sharply, spinning back to face the sheriff. He was shocked at the statement.

"That's right," Starkey said, chuckling after having caught Ramsey unawares.

"What in hell for?" Ramsey asked, still in wonder, but feeling the anger crawling back inside him. To mask his confusion, he pulled out a stick match and picked at a stray bit of food caught between two teeth.

"Well, it was you who killed those three outlaws yesterday."

"Now hold on there, Sheriff. Tice Webb had a hand in that."

"Don't matter none to the folks around here. Tice Webb's been around here from the beginnin'. But you, you're a newcomer. What, four months now, maybe five? And you have a reputation of some note to boot."

"I ain't . . ."

"Hell, it don't matter none whether you deserve that reputation or not. Not to these people. You ought to know that." Starkey spoke sadly, knowing the truth of his words. "What matters to these people is that you *have* that reputation. Deserved or not, it was hung on you, and it'll be with you for all time. There's a heap of rumors circulatin' about you around here, Mr. Ramsey. I expect at least some of 'em's true, or partly true. Maybe all of 'em, for all I know. I don't give a tinker's damn about those rumors. But these people, well, they take 'em to heart and believe in 'em."

"Hellfire and damnation."

"Yeah." Starkey spit again. "Anyway, since they all know Tice and you're the one with the reputation—plus the fact that you carry that God damn funny gun—well, they just figure you was the one sent all three of those owlhoots to their just rewards." He was more than a little sarcastic.

"That's a damn foolish thing to think," Ramsey grumbled.

"And this"—he tapped the checkered walnut butt of the LeMat—"ain't a 'funny gun.' "

"It is to a lot of these folks." Starkey grinned under his mustache. "Of course, it ain't to me. Damn good weapon, the LeMat."

"Sounds like you've used one before," Ramsey said, interested in spite of himself.

"At Fredericksburg and Chancellorsville and Gettysburg. Lost the damn thing retreatin' from Gettysburg. Christ, what a bloodbath that was. Got our asses whupped real good there. We could've won . . ." He trailed off, coughing a bit to cover his embarrassment at having gotten carried away. "I never could get ahold of another one," he said more calmly. "Had to settle for an old Colt Army I grabbed up from some God damn dyin' blue belly." He tapped the one he was wearing. "Still is a damn good gun. More'n once that Yankee's come back from the grave to save this old warhorse." He grinned.

"Hell, that must stick in your craw," Ramsey said with a friendly chuckle.

"Ah hell, I ain't got nothin' against Yanks no more. You?"

"Nope. Never did." Ramsey shrugged and fell silent.

"Anyway, folks here lay the blame on you for killin' those three."

"I'd of thought they'd be happy three of those bastards are pushin' up the daisies now."

"Some folks are. Damn glad. Hell, nearly all of 'em felt that way at first. Then a few got to thinkin' that maybe Roberts might not take too kindly to losin' three men and might be comin' back here, gunnin' for whoever did it. And, of course, if some poor townfolks got in the way . . . well, it might learn 'em to mind their own business."

Ramsey gnawed on his lower lip a minute, trying to keep his volatile temper in check. "And what's your thoughts on such an idea, Sheriff?" he asked tightly.

"I think they're right, Mr. Ramsey." With a commiserating grin, Starkey touched the brim of his Stetson and wandered away, whistling a jaunty tune.

"God . . . damn!" Ramsey hissed, slapping his thigh in irritation. "Of all the damn foolish . . ." He drew in a lungful of air and let it out in a slow, sustained blast. He strode off down the street and into the Cloverleaf Saloon.

He drank more than he should have but stopped himself before he got out of hand. He shuddered in thinking back to not so long ago, when he would have drank himself stupid and then caused no end of trouble for himself, his friends and . . .

He thrust that thought out of his mind. Those days were long over, he told himself firmly as he lurched out of the saloon and up the street. He was still more than a little annoyed, but he kept himself in control and was quite proud of himself for that feat.

Ramsey was still on edge in the morning, as he tried to quiet his mildly sour stomach and throbbing head with several cups of black coffee and a strong, bracing breakfast of fresh eggs, slices of ham, and biscuits slathered in white gravy at Cordelle's Restaurant.

He still looked harshly at everyone he passed on his stroll down to Dodge Carver's shop. He was waiting—almost eagerly—for someone to confront him. But no one did. Most folks offered a friendly "Good morning, Mr. Ramsey." He generally scowled in return.

At the shop, he manhandled an old Springfield rifle carefully into a vise, impressing Carver once again with his ability to accomplish so much—and do it so well—despite his handicap. It took most of the day, but Ramsey finally finished the job of converting the breechloading Springfield from black-powder-filled paper cartridges and round balls to the more convenient metal cartridges that were fast growing in popularity.

He had thought of doing the same with the LeMat but decided against it. Metal cartridges were still too hard to come by out here. But maybe one day, he promised himself.

Ramsey was tired when he left the shop, but a fine dinner at Scheibel's of fried pork chops, yams, and corn, topped off with a large portion of peach cobbler and several cups of coffee, put him in a better frame of mind. Bloated, he wandered down to the Lone Star Saloon and pushed inside.

Abel Jackson saw him coming and had a mug of beer poured and waiting when Ramsey reached the bar. "Evenin', Mr. Ramsey," Jackson said. "You pulled out of here mighty fast last night. Somethin' set wrong in your craw?"

"Hell, I just couldn't take no more of the whinin' and moanin' from those boys I was playin' stud with. Christ, all they did was complain about the things goin' on here in Plentiful and lament

as to how the law can't protect 'em from such things.'' The anger
flared up in Ramsey again, and he tried to wash it away with beer.

"I reckon they got some cause for such thinkin','' Jackson said
innocently.

"Like hell!'' Ramsey snapped. "I'd have thought you were a
better man than to cotton to such thinkin'.'' Real anger bubbled
just below the surface.

"I said *some* cause,'' Jackson said easily. "Those boys ain't
got no more business bein' in a posse lookin' for a bunch of
hardcases like Cotton Roberts and his boys than I do.''

"I never would've took you for a coward, Abel,'' Ramsey said,
rankled.

Jackson's eyes glittered with danger and pride. "Shit, boy, I
was ridin' with posses before you was off your mama's breast.
Lordy, I'm too God damn old for such things now. These old
bones don't set a saddle as well as they did years ago when we
were runnin' down Comanches and such.

"But,'' Jackson added, drawing himself up straight, "those
owlhoots know there's nothin' wrong with my shootin' eye. They
know God damn well that any one of 'em sets foot through the
door of the Lone Star Saloon is gonna get his ass shot dead then
and there.''

"That didn't do a hell of a lot of good for two men who got
killed in the bank the other day.''

Jackson shrugged. "Like I said, Kyle, I'm too God damn old
for posse work. As for the rest of these folks around here, they're
afraid. You can't blame them for that, can you?''

"Reckon not,'' Ramsey grumbled, not wanting to be convinced.
But he had seen it before, even back in New Liberty, Texas. Many
of the folks had been cowed by several men, men most of the
folks in Fannin County had known for years. It took Kyle and his
brother Matt, along with some other veterans, to snap them out
of their stupor and win back their pride for them. The same thing
needed doing here, but Ramsey would be damned if he would
take on that job.

He drank a little more beer, then said, "Hell, Abel, everybody's
scared some time.''

"I know that. So do you. But they don't. Hell, they see you
waltzin' around town with that big old LeMat, or maybe somebody
like John Starkey carryin' his hogleg Army Colt, and they don't
think you boys have ever been afraid.''

"Shit, Abel, half of 'em fought in the War between the States or against Injuns. They ought not to be afraid of a little gunplay."

"Kyle, you're alone. So's Starkey and old man Burch. These other boys all got families to look after. They ain't made their way in life with a gun in years, most of 'em. Now they take people's photographs, or make tinware, or sell ladies' clothes. Hell, they ain't about to risk their asses chasin' after hardcases when the law's supposed to do it for 'em. Besides, most of 'em'd shoot themselves or their friends like as not."

"Lord, Abel, they'd outnumber Roberts's men three or four to one. Might be a few of 'em get killed in the fightin' when they cornered the outlaws, but then they wouldn't have to worry no more about those boys ridin' through here again and raisin' hell."

"You gonna pick the ones they'll plant and then tell it to their wives and younkers?"

"Well, hell no, Abel. But Christ, if they took care of business, it'd be a lot better than settin' here waitin', wonderin' when Roberts and his boys would come ridin' through and who'd be the next to get planted after the visit."

Jackson shrugged. "All that might be true, and I dare say it is. But you'll never be able to convince them of that."

"Shit!" Ramsey mumbled. He drained his beer and tossed a coin on the bar. He left, angry once again.

CHAPTER
★ **4** ★

Time served to ease Ramsey's anger, as it did that of most of the townspeople of Plentiful. As the days passed, less talk was heard of the two lawmen's alleged faults. And less talk was heard about the fear of the outlaws returning to deal reprisals against the town. Indeed, it seemed that the bravery of the average citizen of Plentiful had grown twofold as each day put them further from the last raid.

A week passed, and Ramsey found that he was no longer carrying a chip on his shoulder, practically daring anyone he met to accuse him of something. He worked hard at his job, which he enjoyed except for having to deal with Dodge Carver. And he spent the evenings whiling away his time—and much of his hard-earned cash—at the Lone Star Saloon. He even found it within himself to afford—with some little regularity—the time and cash to spend with the sorrowful strumpet Ada Belle.

Another week went by, and the town of Plentiful seemed to be back to its old self. Business went on, the people did their work, the raid apparently forgotten. To listen to some of the residents, peace had finally been achieved.

Ramsey relaxed, leaving the tenseness he had felt behind as people stopped blaming him for their troubles. It was with much better humor that Ramsey strode the streets of Plentiful these days;

even the rain that had come several days earlier and lasted for two had not bothered him.

Two weeks and three days after the raid by the Cotton Roberts gang, Ramsey was walking up Center Street toward Scheibel's Restaurant. He had worked hard that day, dealing with the detailed work of replacing a trigger spring in an old Army Remington. It was hard, close work, and he had sweated over it in the small, close shop. But finally he was done and now was heading for his dinner. Then he saw Sally Tucker strolling in his direction, not paying much attention. Ramsey tensed immediately. Tucker's usually haughty manner did that to him.

Tucker was unaware of Ramsey's presence until she was quite near him. She was more interested in looking in the windows of the shops that lined the wooden sidewalk. She reached Miss Maggie's run-down bordello and turned her face forward up the street, wrinkling her nose in distaste. As she did so, she saw Ramsey.

Ramsey had been watching her slow, hip-swaying sashay and was enjoying it immensely, despite his dislike of her attitude. Tucker was dressed in a rather plain blue calico dress, with a simple bonnet and drawstring purse, both of which matched the dress. Though the dress was devoid of ornamentation, it clung to her perfect hips and slightly flaring bosom in a way that could raise the passion even in a man three weeks dead. Ramsey was very much alive.

"Good evening, Mr. Ramsey," Tucker said in her sweet, soft tones.

He was surprised at not hearing any condescension in her voice. "Evenin', ma'am," he muttered, a little ill at ease.

"I have not seen you since that day when . . ." she faltered and stopped, casting her eyes downward. Her face came back up and was serene. Tucker smiled, dazzling Ramsey. "Well, I had meant to thank you for what you did for me—and those two unfortunate boys."

"Weren't nothin' to speak of, ma'am."

"I'd not say that," she said firmly in her always perfect diction. "No, not at all. If it were not for you and Mr. Webb, why, there's no telling what might have happened."

Ramsey grew more uncomfortable under the assault of this beautiful young woman's gentle gratitude. He was not used to high praise from such a source. He absentmindedly scratched his right ear, trying to grin. "My pleasure, ma'am," he finally mumbled.

"Please call me 'Sally,' Mr. Ramsey." Tucker was trying her best to keep bright, but the rude Texan was not making her job any easier.

She would have been shocked had she known that this hard-edged veteran of the Civil War and more than a few gunfights was a little afraid of her. He would never admit to that fear, of course, preferring to think of it—if he ever did—as being awed that such a beautiful, cultured, educated woman would look at him—and treat him—as any more than a lowly hired hand.

"All right, Miss Sally."

Tucker was growing a little annoyed at Ramsey's standoffish behavior. She was unable to see it as the natural shyness that made him uncomfortable in the presence of someone like her. "What's your Christian name, Mr. Ramsey?" she asked suddenly, surprising herself with her boldness.

"Kyle, ma'am."

"That's a fine name. Very nice. May I call you that?"

"If you like, Miss Sally." He stared at her perfect face. She had dazzling violet eyes under soft, serenely arched eyebrows. Her nose was small and flawless, with just the slightest upturn at the end. Her full, wide lips, darkly red against the paleness of her delicate cheeks, were parted a bit by the slight overbite of small, pearly teeth. *Good Lord, she's stunning*, Ramsey thought.

Ramsey smiled mightily, hoping she would return the gesture so that he might bask in her staggering beauty for even a moment longer.

There, Tucker thought, proud of herself, *I've finally won him over*. She returned the smile.

His breath caught in his throat, and an aching started in his midsection. He gulped. He didn't know what possessed him, but he suddenly blurted out, "I'm on my way to dinner, Miss Sally. Over to Scheibel's." He realized he was making a fool of himself, but he had gone too far now to stop; he had to plow ahead. "Would you care to accompany me?"

It was Tucker's turn for discomfort. She truly was grateful for what Ramsey had done to protect her, and she wanted him to know that. But to go to dinner with him? Well, that was another matter entirely. He was handsome enough, she supposed, but he was dirty and smelled of oil and guns and beer and sweat. His clothes—denim pants and plain red cotton shirt with the left sleeve pinned up over his arm stump—were soiled and worn.

All that was bad enough, but then there was that large, deadly looking pistol. Such an odd-looking weapon, she thought. And he carried that bone-handled Bowie knife. There was no telling what he did with either weapon. She suppressed a shudder.

Ramsey saw her hesitation and sensed her reluctance. He knew she was trying to find a way to let him down, and it was only a little heartening to him to know that she was trying not to hurt him. *Damn*, he thought, *how could I have been such a fool?*

"I'm sorry, ma'am," he said earnestly, contritely. "I've overstepped my bounds and have offended you somethin' awful. I'm powerful sorry, Miss Sally."

"No, no," Tucker said hastily, trying to assure him while at the same time trying to dodge his invitation. But she wanted to do both as nicely as possible.

"I understand," Ramsey said softly. The initial burst of joy that had flashed through him had been drowned in the brooding, dull acceptance of his lot. He should have known better. "Well," he added, touching the brim of his stained hat with two fingers, "I'll be takin' my leave of you now, ma'am. You'll not have to worry about me botherin' you. That's for sure. Evenin', Miss Tucker."

"Wait!" Tucker called after him as he stepped around her and started up the street. She had the sinking feeling that she had just done something incredibly foolish.

But Ramsey did not stop, and a moment later, a much sadder Sally Tucker continued on her stroll. She was angry, and she nibbled at her plush lower lip a moment. *How dare he ask me such a thing?* she wondered.

Then she stopped. *Good God*, she thought, realization splashing over her. *I'm not angry at him! I'm angry at me. Lordy, why am I so foolish and arrogant?*

She spun and watched Ramsey's broad back moving away from her. For a moment she thought to run after him, grab him, plead for his forgiveness. But she knew that it would do no good. Despair began to settle over her. *Stop it!* she told herself firmly. Suddenly she smiled. This was not the end of things, she knew. She would see Mr. Kyle Ramsey again. And soon.

She turned and moved on down the street, slowly.

Ramsey hardly tasted his food as he shoveled down a meal of

chicken and dumplings. Then, almost defiantly, he polished off a rare treat—a large bowl of fresh ice cream. He settled back with a cup of coffee afterward, his mind awhirl with thoughts of Sally Tucker.

"Bah!" he finally muttered. He strolled over to the Lone Star Saloon, where he occupied his mind with several mugs of beer and several hours of stud poker. He knew he was doing it to keep his mind off Tucker, but as long as he was successful at it, he did not mind.

But after he had crawled into his bed for the night, he knew that the fight was futile. He had won several battles to keep the woman from his mind, but he figured he was about to lose the war. Thoughts of her crowded into his brain, and he tossed and turned, unhappy at not being able to rid himself of the thoughts.

He was in a grouchy mood the next morning at breakfast, and Dodge Carver could tell with one look that Ramsey was best left alone with his work that day. Ramsey worked without let up, repairing the stock of a shotgun, replacing the barrel of a Spencer rifle, and performing several other small repair jobs.

By then dark had started to settle over the town. He rubbed the fatigue out of his eyes and realized that he had not thought of Sally Tucker all day. And as soon as he became aware of that, thoughts of her leaped to mind. "God damn it all to hell and back again," he muttered.

He stepped outside and stood a moment. It was hot and still muggy. He wished it would rain again and clean the air out. But it was still far better outside in the air than in the dull interior of the gun shop. Locking the door to the shop, he stepped off the sidewalk into the street. He took off his hat and plunged his head into the horse trough nearby.

Ramsey whipped his head back up and then from side to side, sending up a spray of water. "Whoo!" he said aloud, not caring if anyone heard him. The dunking revived him some. He clapped his hat back on his hair, which streamed water down his face and the back of his neck into his shirt. It felt good.

"Now leave me alone, God damn it, woman," he muttered under his breath as he headed toward the restaurant. He felt even better after devouring a seared beefsteak, a heaping serving of boiled potatoes, two ears of corn, half a dozen biscuits, a sizable portion of cherry cobbler, and three cups of black coffee.

He headed toward his room, figuring to get an early night's

sleep to make up for what he had lost the night before. But the sounds emanating from the Lone Star Saloon caught his attention. "No harm in seein' what's goin' on," he mumbled, heading for the swinging doors.

The place was in full howl. There was barely room to make his way to the bar. "What in hell's goin' on, Abel?" he yelled over the roar.

"Damned if I know," Jackson bellowed. "There was one or two folks in here. Next thing I know the place is full and everybody's havin' hisself a time. Not that I'm complainin'!" He hurried off.

Ramsey shook his head, grinning as he swallowed a mouthful of beer. This looked to be some good times, he thought. He was always comfortable in a saloon, and when there was this much activity, it was all the better.

He polished off the beer quickly and ordered another. When Jackson plunked the mug down, Ramsey grabbed him and yelled, "Gimme a bottle, too, Abel."

He took turns sipping from the bottle and the mug. Soon he felt a rosy glow forming in his middle and spreading outward. Ada Belle suddenly lurched up beside him. She was flushed, and her usual melancholy was gone, replaced by a half-drunk joy. "Buy a girl a drink?" she asked, slurring the words only a little.

"The hell with the drink," Ramsey shouted into her tiny ear. "Let's just go out back."

"Sure."

Ramsey wasn't sure how long he spent in the small, cramped crib in back of the saloon, but he got bored after Ada Belle fell asleep, snoring softly through half-blocked sinuses. When he returned to the Lone Star, it was still going strong.

He joined in a poker game, but things started to blur considerably after that. He didn't remember how—or when—he got to his room; he was just suddenly aware that he was lying on his back, in his bed, in his room at Parker's Rooming House.

"Damn," he muttered drunkenly. He belched loudly as he tried to get up. He finally managed, though he swayed more than a little before he got himself under control. He unstrapped the belt with the LeMat and the Bowie knife and let it thunk onto the floor.

He started to unbutton his shirt. He never finished. He just toppled backward onto the bed, snoring loudly and regularly.

• • •

Sally Tucker appeared before him, entering quietly through the door. She wore only a cotton nightshift. She was barefoot, and he was rather surprised that he had noticed that.

"I want you, Kyle Ramsey," Tucker said in a voice that was not real. It wrapped around him like an undershirt.

Tucker undid several buttons and then shoved the nightshift down over her shoulders. It floated to the ground at her feet, and she stood before him entirely nude. Then she was coming toward him.

Ramsey tried to get himself undressed but was having a devil of a time at it. Tucker crawled onto the bed with him and began kissing him. He moaned. Tucker began to undo his shirt, then his pants.

Another sound entered into his consciousness, but he could not figure out what it was. He decided it didn't matter. There were more important things to attend to now. Still, the other sounds nagged at him as he gratefully surrendered himself to Tucker.

CHAPTER

★ 5 ★

Kyle Ramsey awoke in a sweat. His head swam and his stomach lurched violently. He was alone in the bed, and he realized that his passionate session with Sally Tucker had merely been a drunken dream. Or maybe a nightmare.

Then he became aware of the sounds that had awoken him, the sounds he had heard and ignored in his dream: pounding horses' hooves, and gunshots. "Shit," he muttered.

He rolled off the bed onto the floor and his stomach protested. Vomit spurted out and he retched, helpless. "Good God damn Christ!" he moaned. "Of all the times to be sick like this. Of all the nights to go out and get likkered up. God damn fool."

He lay there on the floor, sucking in breath and praying that no one would tell an angry Cotton Roberts—if that's who was outside—who had killed his three men. And he prayed, as well, that no one would tell the outlaw where that man lived.

Sides still heaving, Ramsey managed to shove himself up, and he inhaled great rasping clouds of air into what felt liked bruised lungs. He hoped it would settle his roiling insides. Finding a modicum of success with it, he decided he could move. He took a shaky step, then another.

His stomach rebelled again, spewing forth the poisonous contents that lurked there. He fell to his knees, bracing himself up on his arm. His stomach spasmed, clenching and knotting around the sickening emptiness within.

Ramsey moaned, spitting out the residue of his vomit. "Good Christ," he whispered through clenched teeth. "Dumb bastard," he mumbled after a moan. "Promised you'd never do such foolishness again. God damn, serves you right to be slumpin' here on the floor, pukin' your guts out."

It took several more minutes before he could make it to his feet again. When he did so it was with much effort, and he succeeded with trembling knees. The room did a small, slow jig before his eyes, and he clamped his eyes shut. "Lord, this can't be happenin'," he whispered, a small knot of fear growing in his belly.

After what seemed an eternity, he cracked the lids slowly. The room, thankfully, stayed put. He knew he had to move, but the thought did not excite him in the least. But he shoved his right foot slowly forward. It worked, and he did it again, staggering around the foot of the bed and on across the room toward the single small window that overlooked Center Street.

He looked out, his stomach recoiling again. But there was nothing left inside to be emptied. He sank down, resting on his knees and laying his head on the windowsill, and he watched the scene unfolding before him.

Ramsey saw two bodies—townsmen both—lying in the street, their blood soaking into the dust. "Damn!" he mumbled, the sickly sour taste of the vomit still thick in his mouth and throat.

He counted ten mounted men roaming the streets, firing their pistols at anything that moved—or at nothing, since they seemed to be the only things moving out on the street now. Dust curled up into the powerful blue sky from under the horses' hooves.

Most of the outlaws seemed to be facing southward, keeping an eye out for—or on—something Ramsey could not see. A youngster must have been watching from Webb's Mercantile, for he suddenly burst out of the store, heading for the east side of Butler Street, which cut across Center on the north side of the general store.

One of the outlaws—a big, handsome man on a prancing roan—spun the horse toward the boy. He leveled a large pistol and fired deliberately.

The boy—who was perhaps twelve years old—was smashed forward by the bullet, the back of his head gone. He staggered on a few more steps, propelled by the impact and inertia, before falling onto his face in the dirt.

"Jesus God damn Lord Almighty," Ramsey gasped. He had seen his share of horrific actions during the Civil War, but never had he seen such a senseless, wanton killing as this. There was no cause, no reason for this. The viciousness of it—and the killer's absolute lack of feeling at having done it—chilled Ramsey to the marrow.

Sucking in air against the tremors that wracked him, Ramsey shoved the window up. Hot, stale air greeted him, and a moment later the breeze carried to him the odor of powder smoke and fresh-spilled blood.

He realized he did not have his pistol. Disgusted and sickened at his state, he crawled, scrabbled, and lurched to where he had dropped the LeMat as he had drunkenly stumbled into his bed the night before. He wrapped his hand around the butt of the pistol, pleased at its comforting bulk and weight.

As he turned—carefully, so as not to faint from the crashing pain in his head—he heard a muffled scream from somewhere outside.

Throwing caution to the wind, he jerked himself up and ran haltingly toward the window. He saw two men dragging a woman out of the First Bank of Plentiful down the street southward. He could not tell, at this distance, who it was. But it did not matter. He was not the type to sit idly by while any woman was manhandled in such a way.

He raised the LeMat in his one trembling hand and tried to take aim. His eyes were clouded, and he had to blink a few times to clear them. When he did, the two outlaws had already thrown the woman up onto the saddle of a third man, who swatted the woman across the back of the head with the barrel of his pistol. He jabbed his spurs into the horse's flanks, and the animal sped away, southward.

"Damnit, hell," Ramsey muttered, aiming shakily at the fleeing outlaw. But before he could squeeze the trigger, he realized that the man was already out of range.

He shifted his sights to the two who had dragged the woman out of the bank. But they were mounted and spurring their way after the one with the woman. The rest of the gang was heading in that direction too, firing off pistols to keep the townsfolk behind walls.

A searing anger tore through Ramsey, steadying him as he picked out one of the stragglers and aimed at him. He fired off several rounds at the man; then shifted to another and fired off the rest of his nine revolver shots.

The first man he had taken aim at toppled from his saddle and sprawled on the ground. The other jerked in an arch, showing that he had been hit. But he managed to cling to the saddlehorn and race after the others.

"Christ!" Ramsey whispered as the hangover stabbed at him again. He turned to face into the room and sank down, weak and exhausted. The room gyrated, and he moaned as thunder crashed inside his skull. He had not felt this sick and in such pain since he had lost his arm. He closed his eyes, hoping that it would make all his suffering go away. He slumped to the side, asleep before his head tapped the floor.

Ramsey did not know how long he had been out, but he felt mildly better when he opened his eyes and shoved himself up so that he was sitting with his back to the wall under the window. He sat that way for some time, afraid to move and thinking that all this had also been a dream.

Then he smelled the putrid odor of old vomit, masking even the whiskey smell that emanated from each of his pores. He set the LeMat down and rubbed his face. His stomach grumbled from hunger, though at least it was not recoiling on him. But his head still pounded.

"Well, shit," he grumbled softly. "No use in settin' here on your lazy ass no more." He eased himself up after grabbing the LeMat. He stood for a few minutes, rather amazed that he was mostly steady. His head hurt with a vicious intensity, but he could function.

He haphazardly cleaned the LeMat and then reloaded it carefully. He slid it into its holster and then buckled on the belt. He grimaced at the mess he had made on the floor. With a little more certainty, he left the room. Downstairs, he found old man Eli Parker, who owned the boardinghouse. "I was sick up in my room, Eli," he said with a straight face and only a twinge of guilt.

"I'll have it cleaned up for you," Parker said. The old man was a nice fellow, Ramsey thought. He knew damn well that Ramsey had been sick because of an overindulgence in spirituous liquors, something Parker never even touched. But Parker would not throw that in his face. Ramsey knew, though, that he would have to pay an extra dollar or two when his bill came due at the end of the week, to pay for the cleaning.

"You do know what happened today, don't you, Mr. Ramsey?" Parker asked.

"Cotton Roberts and his boys visited again."

"Yep. Took a woman away with them, too."

"I saw that," Ramsey nodded. He glanced over at Parker's large grandfather clock. Three o'clock. *Damn!* Ramsey thought. "Didn't see who it was, though," he added.

"Marshal Burch said it was Miss Tucker who was taken."

"What?" Ramsey asked, shocked.

"Yes, sir. Don't know why, though. It's a terrible business, this. All of it. Terrible, just terrible."

"That's for certain."

Ramsey hurried out. His first stop was at Webb's Mercantile. "You hear about the excitement?" Tice Webb asked excitedly.

"Yep. Now I need . . ."

"Damnedest thing," Webb muttered, shaking his head.

"Watch your tongue, Tice Webb," Mrs. Webb said sharply, but with a slight bantering tone.

"Yes, ma'am," Webb said, rolling his eyes heavenward.

"Look, Tice," Ramsey said, not sharply, but firmly, "I'd love to set here and chat about all this with you. But I got some things to attend to. So I need a few things."

"Sure," Webb said, a little hurt.

"I need some new pants—Levi's, I think, will do. And a new shirt. You still got the sky-blue muslin one I saw the other day?"

"Yep." Webb was still a little irritated.

"I'll take it, then. An extra shirt, too. Whatever you got. And several bandannas. And I'll need some paper cartridges, and ball and caps. I want some bacon, hard tack, coffee, sugar, flour. The clothes I'll take with me. The rest you can send over to Parker's."

"All right." Webb almost forgot his ire as he began to pile up the items and run a total.

As Webb worked, Ramsey asked, "They leave you alone, Tice?"

"Who? Those owlhoots?"

"Yeah."

"Sure. Don't know whether they were afraid of me or just tendin' to other things. But," he added conspiratorially, "to tell you the truth, Kyle, I'm sure as hell glad they did."

"I would say."

It was but a few minutes more before Ramsey had his clothes, wrapped in brown paper, in hand. He paid Webb and left, letting the storeowner gather up the other things in a box to be taken to his room later.

He headed straight for Doc Bedloe's place. The doctor, who was also a dentist, had a couple of tubs in back of his place on the bottom floor. And he gave shaves and haircuts in the room out front. The town, as Ramsey hurried across and up the street, was eerily quiet.

"Phew," Bedloe said as Ramsey swept into the room. "You're as high smellin' as a polecat, Mr. Ramsey."

"I reckon," Ramsey said without humor. "Can you give me a shave and a haircut?"

"Sure."

"I'd like a bath, too, afterward."

"You *need* a bath, Mr. Ramsey."

"Yeah. You got somethin' I can take to ease this painin' in my head?"

"I expect. Those new clothes?" He pointed to the package.

"Yep."

"Put 'em in back, and then take a seat in the chair." He waved a hand at the barber chair. "I'll go on upstairs and fetch a powder for your head pain."

"Thanks, Doc." As the doctor headed up a staircase off to the side, Ramsey went into the back and set his package down. Back in the front room, he looked over the counter. He grinned when he saw some tooth-cleaning powder. There was no brush to use, but he would manage. Ramsey poured some water from the pitcher into a glass. He took a mouthful of water and swirled it around a bit before spitting it out the window into the alley. He wet his index finger and stuck it into the tin of tooth powder. The finger came out coated with powder. Then he scrubbed his teeth vigorously with his finger. He had just ended rinsing and spitting when Bedloe returned.

Ramsey felt almost human as he lowered himself into the chair. Bedloe handed him a glass of milky water. He looked askance at it for a moment before swallowing it down. Then he lay back and relaxed as the doctor-dentist-barber went to work on him.

Ramsey knew he had fallen asleep, but it could not have been for long. He awoke as Bedloe was pulling the towel away. "There, all done," the doctor said. "You ready for that bath now?"

"Yep."

"Good. I had Homer fill one of the tubs while I was working on you. Everything's all set."

Ramsey went in back, stripped off his soiled clothes, and eased himself into the copper tub full of steaming water. Afterward, splashed with lime water and dressed in his new clothes, he felt like a new man. His stomach told him it was time for food. He paid Bedloe and then headed up the street toward Scheibel's.

CHAPTER

★ 6 ★

After filling himself to the point of bursting on ham steak, yams, carrots, brown betty, milk, and coffee, Ramsey was feeling his old self. The concoction Doc Bedloe had come up with had eased the throbbing in his head, and the food served to settle his stomach considerably.

With a growing sense of unease, he strolled over to the Lone Star Saloon. His unease came from the remembrance of last night's episode. But he was not going to the saloon to drink. He wanted information, and he figured that would be the best place to get it.

"Evenin', Kyle," Abel Jackson said, looking at him for the signs of hangover. There were none left, except the bloodshot eyes.

"Evenin', Abel."

"You want somethin'?"

"Just a beer."

Jackson got it and set it down. Ramsey paid for it and lifted the mug. He strolled off, pretending to stop and watch a stud-poker game here or one of draw poker there. But mostly he was listening to those all around him.

What he heard was about what he had expected. Most muttered darkly about making changes when the next election rolled

around—about how they would get a new marshal and even a
new county sheriff, if those two lawmen didn't change their ways
and start protecting the citizens of Plentiful like they were supposed
to be doing. Like they were being *paid* to do.

"Marshal Burch and Sheriff Starkey called for a posse, didn't
they, Adolph?" Ramsey asked Adolph Bock. He had become
annoyed after listening to the heavyset, mustachioed German run
on at length about the lack of adequate law enforcement.

"Ya. Zo?"

"Why don't you get off your fat lazy ass and join in?"

"Dot is not mine line of work," Bock said stiffly. "Dot is for
Marshal Burch and zat other fool, Sheriff Starkey, to take care
of."

Ramsey stood very quietly and very still. The desire to smash
this blubbering oaf in the face with his mug was strong within
him. Finally he brought himself under control. "You, Mr. Bock,"
he hissed, "remind me of a bloated steer carcass festerin' in the
Texas sun: somethin' that's ever present, but of no account, and
to be avoided at all turns."

"I vill not stand here and be inzulted," Bock huffed.

"You get some backbone all of a sudden?" Ramsey asked
sharply. "You ain't shown no signs of it before." He stood easily,
waiting. He wanted the German to come at him, so he could
relieve some of his frustration toward these insignificant people
on one of the main offenders.

Bock sputtered.

Ramsey grinned viciously. "I hope that the next time Cotton
Roberts and his boys ride through here you're the first one to get
plugged. I hope he or one of his men puts a hole in that big fat
windbag of a belly you got."

"They vill not return," Bock stuttered.

"Unless you got some inside knowledge," Ramsey said, drawing a gasp from the crowd, "by Christ they sure as hell will be
back. As long as you fools don't get up the courage to fight 'em
off."

"Dot's not a fair thing to zay, Mr. Ramsey," Bock whined.

"Fair shit," Ramsey growled. He slammed his half-filled mug
on a table. "I am sick to death of you God damn fools—all of
you!—pissin' and moanin' about how beset by these troubles y'all
are when you won't to nothin' to help yourselves. Y'all make me
sick!"

He stormed out, his blood boiling with rage.

"Now you see what we're up against?" Starkey asked quietly as Ramsey leaned against the outside wall of the saloon.

"Some of this is your fault, Sheriff," Ramsey said angrily.

"How so?"

"You know what these people are. What you ought to do is just shanghai a few of 'em for a posse. Just walk up and tell 'em they're deputized and that they're coming with you."

"I can't do that," Starkey said softly. "What could I do if they refused? Shoot 'em?"

"Reckon not." Ramsey sighed. "You ever tried gettin' some federal marshals down here? Or maybe even some army troops?"

"Territorial governor won't allow it," Starkey shrugged. "What about you, Mr. Ramsey?" he asked slyly. "Why won't you join a posse?"

"Ain't been asked. The only time I was here when Roberts's men raided was that one two weeks ago. You didn't even call for a posse then. If you did, I didn't know of it."

"Gave up on such things," Starkey said ruefully. "Wasn't no point no more."

Ramsey nodded.

"Would you join one if I made the call?"

"It's likely I would."

Starkey believed him. He almost grinned. "That'd be one hell of a posse, wouldn't it?" he said sarcastically. "Me, you, and old man Burch."

"Yep. Pure hellacious," Ramsey said in the same tone.

"You know another of them outlaws was killed in that raid today?" Starkey asked, arching an eyebrow in Ramsey's direction.

"Yep," Ramsey said noncommittally.

"Wasn't you responsible, was it?"

"Reckon it was."

"Maybe me'n Royal don't need to go along on a posse with you, Kyle," Starkey said with a short, humorless chuckle. "You seem to be doin' right well handlin' those boys all by your lonesome."

Ramsey shrugged. "Reckon I am. But for every one of them that goes down, it seems at least one of your citizens gets killed too. You want to plant another dozen townsfolk before those outlaws are taken care of?"

"No," Starkey said sadly.

"Didn't think so."

They fell silent. Finally Starkey said, "Well, reckon I'd best be on my way, Kyle." He turned to leave.

"Sheriff," Ramsey called. When the lawman faced him he said, "You best think of somethin' to do about all this. And soon. Roberts ain't about to let this go. The pickin's here are too easy for him. And he's lost at least one more man—the one I killed. I winged another one, too. No tellin' what might happen to him. And then there's Sally Tucker."

"Yeah, there's that." Starkey pulled a bandanna from his right hip pocket and mopped the sweat from the back of his neck.

"You know why he took her?" Ramsey's eyes bored into the sheriff's.

Starkey looked uncomfortable. He fidgeted a bit, replacing the bandanna in his pocket. Then he shrugged the great humped shoulders. "Miss Sally's been widowed more than a year now. As you might expect, every man in this town's tried courtin' her. But she wasn't havin' any of it. Guess she's aimin' on stayin' true to her late husband, Pete."

The sheriff pulled out the bandanna again and loudly blew his nose into it. As he stuffed the cloth away, he continued: "Word has it that Roberts met Sally a few years back and took a likin' to her."

"That's sure as hell understandable."

"Yep. Anyway, some folks think that he took a little too much of a likin' for her and tried to talk her into goin' away with him. Now, old Cotton Roberts is a handsome cuss, I'd have to admit—"

"He a big feller? Rides a roan?"

"Yep. Why?"

"I don't know any of these outlaws, except by reputation. But I saw that one today. He looked to be the leader. Now I know for sure."

"Yep." Starkey shrugged. "Like I was sayin', he's a handsome cuss, and most women'd like to cozy up to him, I guess, if looks was all that counted. But Miss Sally never saw it that way. Took her weddin' vows most seriously."

He stared out into the street for a few moments, then said, "Seems like he approached her several times to go away with him, but she turned him down in no uncertain terms each time.

Then he tried draggin' her away one time. She screamed, and Pete come a-runnin'.

"Now, Pete wasn't no slouch, either. Not in the looks department, nor in size. Every bit as big as Roberts. He come flying around the corner of their house and saw Roberts tryin' to haul Miss Sally up across his saddle. Pete saw red over that."

"I would, too," Ramsey said, grinning tightly. His hand clenched involuntarily as he thought of what he might do to a man who tried to harm his woman—if he still had a woman.

"And me. Well, Pete hauled Roberts down off that horse and proceeded to whale the livin' tar out of him. Eventually, Royal showed up and pulled Pete off Roberts. Sally was afraid Roberts might do something bad to Pete while Royal was talkin' to him. But that bastard just took the opportunity to get away. Two weeks later Pete was killed—shot in the back of the head while he was out in the barn, tending to the stock of an evenin'. After that, Miss Sally moved on into town from the farm they had."

"And nobody could prove Roberts did it, right?" Ramsey asked shrewdly.

"Never really tried. Then, as now, nobody wanted to get a posse up. There was little to connect him with the death anyway, except that they had that fight—if you could even call it a fight—a couple weeks before Pete died."

"Why hasn't Roberts tried to take her away by force before now?"

Starkey shrugged. "Reckon it's a couple things, but I can't be certain, you understand. First off, when Pete got killed, Roberts only had three or four boys who rode with him regular. Enough to frighten the townsfolk into not sending a posse after him, but not enough for him to feel too brave, either.

"I reckon Roberts was some wary, too, for a long time, worried that if he came in here and tried takin' Miss Sally, we might well lay a trap for him. I did have a deputy watchin' over her for a spell. But she didn't like it, and since Roberts never did try anything, I pulled him off. He's runnin' the office over to Sagauche now."

Starkey pulled out his plug of tobacco and sliced off a hunk. He was silent as he chawed it down to a consistency he was comfortable with. He spit, making sure all was right before continuing.

"He raided here maybe a year ago, that time with half a dozen

men. When he got away with that, he got a little bolder. A few
more men joined him and he raided again, with close to a dozen
hardcases ridin' with him. And again, each time gettin' more
darin'. I reckon he was testin' his power over us, waitin' for the
day when he could take Miss Sally without worryin' about any
consequences.''

"And that was today?"

"Seems like it."

"What are you goin' to do, Sheriff?" Ramsey asked.

"Ain't sure." He stared into the dark again for some moments.

"You can't let her stay with those bastards." Ramsey realized
he cared more about this woman than he should, than he had any
right to, than he wanted.

"That's a fact." Starkey grunted. "You got any ideas?"

"We go get her," Ramsey said firmly, without hesitation.

"What do you mean?" Starkey asked, interested and worried
at the same time.

"Just what I said. It's simple enough."

"What do you mean by 'we'?" Starkey's curiosity was piqued.
He had been a wild young man in the Civil War, reckless and
ready to throw himself into danger for a good cause. He had gotten
away from that in the seven years since that war had ended.
Perhaps, he thought, it was time to regain some of that youthful
glory.

"You and me," Ramsey said bluntly. "Marshal Burch, if he's
of a mind to come along. Anybody else who takes it into their
head to put an end to those bastards for all time."

Starkey stared at the Texan for a bit. A grin started slowly
beneath the mustache and grew and grew. "You're *loco*, Mr.
Ramsey," he said, chuckling. "You know that, don't you?"

"Yep." Ramsey smiled.

"It's a good way to be, boy. I like that. But ain't you worried?"

"About what?" Ramsey shrugged. "I've been in far worse
spots. Am I supposed to be worried because these boys are hardcases? Or because there might only be the two of us? Hell, that
don't mean mule shit to me. Now, was you to ask me if I was
scared, I might have somethin' to tell you."

"You scared?" Starkey asked, still grinning.

"Damn right. Only way to go into battle of any kind is with
your stomach all tied up in knots from fear. Keeps your mind
clear and gives you an edge."

"You really believe that?"

"Yep."

"Me too. When do we leave?"

"I'm fixin' to be out of here by first light. You aim to come, best be in front of your office before then. You want to rustle up some others to go with us—if you can—best get started on it. They ain't gonna have time to prepare."

"I'll have to deputize you."

"There's time in the mornin' for such foolishness."

Starkey nodded. He grinned once more and then hurried off, his bulk making him look awkward while doing so.

Ramsey watched him fade into the darkness. *Now what in hell have you gotten yourself into?* he wondered. *Lordy, you got to stop these foolish heroics.* He really did not know why he got involved in such things, only that he seemed to be drawn into them against his will. He had long before given up trying to fathom it. He just accepted it and went along with it.

CHAPTER

★ 7 ★

Kyle Ramsey looked down Center Street as he stepped out of Parker's Rooming House and stopped beside the big, black mule. It was light now, but the temperature was still pleasantly cool. Ramsey hung the burlap sack filled with food on the saddlehorn and awkwardly tied his blanket roll behind the cantle.

Though it was early, Ramsey had been up for more than an hour. He had eaten a filling breakfast of eggs, steak, biscuits with honey, and coffee. Then he had walked to George Port's Livery and saddled up his mule—a cantankerous, belligerent beast named Sunshine. He walked now, towing the mule behind him, the short distance to Dodge Carver's gunsmith shop. He saw a lantern on inside and was surprised when Carver greeted him. It was odd that the gunsmith was here at such an hour.

"Mornin', Dodge," Ramsey said quietly, stepping inside the wooden building.

"Mornin'. I hear you're planin' on makin' a trip, Kyle."

"I might."

"You got a heap of work to do here."

"It'll hold."

Carver stared at Ramsey. Though he had never let on, the burly, gray-haired gunsmith liked the Texan. "I reckon it will," he

43

murmured. Then, a moment later, "Anything I can do for you?" he asked more strongly.

"You can come with me," Ramsey said levelly.

"Hell," Carver chuckled, not very humorously, "if the outlaws didn't kill me, my wife would certainly do so when I got back. Seriously, I got her and the five young'uns to think about. A few years ago I might've . . . certainly I would've . . ." He could not finish. He cast his eyes down, ashamed.

"Yeah," Ramsey said.

"Anything else I can do?"

Ramsey thought for a moment. He was rather surprised by Carver's unaccustomed friendliness, but he decided right off that the man's amiableness was not false. "I could make use of that 10-gauge scattergun I reconditioned the other day."

"That shotgun belongs to Mayor Aldridge, Kyle, as you well know."

"So?"

"Well," Carver said with a spreading smile, "I reckon that since he ain't paid me yet—and shows no signs of doin' so any time soon—maybe it does need some field testin'." Having decided, and happy about it, Carver smacked his palm loudly on a workbench, making small tools and parts jump. "No, by God, I don't see no problem with field testin' that gun at all."

Ramsey nodded, amazed. It was the first time he had ever seen Dodge Carver smile. Mostly the gunsmith just scowled. "I'll need some shells you got for it, too."

"Done. Anything else?"

"Not that I can think of."

As Carver headed toward the back of the room and the small safe in which he kept his ammunition, Ramsey picked up the scattergun. It had been made about 1868, Ramsey guessed, and was a fine weapon now that he had reconditioned it. It was powerful and sturdy, and it would be quite deadly at close range. Carver came by and dropped two boxes of shotgun shells—00 buckshot—on the workbench. Ramsey nodded and cracked the shotgun. He stuffed two shells in and snapped the weapon shut.

"You got a rifle?" Carver asked.

Ramsey nodded. "Yep. A Springfield. It's old, but it does the job." He thought for a moment. "I could use some cartridges for it—.50 caliber."

Carver returned to his safe and came back with two boxes of

metal cartridges. Ramsey set down the shotgun and picked up the shells for it and walked outside. Carver followed him out, carrying the ammunition for the Springfield. "Thanks," Ramsey said, taking the boxes and stuffing them in his saddlebags—those for the rifle on the right, those for the shotgun on the left.

Both men returned to the shop. Ramsey picked up the scattergun from where it was leaning against a workbench.

Carver rummaged around behind the old desk he used. The desk was piled high with papers, small boxes, parts of weapons, several pistols, and other assorted junk. "Ah-ha, here it is," Carver muttered. He straightened, holding up a dusty saddle scabbard.

They went out into the budding dawn, Carver wiping the scabbard as he walked. He hung it on the left side of the mule's saddle—the rifle was on the right side—and Ramsey shoved the shotgun into it.

"You got all you need?" Carver asked.

"Yep. Except maybe some help."

Carver shrugged. "I've done all I could. Well," he added gruffly and embarrassed, "you take care of yourself out there. Good help's hard to come by, and you ain't half bad." He stuck out his right hand.

"Yeah," Ramsey mumbled, shaking the proffered hand. Then he mounted the mule and rode up to the boardinghouse at the other end of Center Street. In his room, he loaded into a burlap sack his powder and ball for the LeMat, plus the food he had bought.

As he hung the sack on the saddlehorn outside, he looked down Center Street. A crowd was growing in front of Town Hall, about halfway down the block, on the east side.

Ramsey took the reins to the black-bodied, white-faced mule and led it down the street toward the crowd. He stopped behind the last of the people. He stroked the mule's thick, powerful neck and listened as Marshal Royal Burch exhorted the crowd.

Burch was an old man. About sixty, Ramsey would have guessed. Arthritis had slowed him some but had done little to dim his spirit. He was a sprightly man, five-foot-eight and spare of frame. A fringe of gray hair hung out from the back of his hat, but Ramsey knew the rest of his head was bald. He still had piercing blue eyes and steady hands.

"We all know there's been a wagonload of troubles fallen on Plentiful of late," Burch said in a powerful voice that belied the years and danger the marshal had seen. "But lordy, folks, there ain't a hatful of things me and Sheriff Starkey can do about it on our own. You all should know that. You people want to be shed of Cotton Roberts and the scourge he brings, you're gonna have to throw in with me and the sheriff."

There was a sick silence, until someone in the crowd shouted, "We ain't gettin' paid to do such work."

"That's true, I reckon," Burch said. He was angry and frustrated, but so far he had been able to contain it.

"We're payin' *you* to do such things," someone else yelled.

"That's true, too." He paused, then added, "but you people are payin' more than money."

He looked almost pleased by the excited rumble that made its way around the crowd. "You people are payin' in blood. Every time Roberts and his boys ride through here, another couple of you die."

It was cruel, but he no longer cared. He waited quietly as the angry buzz hummed through the assembled clot of people.

Sheriff Starkey had not moved. The huge county sheriff still leaned back against the wall, watching warily without seeming to do so.

When the grumbling had run its course, Burch said, "And you're gonna keep on payin' with your lives till you rise and smite down this devil that's been plaguin' Plentiful." He felt sure that the Reverend Worcester would approve.

"I'll go," a quavering voice shouted, startling everyone for a moment. Then the frailty of the voice struck home, and there were scattered chuckles.

"Who said that?" Burch demanded—knowing, but wanting to expose the old fool for what he was.

"Me, God damn it." An old man shoved his way forward.

"Now Three Fingers, you know that's plumb foolish. Out of the question," Burch said softly, trying not to hurt the old man's feelings.

Three Fingers Monroe—who had gotten his nickname when a six-shot cap-and-ball revolver blew up in his hand, taking two fingers with it, back in the late '40s—was at least seventy years old. No one knew for certain. But he knew things about people and places going back to the days of the mountain men. Most folks didn't believe half his tales, but he talked with a knowing tone of men who had lived years before. Monroe was stronger than he looked, but he was in no condition to sit in a saddle for several days of rough riding while chasing after owlhoots.

"I'm ready to leave now, God damn it," Monroe said, his toothless mouth making whistling and flapping sounds when he spoke. He shoved a gnarled hand through the flowing mane of matted white hair. It matched the beard, though the latter was stained with tobacco juice and food. He looked quite foolish, standing there with an old Leman rifle in his trembling hands.

"No, Three Fingers," Burch said sharply. "That's final." Burch felt bad about all this. Before too many more years, he would be in Monroe's position. It was not something he looked forward to.

Burch looked out across the small sea of mostly hostile—and fearful—faces, then said with a sneer, "But it's nice to know we got at least one man here's got some gumption."

The crowd was silent, but Burch could feel their anger. *Lord, he thought, how could these people be so docile and complacent? Didn't they have any pride?*

The silence seemed to weigh over the town like a thunderhead. It was broken only by the small sounds that never stopped—a horse snorting or shuffling, a nervous cough, the wail of an infant quickly quieted by its mother's breast, the soft remonstrance from a mother to a child.

Ramsey swung himself up onto Sunshine's broad back. "You're wastin' your breath on this rabble, Marshal," he hollered, his tone cold. The crowd began to turn toward him. "You could take 'em all together and still not find one backbone. Only thing you'd find would be a big heap of yellow."

The crowd was facing him now, their anger radiating hotly toward him. Ramsey grinned in devilish delight. "Bunch of pukin' cowards you got here, Marshal. All they can think of is keepin' their scrawny, lice-infested, no-'count hides safe at home."

The crowd's grumbling grew in tone and intensity, and angry babbling lofted up into the hot morning air. A woman's voice cut through the deeper hum as she shrilly accused her husband of cowardice. Then the voice dimmed as he growled something at her.

"All they can do is set here in their fright, pulin' about how they've been set on by devils and demons and such. And how the law can't do nothin' for 'em." He spit in the dirt. "Cowards, pure and simple, each and all of you."

There was little grumbling now as a cloud of shame emanated from the crowd. One young man of about eighteen looked ready to step forward, but an older man—his father, presumably—clamped a hand on his arm, preventing him.

Ramsey was truly disgusted. "Y'all know," he said sharply, "that was it not Miss Tucker that was stole away, it might've been your wife or daughter. Or maybe it'd be your son that got shot down in the street like a rabid dog. Then what would you do?" He paused and spit again. "Most likely nothin'. Just like now."

He looked up at the clear blue of the sky, wondering why he was getting so worked up over all this. He had seen this before. He never could understand it, but he had seen it. He blew out a breath and looked toward Burch and, behind the marshal, Starkey.

"Well, I aim to be leavin' out after those murderin' critters. Any of you care to ride along?"

"I'm ready," Starkey said, shoving away from the wall. His face was flushed with anger. He stepped directly from the raised wooden sidewalk into a stirrup and pulled himself onto his horse.

"And me." Burch stepped up and mounted his horse next to Starkey.

"Then let's ride," Ramsey growled. He was angry at the people of Plentiful, and he wanted to be away from them, at least for a spell.

"You got to be deputized first," Burch said. He and Starkey moved their horses through the throng, which parted worriedly.

"Then get it done."

"Hold up your right hand," Burch said. When Ramsey did so, Burch said, "Do you, Kyle Ramsey, promise to uphold whatever laws we got and try to catch these infernal devils who have set upon this town more times than anybody'd like to remember?"

"If you say so."

"Good. Here." He held out a badge.

"Pin it on, Marshal," Ramsey said quietly. "I have trouble doin' such things by myself."

Burch nodded and pinned the tin star to Ramsey's new blue shirt.

"Let's ride," Ramsey growled, spurring his mule forward. People scattered out of his way as he charged down Center Street. Burch and Starkey were right behind.

CHAPTER

★ 8 ★

The outlaws were not hard to track, since Cotton Roberts and his men were not worried about being followed. As soon as Ramsey and the two lawmen had passed the southern edge of Plentiful, they had slowed their animals to a walk. The road here was wide and well used, lined with pines, aspens and cottonwoods. The three men caught glimpses of Sagauche Creek off and on through the trees and brush to the west. The road narrowed quickly.

Four miles on, Ramsey, who was leading, stopped his mule and climbed down. Carefully observing the side of the road to his right, he nodded. He left the reins to Sunshine dangling and moved onto a small path that cut the road from the west.

He was back a few moments later. "This way," he said, climbing onto the mule and heading down the path.

As the day grew older, he had a little more trouble following the trail. Not so much that it was hidden, but that the gang used this path frequently, and tracks were all over. It made it hard to distinguish which ones were made when.

Adding to the confusion were the numerous smaller trails that cut this main path. Each had to be explored and checked. They splashed across cold Sagauche Creek several times as the creek bent around and back on itself. Or, Ramsey thought, maybe it was just the path that meandered crazily, possibly a ploy by the outlaws to throw off pursuit.

But Ramsey was always able to pick up the right trail, though it sometimes took a while to do so.

During the times when the track was easier to follow, Ramsey questioned the two lawmen on the gang.

"Roberts is a mean bastard," Starkey said at one point.

"I saw evidence of that yesterday," Ramsey said with a knot of rage in his gut.

"The boy?"

"Yep."

"That's typical of Roberts," Starkey said. "That God damn Yankee's got a mean streak a mile wide."

"Yankee?" Ramsey asked.

"Hell, yes. He was thrown out of the regulars back during the war, from what I hear. Was too fond of terrorizin' towns rather than fightin' Rebs. He got to thinkin' that if Quantrill and his ilk could raid for the South, he might as well do the same for the North."

"Quantrill weren't no real Southerner," Ramsey said. "Not in his heart, anyway." He hated men like Quantrill. Such blood-thirsty rogues gave the South a bad name.

"The same could be said of Roberts and the North," Burch said.

"Royal's a blue belly through and through," Starkey confided with a grin.

"That right?" Ramsey asked.

"I'm a Northerner," Burch said proudly. "Served as a supply officer for the Union Army during the War of the Rebellion." He was almost defiant. "I was a little old to be totin' weapons against the likes of you and John here. That bother you?"

"Not in the least. I never hated Yanks just for bein' Yanks. There are a few individuals, though . . ." He chuckled low, though it was true, and if he dwelled on it, he could work up a pretty good hate for those individuals.

"Sorry I asked," Burch said seriously. "I get my hackles up sometimes when I shouldn't when the subject comes up. Seems a mighty lot of you Rebs can't get over the fact you lost the war."

"I ain't one of 'em," Ramsey said sourly. He didn't worry overly much about the South having lost, but, then again, he didn't much like having his nose rubbed in it either.

"Anyway," Burch said, knowing how Ramsey must be feeling, "Roberts got up a bunch of blue bellies and began raiding. After the war, he was caught, tried, and sentenced to hang, along with some of his boys. But some others managed to break him out of jail. He headed west, into the Indian Nations, and spent some time raidin' there."

"He wasn't the only one doin' that," Starkey said, an eyebrow raised.

"That's a fact. After a couple, three years of that, several federal deputies were hot on his trail."

"So he came up here?" Ramsey offered.

"Yeah. After spending some time in Kansas and Nebraska, from what I hear."

Ramsey stopped to check conflicting trails again, and soon he had them following the right path once more. They walked their animals across Sagauche Creek again, letting the animals drink some as they did. The sun was setting, and the light was growing too dim for good tracking.

"Reckon we ought to call it a night," Ramsey finally said. "We'll make camp here and pick up in the mornin'."

The two lawmen had no objections. "You see to the animals, Kyle," Starkey said. "I'll get firewood, and old Royal here," he added with a grin, "is a fine fair cook when called upon."

Ramsey nodded. He led the two horses and one mule away to the side. He turned the sacks of supplies over to Burch and then hobbled the animals. He hated saddling and unsaddling animals because of the difficulty in doing so with only one arm, but he kept his peace and struggled.

He set the three saddles and bedrolls aside before currying each animal, starting with Sunshine. By the time he had finished the mule, Burch had a fire going, a coffee pot on the fire, biscuits frying, and meat—Starkey had shot a small deer that morning—roasting.

Ramsey hurried in his work, the smell of the food enticing him and encouraging haste. He was just about finished with Starkey's horse when Burch called, "Dinner's ready."

Ramsey washed his hand and face in a quiet pool in a shallow curve of Sagauche Creek and hastened to the fire. The other two men were already digging in, and Ramsey wasted no time in grabbing his share. When they had finished, Starkey cut off some tobacco for chewing, and Burch filled and lighted a small corncob pipe. They sat back, leaning against their saddles.

"Where you from, Kyle?" Burch asked through the cloud of pipe smoke.

"New Liberty, Texas. Down in Fannin County. You?"

"Ohio. What are you doin' up this way?"

"None of your business, Marshal," Ramsey said calmly. "No offense, but . . ." He shrugged and lifted up his shoulders.

Burch nodded and said softly, "It's my job."

"Like hell," Starkey said with a laugh. "You're just a nosy old coot."

"Damnit, don't make light of me, John," Burch snapped. "I was fightin' Mexicans durin' *that* war when you was still pissin' on your ma's lap."

Starkey was taken aback. "Didn't mean nothin' by it, Royal," he said easily. There was contriteness, but no deference, in the voice.

"That's not the way I took it. I know my years are catchin' up on me, John. I don't need to be reminded of it by you, nor anyone else. But I can still do my job well."

"I reckon," Starkey said noncommittally.

"The reason I was askin' questions of you, Mr. Ramsey," Burch said, turning angry eyes on Kyle, "is that I got me a hunch someone in town's connected with Roberts somehow."

"What?" Starkey asked sharply, surprised.

"What's the matter, Sheriff?" Burch asked sarcastically. "The old fart come up with somethin' the bright young buck of a county sheriff ain't seen yet?"

"What in hell are you talkin' about, Royal?" Starkey asked, ignoring the insult.

"Roberts has got to have a man inside town. I got no idea who. I just know it's got to be."

"Why?" Ramsey asked, interested. Starkey sat brooding but listening.

"They always know when to hit Plentiful. Except for this last time, they've raided us every time the bank had a shipment of silver and gold from up in the mountains waitin' to be sent on. And when they raided this time, they knew exactly where Miss Tucker was. I was watchin' 'em, and they knew what they were goin' for."

"By Christ, I think you're right," Starkey said in deferential agreement. "Christ, how could I not have seen that?"

"Takes time to learn to watch for such things," Burch said quietly. He had made his point and was not the type of man to rub salt in someone's wound.

"You got any ideas on who it might be?" the sheriff asked.

"Nope." Burch knocked the ashes out of his pipe on the heel of his boot. He poured another cup of coffee. "I know a few folks it ain't."

"But you thought I might be the one?" Ramsey asked astutely. He was not sure whether he wanted to be angry about it or not.

"Didn't necessarily think so. Just considered the possibility. Reckon if I asked you a few questions, I might learn somethin'." He shrugged. "Like I said, doin' my job."

"Well, I ain't the one," Ramsey said firmly, deciding he would not be angry.

"I didn't reckon you were, but you never can tell," Burch said with a grin. "You're too new to Plentiful, for one thing. They hit the town a couple times before you showed up. And after all my years, I think I can judge men fairly well. I reckon you're on the up and up." He smiled. "Even if you are a Reb."

"High praise from a blue belly," Ramsey said, grinning.

"Who do you know it's not?" Starkey asked.

"Us three, for starters. Tice Webb. Miss Tucker. A couple others."

Starkey nodded. "You have any thoughts at all on who it might be?"

Burch shrugged. "Could be damn near anyone. I suspect that gambler Alabama might be involved. But that could just be my dislike for people like him. Adolph Bock acts some suspicious on occasion. Even your boss, Kyle, Dodge Carver, acts queersome of a time."

Ramsey was about to object but decided to stay silent. He didn't know Carver all that well, and his newfound friendliness still seemed out of place. *Maybe Carver did that to throw me off the scent,* Ramsey thought. If it were true, though, he and the two lawmen could be in serious trouble when they caught up with the outlaws. He shook the feeling off. It was too preposterous, he thought. Still, he would be extra wary.

"How many men does Roberts have ridin' with him?" Ramsey asked.

"Dozen, maybe a few more," Starkey said. "Includin' Roberts himself, there was fourteen or fifteen, I reckon. Till you killed those four of them." He snapped his fingers, "That reminds me." He rummaged in his saddlebags for a moment before pulling out a small roll of bills. "This here's yours," he said, handing it to Ramsey.

"What for?" Ramsey asked, taking the roll and counting it: two hundred and fifty dollars.

"Reward money. Just wired yesterday. Fifty dollars each for Philbin, Wade and Bruckner. Those were the three you killed the first time over in Webb's store. Patricio Zayas, the one you shot in the street day before yesterday, had a hundred dollars on his head."

"I reckon I can find some use for this," Ramsey said with a grin, stuffing the money in one of his own saddlebags. "You know who it was I winged the same time?"

"Gettin' greedy?" Starkey asked with a grin. "Ain't sure. But I think it was Louis Lambert. Nasty little bastard who's due for a hanging in New Orleans, as well as half a dozen other places if they ever catch up with him."

"Maybe you cheated the hangman, eh, Kyle?" Burch chuckled.

"We can always hope." Ramsey did not like killing, but he held no remorse for anything he had done to members of the Roberts gang. They were, he figured, worse than rabid wolves and to be treated with the same disgust, caution, and coldness. "How far from town you think they're stayin'?"

Starkey shrugged. "We have no idea where they're hidin' out. But it can't be too far, I'd say."

"Looks like we're headin' for Lost Canyon," Burch said. "I reckon that's the only place reasonable out this way they could have a decent hideout."

Ramsey was impressed with the old man's astuteness. "How far?"

Burch wriggled his mustache as he thought. "Ten, fifteen miles from here. I reckon Roberts and his men can do the distance from there to Plentiful in a hard day's ride."

"Which way's the canyon?" For some reason, Ramsey was excited. Maybe it was the thought of seeing some action. He wasn't sure.

Burch pointed in the general direction they had been going—mostly southwest. There was a gap in the mountains there.

"Through Sentry Pass. A few miles to the other side, the canyon branches off into the mountains there."

"I say we give up this here lookin' for signs," Ramsey said, not expecting nor wanting argument, "and just head straight for the canyon. What do y'all think?"

"Sounds right to me," Starkey said, yawning.

"Me too," Burch agreed.

Ramsey stood up and started to unroll his blankets. He stopped suddenly and spun around. "Why didn't you think of this before, Royal?"

"Had it in mind since we cut off the road onto this path. But it took a spell before I was fairly certain that's where this was headin'. I still ain't for sure certain, though. But I wanted to be as sure as I could."

Ramsey nodded. *Yeah,* he thought, *and you wanted to see how long it would take me and John Starkey to think of it too, you old coot.* With his back turned to the others, Ramsey grinned. He was beginning to like Marshal Royal Burch quite a bit. Finished with his blankets, he tossed the last dribbles of his coffee on the small fire, where they sizzled momentarily. "Well," he finally said, setting the tin cup down, "I don't know about you boys, but I'm bushed. You can set here and chat through the night, if you want, but I aim to get some shuteye."

He kicked off his boots and stretched out on his blankets.

CHAPTER

★ **9** ★

Ramsey sat on the spine of the world and looked around. It was breathtaking, and it made a man—even one like Kyle Ramsey—believe in God. His parents—well, his mother mostly—had tried to instill in him and all his brothers and sisters the fundamental tenets of bedrock Methodism. While Kyle had made the motions when he was younger—going to church, showing deference to the minister when that pious, pompous soul came for his free Sunday dinner once a month or so—he had given up such things the last several years.

It wasn't so much that Ramsey no longer believed in God. Anyone sitting here looking at the magnificent splendor of the snow-covered peaks towering alongside the pass, the thick stands of pine, or the thin, glittering ribbon of Sagauche Creek far below could not help but believe. It was just that Kyle had no patience for religion.

In addition, he figured he was so far fallen that even God Himself couldn't save him. He had, he guessed, broken all Ten Commandments, many of them numerous times. He reckoned that repentance was not in his nature anymore and redemption not in his future.

"Lost Canyon's over that way," Burch said, pointing.

Ramsey shook himself from his foreboding musings. *Damn, but if this country doesn't make a man feel small and inconsequential,* he thought. He looked to where Burch was pointing, and he could see the slashing indent that was the canyon. "You see smoke coming from the canyon?" he asked, unsure.

Starkey and Burch stared out past the brilliant blue of the sky toward the rocky defile. The air was crystalline in its purity and made breathing hurt just a little.

"I reckon I do," Starkey said, nodding.

"I don't see nothin'," Burch grumbled.

"If you'd put on your spectacles, God damn it, you'd be able to see," Starkey said with a friendly chuckle.

"Bah," Burch snapped.

"Let's go," Ramsey said, a sense of dread urging him to haste. He had the easiest time of it, as the mule sure-footedly picked its way along the rock-strewn path with a high mountain wall on one side and a sheer drop-off on the other.

Ramsey licked his lips, not wanting to admit to a bellyful of fear. But he did not like heights, and the emptiness to his right made him rather queasy.

It took only a couple of hours before they were down on a meadow and pushing their animals faster, heading for the mouth of the canyon.

"Reckon we ought to stop for some grub?" Starkey asked just after they had entered the narrow ravine.

"You hungry?" Ramsey asked, trying to grin but not succeeding. He was hot and tired and felt himself forced onward, as if he had some kind of deadline.

"Yep," Starkey said, also failing in his attempt at humor. "And it might be a while before we get another chance."

"We meet up with Roberts's bunch, and you'll be glad you weren't weighed down with food," Ramsey said a little crossly.

"Somethin' eatin' at you, Kyle?" Burch asked.

"None of your God damn . . ." He stopped and inhaled. Then he let the breath out slowly. "I don't know what it is, Royal. It's almost as if . . . Ah hell," he spat, "I don't know."

"Well, I don't know as if we need to stop and feed our faces," Burch said. "But the horses need a rest after comin' through that pass. And I reckon we can all use some water. The animals, too."

Ramsey nodded. He walked his mule down to the bank of the stream. It was narrow here, and the bank was muddy and thick with brush. The mule began drinking as Ramsey climbed down off the animal. He took off his hat and dunked his head in the water, pleased by its coolness.

After drinking his fill, he loosened Sunshine's saddle, letting the animal breathe. He pulled three pieces of beef jerky from his saddlebag and passed two around, saving one for himself.

Ramsey was itchy to be on the move, and he paced around. Finally he could stand it no longer. "Time to ride," he said gruffly, recinching the mule's saddle.

All three were more cautious as they worked deeper and deeper into the canyon. Thick stands of pines and aspens periodically gave way to small meadows. In one such glade, they carefully made their way around a grizzly sow and her three cubs. The grizzly stood upright and grunted in irritation but did not attack, though she did make the mule and the two horses rather nervous.

By midafternoon, they could clearly see smoke and knew they were getting close to a cabin or camp. They were in another of the interminable stands of trees, but they could see its end close by. Stopping there on the fringe of trees, Starkey pulled out a looking glass and gazed across the meadow.

"Can't see nothin'," he grumbled.

They moved on and through a small copse of aspen. Out of that, they could see a camp half a mile away across a narrow glade, broken only by a small thicket of brush and spindly aspens that ran right up to the canyon walls on each side.

Starkey climbed atop a large boulder and took a look through the glass. He was grinning when he scrambled down from the rock. "It's them," he announced.

"You sure?" Burch asked.

"Yep."

"How do we do this?" Ramsey asked.

"I think we've got to be careful with Miss Tucker in there," Burch said. "We might be here to clean up these scum, but we don't want her—or anybody else who's not part of the gang who might be in there—to get hurt."

Ramsey nodded. "What's the camp look like, John?" he asked.

Starkey described what he had seen through the glass. The camp consisted of a large cabin backed up to the stream that ran along the boxlike rear wall of the canyon. On each side of it and just a little forward was a tent. In front of each tent was a small fire. Behind the tent on their left, in a slight depression in the canyon wall, was the horse corral. Men moved about all through the camp. To their left, forty or fifty yards in front of the camp, was the thicket of white aspens and various brush. It was the only cover between where they stood and the camp.

"I reckon Miss Tucker's in the cabin."

"It would figure," Burch agreed.

"Damn, they picked a good spot to defend, didn't they," Ramsey said rhetorically. He paused a moment, then said, "I reckon we'll ride on up alongside the left wall of the canyon here. That'll keep those trees between us and Roberts's men.

"Once we get into that thicket, behind cover, we'll work up as close as we can without exposin' ourselves. Soon's we're set, John, you and Royal start up a ruckus of some kind. I'll slip up to the corral and stampede the horses. Then I'll try to get into the cabin and see if I can find Miss Tucker."

"That's a damnfool plan," Starkey snapped.

"You got a better idea?"

"Nope," Starkey admitted.

"You?" Ramsey asked the marshal.

"Nope," Burch answered.

"Then let's go get it done. And if either of you looks like you're gonna be overrun, turn tail and run. Don't hang around."

"What'll happen to you?" Starkey asked.

"Most likely I'll be pushin' up flowers come mornin'. But if I get a chance, I'll try to get out the back way. It looks like there's a path headin' up the canyon wall. If there ain't . . ." He shrugged.

There was nothing more to say, so they rode off, walking their animals slowly so as not to raise dust. Their stirrups scraped the canyon wall on their left sometimes, though they often had to move out a few yards to get around brush or rocky outcroppings.

The camp, they saw when they had worked their way through the trees, was mostly quiet, with men napping in the shade or working at various chores. Four sat at a makeshift table playing cards. The cabin seemed to be silent.

Ramsey tied Sunshine to an aspen. "Give me a minute to move up a little more," he said. Burch nodded while he unlimbered a Henry repeating rifle. Starkey just pulled out his heavy Spencer rifle. Ramsey worked his way forward, slipping from tree to tree, so silent he seemed to be part of the dappled shadows. He finally stopped and looked back. Burch was staring at him. He nodded. A moment later the Henry opened up and, seconds after that,

Starkey's Spencer. Ramsey did not hesitate to watch the outlaws scrambling for cover. He dashed across twenty yards of open ground before he found three aspens together. He stopped to catch his breath.

Looking back, he saw two outlaws on the ground. He did not know if they were dead or only wounded. Another was heading for the horses. "Damn!" Ramsey muttered. He sprinted out from behind the trees, angling toward the outlaw. He slammed into the man, knocking him down. Ramsey leaped up and stomped a boot-heel into the outlaw's stomach. The man's breath burst out in a *whoosh*. Ramsey kicked him in the face and then ran on the few steps to the corral.

The back of the corral was formed by the canyon wall just past the stream. Half of one side was also canyon wall. The rest of the barrier was a haphazardly fashioned fence of logs. Ramsey kicked several logs down and then some more. Horses whinnied and snorted, rolling their eyes nervously at these strange antics.

Ramsey clambered over the fallen logs and into the corral. He worked his way quietly but quickly until he was standing in the few inches of water in the stream. "Go on!" he shouted, smacking the horse nearest to him on the rump. "Git!" he roared.

He pulled off his hat and waved it frantically, yelling some more. A big chestnut stallion snorted and rose up on its hind legs, its front hooves flashing. Then he landed and raced off, leaping over the pile of fence poles Ramsey had knocked down.

The other horses crowded after the stallion, racing off across the glade. Several outlaws used the horses for protection as they ran out of their tents, trying to stop the stampede. Two men went down, hit by gunfire.

Ramsey grinned. Burch and Starkey were doing even better than he had hoped they would. He just prayed they could keep it up a little longer. He dashed to the back corner of the cabin and stopped again to catch his breath. His heart pounded from the exertion, but it was almost a comforting feeling.

The cabin was made of rough-hewn logs, laid even more carelessly than the fence. Gaps showed where the outlaws had been too lazy to replace the chinking mud. The back wall was only five yards or so from the stream. A window had been crudely hacked out in the back and was covered over with badly hung oiled paper.

Ramsey slid along the rear wall, his back against the logs, and headed toward the window. The bottom of the window was at chin level. He pulled his Bowie knife and ever so cautiously made a small slit in the oiled paper. Using the blade to pry one side of the slit away, he put an eye up close and peered inside.

The room was sparsely furnished, with a rickety cot, a crate used as a table, and several trunks. Sally Tucker lay on the cot. She looked frightened, but she was alive. No one else was in the room.

Ramsey pulled the knife free and slid it away. He glanced around, checking to make sure no one was around, though gunfire still sounded from out front. He found a stump someone had used for chopping wood.

Sweating with the exertion, Ramsey manhandled the stump to the wall under the window. He wiped his sleeve across his sopping brow and breathed heavily, trying to catch up.

He was just climbing onto the stump when an outlaw flew around the corner. They saw each other at the same moment. The outlaw, who already had his gun drawn, fired.

Ramsey fell off the stump, feeling the outlaw's bullet burn across a rib on his left side. It would have caught him in the chest had he not moved. He landed hard, grunting under the impact, and felt the sharp pain of a rock gouging into his flesh just over his kidney.

The outlaw was swinging toward him, and Ramsey frantically scrabbled to draw the LeMat. He got it out and fired without aiming, using the barrel of buckshot. The outlaw fired again just as the blast from the LeMat ripped into his chest and stomach, knocking his aim far off.

Ramsey stood up and walked a little shakily toward the outlaw, his LeMat ready. But the outlaw was dead, his whole front a bloody mass of torn flesh and mutilated organs. Ramsey shook his head. He had seen worse. He slipped the LeMat back into his holster. And, just to be safe, he picked up the outlaw's Colt and heaved it into the stream.

He hurriedly moved to one corner of the cabin and checked along the side. He saw no one. He did the same on the other. Again, no one. He went back to the stump. Using his knife again, he cautiously looked through the slit he had made in the window covering. All was as before. He climbed onto the stump.

Ramsey heard a frightened gasp from inside the cabin as he punched through the soft covering. He ripped and tore at it until the oiled paper was gone. Warily, but hastily, he climbed into the room.

Tucker was still on the cot, tied to the four corners. She had scrunched up as best she could to get away from whatever new horror was to come at her now.

Ramsey ignored her for the moment. Across the room was a doorway to the main part of the cabin. It was blocked off by a blanket nailed to the ceiling. He stepped up to it and pried an edge of the blanket away. Two men were in the room. One lay on the floor, covered by a blanket. Ramsey could not be sure, but he thought the man was the one he had wounded during the raid on Plentiful the other day. The other man, who was at the one poorly made window in front, was Cotton Roberts.

Ramsey eased the LeMat out of the holster. It was almost too easy, he told himself. Trying to make no noise, he cocked the pistol. Just as he was drawing a bead on Roberts's back, the outlaw leader shouted something out the window and leaped up. Ramsey fired once as Roberts bolted for the door. The bullet thunked harmlessly into one of the logs as Roberts disappeared outside.

With a sigh, Ramsey turned back into the small room, angrily jamming the LeMat into its holster. He walked to the cot. The woman, hearing him but not watching, whimpered.

"Miss Tucker," he said softly. "Miss Tucker, it's me, Kyle Ramsey. I've come to take you home."

CHAPTER

★ 10 ★

Sally Tucker opened her eyes slowly, not wanting to believe her ears. She was certain, despite the evidence, that another demon was coming for her. One like the many who had kept her captive these last . . . *How many days had it been*? she wondered. *A week? No*, she told herself firmly, *only two days.*

She felt immeasurable relief when her wide violet eyes were fully open and she saw an anxious-looking Kyle Ramsey standing before her. For a moment she had a flash of dread. *What if he's one of them*? she thought in horror. Then: *No, he can't be. He can't.*

He was saying something, but Tucker was so wrapped up in her fear and worry that she did not hear him. She made a conscious effort to tear her mind away from the horrific thoughts and focus on what he was whispering.

"... now. Come on, Miss Sally, we really got to move. Are you all right?" Ramsey was worried, too, and sick at the thought of what Tucker might have gone through at the hands of this gang. And he thought she might be hurt. She had such an odd look on her face, as if she had seen a ghost.

"I'm tied up," she finally gasped, jerking her hands at the ends of the short ropes to show him.

He nodded, holding a finger to his lips. "We don't want to attract undue attention," he whispered. She nodded acceptance, though fear lurked in her violet eyes. In a moment Ramsey had sliced through both tethers. "Feet, too," she mumbled, embarrassed. Two more quick flicks of the Bowie and Tucker was free. She sat up, rubbing her wrists. She was afraid—of that much Ramsey was certain. But he could not blame her. He felt a little better since animation had returned at least in part to her otherwise deathly pale face. Her clothing was soiled and a bit tattered but intact, and he hoped it indicated that the gang had left her alone.

"Can you walk?" he asked into her ear.

She bounced off the cot and onto her feet. She staggered and would have fallen if Ramsey had not caught her. "Thanks," she muttered, feeling her face redden in shame.

Ramsey grunted an assent. Still holding Tucker, he glanced toward the blanket, worried that someone might have heard. But he guessed not, with all the gunfire out there. But they had to get out. And soon. Still, he could not rush the frightened woman.

Within moments, though, she said softly, "I think I'm ready."

He nodded and led her to the window. He looked out, assuring himself that no one was around. "Me first," he whispered. "Soon's I'm outside, I'll help you. If someone starts to come into the room in the meantime, you jump out this window."

Tucker jerked her head up and down in assent. Her full lips looked ghastly, as if painted across the milk-white face.

Ramsey clambered out awkwardly. Standing on the stump, he hissed, "Come on, Miss Sally."

Embarrassed, but not willing to let it make a difference, Tucker hiked up her long black calico dress and petticoats, exposing a trimly formed calf encased in a plain cotton stocking. She slid the leg over the windowsill, and Ramsey grabbed her around the waist with his strong right arm and pulled.

Tucker yelped in surprise but allowed herself to be hauled along. Swinging her around outside the window, Ramsey set her on the ground next to the stump and jumped down after her. Thoughts of Tucker's stocking-clad calf—and the briefly enticing glimpse of thigh above that he had caught—burned in his brain as he pointed to where the horse corral had been.

She nodded, but then gasped when she spotted the bloody body of the outlaw Ramsey had gunned down earlier. She tore her gaze away from the wretched thing.

Ramsey checked around the corner of the building. No one was coming. "When I tell you to," he whispered, "head for those trees over there." He pointed again. He noticed that the man he had encountered and flattened was no longer lying by the horse corral. That worried him a bit.

Once more she nodded. She grabbed her skirts in one hand, holding them so they would not interfere with her sprint. "Run," Ramsey hissed, shoving her forward.

She did not hesitate, even though she stumbled a step from his push. Then she was racing across the manure-strewn corral. She realized with a shock that she felt no fear for the moment. Only an odd exhilaration. She could hear Ramsey's boots thumping along behind her.

"Stop!" Ramsey yelled when they had reached the three trees. She did, breathing heavily. She was not used to such things. Women did not run around, as a rule, especially with their skirts held up. She was surprised that she had done so well, considering that she had not run since she was a child, and she was wearing high-top, side-button shoes with short, spiky heels.

"Soon's you catch your breath," Ramsey said, "we're gonna run across this open section. That's the hard part. It's only twenty, maybe thirty yards that we have to go. But we'll be in range, and in sight, the whole time."

"It can't be any worse than what's happened to me already," Tucker said bravely.

"Good. Ready?" Ramsey asked. But he wondered what, exactly, she had been through.

"Yes," Tucker answered, feeling the bile rise slowly into her throat.

Ramsey looked to his left, toward the outlaw camp. The two bodies had been joined by another. Firing still came readily from the outlaws, as well as from John Starkey and Royal Burch.

The outlaws seemed preoccupied. "Go," he said without preliminary, once again pushing Tucker forward.

She ran as fast as she could, oblivious to most of the world around her. Only dimly did she note that Ramsey was galloping just to her left, where he would be in the line of fire should the outlaws see them and shoot. She ran on, her lungs aching, as if ten wild grizzly bears and five hundred Cheyenne warriors were right behind her. She was too intent to be frightened. A stitch developed in her side, but she ignored it.

Then she was in the first light scattering of trees. The copse became denser, and Tucker was aware of the loudness of a rifle firing nearby. When she tripped over a tree root and went sprawling forward, her skirts and petticoats flew up over her back. She was more concerned at the moment about possibly being hurt, rather than showing a bit of stocking. She only hoped Ramsey and Marshal Burch—whom she had recognized in a fleeting moment while falling—were gentlemen.

Tucker lay for a minute, catching her breath and letting the pain in her lungs and side dissipate. She was not hurt, she realized thankfully. Then it dawned on her that she was still lying there with her skirts and petticoats up, and she brushed them back as she stood. She slapped the twigs and dirt and leaves from the front of her dress. She was thankful for not having been hurt. She turned to watch Ramsey and Burch. And for the first time, she noticed Sheriff Starkey.

"Get behind a tree," Ramsey ordered. She did as she was told.

Ramsey had pulled out his Springfield and had joined the other two men in was laying down a slow, steady fire. But the outlaws were well hidden behind rocks, crates, tack, and anything else that had come to hand. The gunfire was more to keep the outlaws pinned down than to kill any of them.

"You realize," Burch said over the sporadic rattle of rifle fire, "that we are gonna have a hell of a time gettin' out of here."

"Yep." Ramsey had tried all along not to think of that. He had mostly been interested in getting the woman out safely. Now there was no putting off the problem. "I reckon we ought to just bust out of here and ride like hell."

Starkey snorted at the suggestion. But he said, "I managed to grab one of the horses you set free. You can use that. Let the woman ride your mule."

"All right. But what about you and Royal?"

"We'll lay down a cover fire till you get out a ways. Then we'll follow along as we can."

Ramsey didn't like it, but there seemed to be little other alternative. "All right, but keep your fat ass down so it doesn't get shot off."

"You just take care of Miss Tucker," Starkey grumbled. "Or you'll answer to me."

"Or what's left of you when I get finished," Burch said smartly.

Ramsey checked his pocket watch. They had been there less

than fifteen minutes. He slipped the Springfield back into the scabbard and dumped the rest of the cartridges into his pants and shirt pockets. "You ever ride astride, Miss Tucker?" he asked.

"No, but I can sure learn fast," she answered with fervor.

Ramsey actually grinned. There was more to this prim, fancy-looking woman than he had imagined. Color had come back into her face and, despite the smudges of dirt and some small scratches, she looked, at least to Ramsey, quite ravishing.

"All right, come on, then," he said. He made a cup of his hand just above his knees. "Put your foot in," he ordered.

She placed her tiny, muddy boot in the large, curved palm, and Ramsey hoisted her up onto the large mule. Tucker squiggled and adjusted until she was settled in the saddle.

Only an occasional shot popped now, as the men—lawmen and outlaws both—tried to conserve ammunition and not expose themselves to enemy fire.

Ramsey went to the pinto Starkey had captured. It was a small, sturdy animal, with patchy fur not completely shed after the winter. "I hope this horse you caught is a broke, John," he said.

"If he ain't," Starkey grunted, "you're in a heap of trouble."

"That's a fact." Ramsey tied a short length of rope to the horse's lower jaw, figuring to use an Indian-style rein. It was the best he could do for now, and he hoped it would work. "You boys best get mounted up too," Ramsey said as he vaulted onto the pony's bare back. The animal skittered a moment but then settled down. He would be fine, Ramsey decided.

"I can shoot better from a stand," Burch said.

"That might be," Ramsey said. "But none of us can do the others any good if he's too far behind here. You get mounted. Give me and Miss Tucker a hundred yards or so head start, then you turn tail and run."

"He makes sense, Royal," Starkey said.

The old marshal snapped off another shot. "Reckon you're right." He climbed up on his horse and then fired again. "Don't want them boys thinkin' we've gone," he said with a grin.

Starkey hauled his bulk up onto his big black gelding. "All right, Ramsey," he snapped. "Git ready."

"You set, Miss Tucker?" he asked.

"Yes." She was pale again, but her fright was considerably less than it had been in the cabin a short while before. She actually began to believe she would get away alive. And all because of this one-armed Texan. She looked at him with new understanding—and with something lurking inside her that she would not admit to.

"See you boys soon," Ramsey said almost cheerfully. He walked the pinto through the trees, the mule following. He came to an impassable section of brush in front of him and stopped at the edge of the trees on the left.

Tucker moved up next to him. "Scared?" he asked.

"Yes," she whispered. "I'm not very brave, I'm afraid."

"I'm scared, too. So're John and Royal."

"What?" she asked, eyes wide with surprise.

"That's right." He smiled.

"But . . ."

"It ain't so much not bein' afraid as it is what you do about the fear. It controls people sometimes. Like the people in town. I imagine there's some of 'em brave enough. But they get to thinkin' they could get killed or somethin', and that fear grows and grows till it takes 'em over. Then they're useless."

"How do you control it?" Tucker asked, interested. She forgot for a moment where she was.

"I don't rightly know," Ramsey said with a shrug. "I just do it. Most folks who do that don't know how. Well," he added gruffly, "we best be on our way."

Suddenly he smacked Sunshine's rump. The mule brayed and shot forward, out of the thicket and into the open. Ramsey jabbed his spurs into the pinto, and the animal started running with a burst. He maneuvered the pony so it was running with its nose almost on Sunshine's tail. It was the best protection he could give Tucker under the circumstances.

Ramsey heard a blazing fusillade from back in the trees. He raced on a litte longer before he looked quickly back over his shoulder. Starkey and Burch were rushing side by side out from the same spot Ramsey and Tucker had left. He glanced ahead.

Tucker was bouncing in the saddle like a drop of water on a hot griddle. She clung on for dear life, scared to death she might fall off and be trampled. Her behind was already sore from the pounding, and the insides of her thighs were rubbed raw and felt like they had been stretched beyond redemption. But still she clung on.

Ramsey grinned, and it came out like a grimace as he gritted his teeth and slitted his eyes against the rushing wind. He took a

chance and looked over his shoulder again. He could see that at
least some of the outlaws had come out from their hiding spots
and were firing in their direction. He and Tucker were almost out
of range, but Starkey and Burch were still within easy range.

"Ride, damnit, ride," Ramsey hissed through his teeth. He
looked forward again. The large stand of aspens was only a quarter-
mile away. Looking back, he saw Burch throw up his arms.
"Damn, no!" he muttered, knowing the old lawman had been
hit.

Burch almost fell off his horse, but Starkey was quick enough
to grab him. With one powerful arm, he held Burch on the horse
as the two animals raced along within inches of each other.

Maybe he's just wounded, Ramsey thought. Then he saw Starkey flinch, and he swore again. He started to slow the pinto,
figuring to go back and help his two friends, but Starkey saw it
and waved at him to keep going. Ramsey looked forward. The
mule, still carrying a flopping, squealing Sally Tucker, had
pounded into the trees. Ramsey knew his first responsibility was
to the woman now. Starkey and Burch could fend for themselves.
He hoped.

The pinto crashed into the trees and onto a small, worn path.
He flattened himself on the horse's neck and yelled at Tucker to
do the same. But either she did not hear him or she was too afraid
to move.

"Hell!" he muttered, as the horse pounded on in the wake of
the mule.

CHAPTER

⋆ 11 ⋆

As Ramsey burst into the trees behind his mule, which carried a frightened Sally Tucker, he glanced back one more time. He could see, barely, Sheriff John Starkey and Marshal Royal Burch racing along. He could not tell at that distance and speed how badly hurt they were, only that they were heading his way.

And there was no sign of pursuit. Ramsey had counted on that. It's why he had scattered the horses. He hoped it would take the outlaws hours—maybe days—to round them up again and begin the chase. He also hoped, looking forward again, that his horse knew what it was doing. Apparently it did.

A few minutes later, Ramsey yelled, "Miss Sally! Slow down!" He thought she did not hear, but suddenly she started, as if waking up.

Scared out of her wits, Tucker yanked hard on the mule's reins. The animal brayed and fought against the reins. Tucker yanked again, harder and determined not to give up. Slowly the great black beast slowed. Just ahead was another glade, glimpsed past the straggling line of trees.

Ramsey slowed his horse too and moved up alongside Tucker. It was a tight fit on the path, and branches slashed at their faces. "We'll stop just into the meadow," he said, loudly enough to be

70

heard over the blowing of the horses and his own wind-plugged ears. "Then go east a bit just to get away from the path. We'll wait for John and Royal there."

"Aren't you afraid the outlaws will come after us?" Tucker asked, terror evident in her voice and face.

"Not for a spell."

"Why?" She was rather surprised.

"I stampeded their horses. It'll take them a while to round up even a few of them. We'll be all right for a while, though I ain't fixin' to spend too long a time settin' here."

Tucker nodded, and she seemed to relax. Her shoulders were not as stiff and her face more serene.

They reached the far end of the trees, though there were still a few solitary aspens standing in the glade, and turned east. They rode only a hundred yards or so and then pulled back into the cover of some thick-boughed pines.

After they had dismounted, Ramsey loosened the saddle on the mule. He hobbled both horse and mule and let them crop the carpet of grass, laced with purple and yellow wildflowers. As he reloaded the one barrel of the LeMat with buckshot, he asked, "You all right, Miss Sally?"

"Oh, yes," she said. She looked—and felt—almost happy. She was out of the clutches of the outlaws, who could not follow, and she was protected by this handsome, brave . . . She stopped those thoughts right off. *Such thinking will get you nowhere,* she scolded herself silently.

Suddenly he hissed, "Get down!"

Startled, she sank to her knees and cowered behind a tree trunk. "What is it?" she asked in a whisper.

"Someone's comin'."

"Who?"

"I reckon Royal and John. Can't be sure, though, and until I am, I figure to be cautious." He waited, wiping sweat off his face with the pinned up sleeve over his stump. It was blistering hot, and the humidity was nearly thick enough to cut with his knife. Thunderclouds hung like clotted cheese overhead.

From his position, Ramsey could see where the trail entered the glade. Starkey and Burch appeared, Starkey on the east side. They were still riding next to each other. Ramsey let them get a few yards out into the glade, trying to make sure the two lawmen were not followed, before he relaxed. Standing up, he yelled, "John! Over here!"

Starkey paid him no mind, as if he had not heard. Ramsey shouted again and still got no response. "Damnit!" he muttered. "Stay here, Miss Sally," he said, urgently heading for the pinto horse. He leaped on and trotted after the lawmen.

"John!" he shouted as he drew near. "John!" He noticed the large stain of blood spreading across the back of Starkey's shirt.

Starkey swiveled his large head and stared with unseeing eyes at Ramsey.

"Jesus, John," Ramsey gasped. "You hit bad?"

"Yep," Starkey croaked.

"How's Royal?" He stopped himself. It was evident now that Burch was dead. "Shit," he muttered. "Well, come on," he said firmly. "Miss Tucker's waitin' over yon a bit. We'll go there, and I'll see what I can do to patch you up."

"No," Starkey said, his voice cracking.

"Why?"

"Wound's too bad." He grimaced as a new jagged edge of pain lanced into him. "And Roberts will be comin' soon."

"The hell with Roberts," Ramsey growled. "He ain't gonna be comin' after us for a good long time. And maybe that wound ain't as bad as you think."

Starkey tried to shrug but blanched when the action sent a wave of agony through his midsection.

"I'll take care of Royal," Ramsey said. Starkey objected, and Ramsey was about to argue when he realized that Starkey was afraid to take his hand off Burch's body because he had fixed in his mind the thought that as long as he kept one hand on Burch and the other on his stomach, he would be all right.

Ramsey nodded and rode slowly back toward where Tucker waited. The smile dropped from the young woman's face as soon as she saw Starkey's pain-etched countenance—and then Burch's body. She gasped.

Ramsey dismounted and rehobbled the pinto, turning it out to graze again. With difficulty—and without Starkey's help—he eased Burch's body down and stretched it out on some pine needles. He had still harbored some hope that the old marshal lived, but Burch was already turning cold.

Ramsey ignored Tucker's racking sobs as he helped Starkey off his horse. The bulky lawman was weak from loss of blood, and with only one arm, Ramsey had a deal of trouble. Starkey fell, knocking Ramsey down, but the Texan got up unhurt. Starkey could not rise, though. Ramsey thought that just as well.

He bent over Starkey and sliced through the back of the sheriff's shirt, exposing the oozing, ugly wound. "Miss Sally, get me a canteen, please." When she made no move, he said harshly, "Get me a God damn canteen, Miss Sally! Now!"

Her sobs stopped midway through one, and she looked funny for a minute sitting there, her face covered with glistening tears and her mouth gaping. Her lips slapped shut, and she nodded. "Right away," she said, getting up.

She brought Ramsey a canteen, and he nodded his thanks. She had recovered herself and could now look down almost dispassionately on the wounded sheriff. "It's bad, isn't it?" she said in a frightened voice.

"Yep."

"He going to die?"

"Don't know. He's in a bad way, that's certain."

"Can you do anything for him?"

"Not a hell of a lot," Ramsey said in irritation. He was irked by the situation—and by his helplessness. "Just wash it off some and try to get the bleedin' stopped. Then I'll bandage him. I wish there was somethin' I could use as a poultice, but if there is around here, I ain't familiar with it."

She nodded. Reaching down, she pulled up her skirts and grasped an edge of one of her several petticoats—one near the middle, since it would be cleaner than those either nearer her skin or the outside dirt. "Give me your knife," she ordered matter-of-factly.

"What in hell are you doin'?" he asked, startled.

"Cutting off a piece of petticoat," she said, with only a small blush. "You'll need a rag for washing off the wound. I'll cut another piece for a binding. Now, give me your knife."

Ramsey pulled out the Bowie, but before he handed it to her he asked, "Are you sure you know what you're doin'?"

"Of course I do, Mr. Ramsey."

"But . . ."

"But what? Do you think it's not right? Is that it?" When he sort of nodded, she said, "Sheriff Starkey is hurt bad, and the longer you sit here arguing propriety with me, the worse he's liable to get. Now, I don't usually hike my skirts up in front of anybody, let alone a man I don't know all that well," she snapped. "But these are not normal times. Besides, you saw a good portion of my leg when I was climbing out that window—and later, when I fell. If that has raised your blood to a boil, Mr. Ramsey, I cannot be responsible for that."

"But . . ."

"Maybe," she said with a sigh, "your plan is to see more of my leg. Maybe that's why you're sitting here arguing when our friend is hurt, so that I'll stand here with my dress and petticoats up in the air. Is that it?"

The thought had not entered his mind, but now that she had drawn his attention to it, he tried to sneak a peak at her legs. Little enough was to be seen other than a trim ankle just above her shoes.

"Well then, take a good look, Mr. Ramsey," she said harshly. "And then maybe you can get your mind back to the business at hand, which is tending to Sheriff Starkey." Her face and neck pinking only slightly, she grabbed her skirts and all her petticoats right at the bottom and hauled them up as one, straight to her chest.

Ramsey gulped as he stared—unwillingly, almost—at her. He was drawn to looking at Tucker's slim, finely shaped legs covered by the coarse stockings and the knickers above. He wet his lips and tore his gaze away. He looked steadfastly at Starkey's wounded back as he held the knife out.

"Thank you, Mr. Ramsey," Tucker said with a distinct chill in her voice.

He heard the knife slice through material, then a ripping noise. "Here, Mr. Ramsey," she said, her voice thawed not a bit.

He looked up and took the proffered piece of cloth. Without a word, Tucker knelt next to him and picked up the canteen. She tilted it so water poured over the small piece of petticoat Ramsey held.

As if waking from a dream, Ramsey bathed the wound. It was still bleeding some but was nearly stopped by coagulation. Starkey, unconscious since he had fallen, fidgeted a bit under the cool water but then settled down.

"Think you ought to try to get the bullet out?" Tucker asked.

"Not here. It'd most likely kill him."

She nodded. "If you can prop him up, I'll do the bandaging," she said calmly.

"Yeah." Ramsey wrestled Starkey's inert form up, until it was sort of sitting. As he held the comatose man up, Tucker quickly and agilely wrapped the bandage round the big man's chest and back. "Done," she finally said. With a wrist, she shoved some stray hairs back from her face, then wiped her runny nose with the same hand. Absentmindedly, she cleaned her hand on her dress.

She was a mess. Her hair was matted, and it fell around her face in tangles. Her face was scratched and covered with streaks of tears, sweat, and dirt. Her eyes were bloodshot, and dark arcs curled under them. Her clothes were ripped and spotted. Her hands were covered with dirt, and several of her short nails were cracked. Ramsey thought she was still gorgeous, and he had to struggle to keep out of his mind the thoughts of her standing with her dress pulled up to her bosom.

"I'm sorry, Miss Sally," he said quietly. "About before. I . . ."

"It's my fault, Mr. Ramsey—Kyle. I have, of course, been under considerable strain and so have acted most unlike myself."

"I . . ." He stopped when he heard Starkey moan.

"We'd better be going, shouldn't we, Kyle?" She looked at him expectantly.

Ramsey stared at Tucker for just a moment, a burst of lustful thoughts tearing through his brain. Then he forced them away. This was not the time nor the place for such thoughts, he told himself sternly. "Yep."

"What can I do to help?"

"Help me bring the animals in."

Ramsey tightened the saddles and got two more ropes when he was done with that. "I reckon you can ride Marshal Burch's horse. It's a heap smaller than Sunshine, and I'll be more comfortable on the mule. I'll put Marshal Burch on the pinto."

Tucker nodded, queasiness threatening her. She swallowed it down.

Ramsey struggled to get Burch's body up onto the pinto, until an exasperated Tucker threw in her help. "Thanks," Ramsey gasped when it was done. "Now, how about you tie him down?"

Tucker gulped but took one of the ropes and did as she was told. As she worked, Ramsey managed to rouse Starkey. Through sheer muscle and sweat, he managed to get the broad sheriff up into his saddle. "Tie him down too, Miss Sally," Ramsey said, panting from all the exertion. "So he don't fall off while we're ridin'."

Within minutes she was done, and Ramsey had caught his breath. "Ready," she said.

"Thank you, Miss Sally," he said seriously. "You've been a big help here, and I'm obliged."

"On the contrary, Kyle, I'm the one who's obliged. You saved me. You and . . ." She cried softly.

He didn't know what to say, so he patted her shoulder softly.

"I'll be all right," she mumbled, angrily wiping her nose and eyes with her hand. "Let's go."

Ramsey mounted the mule and took the ropes to the pinto and to Starkey's horse. "I hate to have you do this, Miss Sally," he said, "but you'll have to bring up the rear. Don't be too fretful, but look on our back trail occasional to make sure we ain't followed."

Tucker nodded solemnly. Ramsey clucked to his mule, and they moved out.

The first part of the trip wasn't bad, except for the driving rain that began less than an hour after they had left the meadow. But recrossing the Continental Divide through Sentry Pass was harrowing. It was already dark when they started the long climb up through the pass, and there was no help from the moonlight or stars, since the clouds blocked them out. Ramsey had to admit to feeling a healthy dose of fear. More than once he called back, "You all right back there, Miss Sally?"

And the small voice would drift back to him, "Doing just fine, Mr. Ramsey."

It was near midnight when they made it down the other side of the pass. Ramsey was tired, drenched, and hungry. But they could not stop for more than a short while for a cold meal of jerky and two cans of peaches. They covered a moaning, groaning Starkey with Ramsey's waterproof slicker, but that left Ramsey and Tucker without protection from the sheets of rain that fell.

They pushed on, through the booming rolls of thunder and the sizzling show of lightning. Ramsey tried to doze in the saddle but was too uncomfortable to do so. With more and more frequency, he would look back toward Tucker and ask how she was doing. Still the small, tiny voice, sounding almost lost in the crash of the weather, came back, "Just fine, Mr. Ramsey." He was amazed by her stamina.

Ramsey had hoped to make better time on the way back to Plentiful than they had going out. But Sagauche Creek, swollen by the rains, hindered them, and several times they had to ride well out of the way they were supposed to be going to avoid flash floods that roared down sharp little gullies.

Mud pulled at the animals' feet, making it hard for them to walk, especially after so little rest. But Ramsey was afraid Starkey would die if they stopped for more than a few minutes at a time.

Just after dawn—at least he thought it was dawn; it was hard to tell with the black clouds overhead—Ramsey found the road leading to Plentiful. "We're almost home, Miss Sally," he called back in a strong voice, encouraged.

"Let's hurry," Tucker yelled. She was so tired she thought delirium was about to set in.

He grinned as a spectacular burst of lightning dazzled them and left a lingering smell of ozone in the chill air. Ramsey stopped and went back to check on Starkey, as he had done periodically throughout the frantic trek. The sheriff was alive and still wavering between consciousness and unconsciousness. But his being alive was the most important thing right now.

Ramsey touched his spurs to the mule's sides. "Come on, Sunshine," he said, urging the mule into a shuffling trot.

CHAPTER
★ 12 ★

They slopped up Center Street, and even the downpour could not keep the people from peering out windows to watch the slogging-wet progress. By the time Ramsey stopped in front of Doc Bedloe's, a small crowd—one that was growing steadily—had gathered.

An exhausted Kyle Ramsey slid off the mule, leaving the animal ground staked. He pulled on the rope and the pinto moved up. Ramsey looped the rope over the hitching post, then repeated the procedure with the reins to Starkey's horse.

Sally Tucker was more tired than Ramsey, but she held her head high as she pulled up alongside the Texan and threw her leg over the back of the saddle, tantalizing more than one man with her disregard for convention—and the brief glimpse of stocking she allowed.

Arvil Bedloe stepped out of his barber shop, and stood under the overhang. "What in blue thunder's going on out here?" he demanded. Then he spotted the two men tied to their saddles. "Mr. Ramsey? What's wrong here?" He pointed, a chill creeping down his back.

"Give me a hand here, Miss Sally," Ramsey said quietly. As he and the woman began loosening the ropes holding John Starkey to the saddle, Ramsey said, ''Sheriff Starkey will be needin' your help, Doc. He's hurt some bad.''

''And Marshal Burch?'' Bedloe asked, sure he knew the answer.

''Ain't a thing you or any other man can do for him, Doc.''

Most of the people in the crowd gasped. Several women began to cry.

''Damn,'' Bedloe snarled. ''Well, let's get John into my office upstairs.''

''Some of you people give me a hand here,'' Ramsey ordered. When no one moved, he roared, ''Give me a hand with the sheriff, God damn it!''

Three men, including Dodge Carver, hurried forward. They eased the big block of a sheriff off the horse. Starkey groaned, his head snapping from side to side in delirium.

''Hurry, boys,'' Bedloe said urgently, getting a good look at Starkey's shock-white face. ''But go gentle.''

Bedloe hurried off the sidewalk at the corner of his building and around to the stairs on the side. The three men struggling to carry Starkey followed. Ramsey, his face ashen from fatigue, and Tucker, who looked ready to collapse, came last.

The crowd gathered at the bottom of the stairs, standing there in the pouring rain to wait, hushed and worried.

''What happened, Mr. Ramsey?'' Bedloe asked as the three sweating men carefully placed Starkey on the table in the doctor's office.

Ramsey explained it quickly and flatly. Tucker tried several times to expand on what he was saying, but the Texan cut her off at each instance. By the time he was finished with his short narrative, Bedloe had cut Starkey's shirt off. The big sheriff was shaking, both from delirium and the chill that had come over him.

''Anything I can do, Doc?'' Ramsey asked, leaning gratefully against a wall.

''Not here. You'll just get in the way. But either you go fetch my assistant or get someone else to fetch him. And *pronto*!''

''Will he live, Doctor?'' Tucker asked, biting her plush lower lip in worry.

''Not if you both don't get out of here and let me work on him. Now go on, get!''

''Where's Harry?'' Ramsey asked.

''Supposed to be in Cordelle's.''

"We'll fetch him. You'll let me know soon's you know somethin' about John, Doc?"

"Yeah," Bedloe said, not looking up from where he worked on the stricken sheriff. "Now get the hell out!"

Ramsey opened the door next to where he was leaning. Tucker went to say something to the doctor, but Ramsey grabbed her by the arm and propelled her out onto the wet landing. The rain had slowed to a drizzle. "What are you . . ." she started.

"He don't need more questions now, Miss Sally," Ramsey said harshly as he closed the door. He was too tired to deal with nonsense.

"But . . ."

"We got other things to do, woman," he growled. "You want Sheriff John to live, we better find Harry. Doc'll need what help an assistant can give him. He don't need two people who don't know beans hangin' around and gettin' in the way."

Tucker was more tired than she had ever been. She did not know how she was still on her feet. And it made her crabby. Still, the significance of what Ramsey was saying got through her anger, frustration, and exhaustion. She nodded, her head suddenly seeming very heavy.

At the bottom of the stairs, they were confronted by Mayor Marlin Aldridge and the other two members of the town council—Antoine Devreaux and Willy Kreuger. "What is going on here?" Aldridge demanded, huffing up in self-importance like he often did.

"I ain't got time to answer your questions, Mayor." Ramsey started to move around, but the town official blocked his path.

"I asked you a question, Mr. Ramsey," Aldridge said harshly. "I expect an answer."

"I don't give a shit what you expect!" Ramsey snarled, eliciting a gasp of shock from nearly everyone. "Now I got business that needs tendin'. I ain't got the time for jawin' with you."

"But I've heard Sheriff Starkey is badly wounded. And Marshal Burch is dead here. I demand to know what's going on."

"John Starkey is gonna be dead, too, you don't get your ass out of my way and let me go on about my business! Doc Bedloe needs Harry to assist him in workin' on John. I got to go find him."

"Where is he?" Aldridge asked sharply.

"Cordelle's."

Aldridge spun around. "Joshua!" he yelled. When the tall, well-muscled young black man had shoved himself through the crowd, Aldridge said, "You know Harry Laird, Doc Bedloe's assistant?"

"Yeah," the black grumbled in a deep basso.

"He's supposed to be down to Cordelle's Restaurant. You run on down there and fetch him fast."

"They won't let me in there."

"You tell Asa Cordelle that if he gives you any trouble, I'll have you whup him with a buggy whip in front of Town Hall tomorrow at noon."

Joshua Cord grinned. "And if Mr. Laird gives you any trouble, you lift him up by his scrawny neck and cart him here, pronto. You got that?"

"Yassir." Joshua spun and ran, the crowd parting in front of him like the Red Sea before Moses.

"Now," Aldridge said, turning back to face Ramsey, "that's taken care of. I'd like some answers."

Ramsey stood looking at the mayor for a moment. Aldridge was nearly as tall as he, broad of shoulder and slim of hip. He was about forty years old, lean and fit. He wore a long black frock coat, buttoned up to the neck against the chilling drizzle. Underneath that coat, Ramsey knew, the mayor would be wearing a crisp white shirt, a brocade vest, and a tightly knotted string tie. He carried an umbrella as protection against the elements, and he wore a sharp black bowler. He was rather handsome, with open, dark-brown eyes, slicked-back hair, bloodless lips, a pencil-thin mustache, and great bushy sideburns.

"You mind if we go stand on the sidewalk, out of the rain?" Ramsey asked, mild sarcasm in his voice.

"Of course not," Aldridge said, shocked at his own ill manners.

They ducked under the overhang in front of Bedloe's, and Aldridge closed his umbrella. "Now, Mr. Ramsey, please tell me what happened."

Ramsey went through it again, a bit more slowly than with Bedloe but not much. Tucker, somewhat in awe of the mayor, kept her peace.

"I see," Aldridge said, nodding when Ramsey had finished. "And what are the chances . . ."

He broke off as he noticed Cord shoving his way through the crowd. In his wake came a young, timid-looking man dressed in once-fine clothes that were turning shabby. ''Mr. Laird,'' Aldridge said, doffing his bowler.

''Mayor,'' Laird said. ''What the hell's going on here?''

''You better let Doc Bedloe tell you. Now hurry on upstairs.''

Laird ran off, taking the stairs two at a time. He disappeared inside at the top.

''Now,'' Aldridge said, ''where was I? Oh, yes. Do you think Sheriff Starkey has much chance to survive?''

''Hell if I know, Mayor.'' Ramsey shrugged. He wanted a bath and clean clothes and a shave. But most of all he wanted some good hot food and coffee. And sleep. ''I ain't a doctor, but he looked bad.'' He shrugged again. ''But I've seen men recover from worse.''

''Hmmm. Well, what . . .''

''Mayor,'' Ramsey said, feeling his heat rise, ''Miss Tucker and I have been up goin' on two full days now. We've covered a fair piece of country under some hellacious conditions. We got one friend dead and another one knockin' on heaven's door. We ain't had a real meal in God knows how long. We're cold, soaked through, and hurt. I—''

Tucker snapped her head up to look at him. ''You're hurt?'' she asked, fear coursing through her quavering voice.

''Just winged, Miss Sally. Nothin' to fret over. But I'd like to get a bath and clean it up.''

''You go right upstairs and have Doc Bedloe—or even Harry—work on it.''

''They've got their hands full with John. I'll keep. It's just a scratch.''

''Are you sure, Mr. Ramsey?'' Aldridge asked.

''Yes, sir. But I would like to get some food and a shave and such. We can jaw about all this tomorrow, after I've caught up on my sleep.''

Aldridge rubbed his pointy chin for some moments. ''Reckon there's nothin' more needs to be done now.''

''Yeah, there is.'' Answering Aldridge's questioning glance, Ramsey jerked his chin toward the pinto and said, ''Marshal Burch needs to be taken care of. I reckon you can find somebody to take him down to Black's Mortuary.''

''It's your duty, Deputy,'' Aldridge said, pointing to the dripping badge on Ramsey's chest.

Ramsey reached up to unpin the badge, but Aldridge said hastily, "No need for that, Mr. Ramsey. We'll see to Marshal Burch straight off. But I have just one more question."

"Yes?" Ramsey asked, straining to keep his temper in check.

"You think Roberts and his men will come riding down on Plentiful any time soon?"

"No, sir. It'll take him some time to get his horses gathered for one thing. And"—Ramsey grinned maliciously, making Aldridge squirm just a bit—"I reckon he'll set and lick his wounds a spell before he comes on us again."

"Very well, Mr. Ramsey," Aldridge said in bloated self-importance. "You may leave." He tried to ignore Ramsey's arched eyebrows. "But I'll want you to see me in my office first thing tomorrow morning."

Ramsey shoved past the mayor without another word. An irritated Tucker moved in his wake, and she cast a withering glance at the town officials. When they reached their animals, Ramsey said, "I'll escort you home, Miss Sally, if that would suit you."

She nodded and smiled. "That would be very nice, Mr. Ramsey."

Ramsey pulled himself up on the mule and Tucker—self-consciously, now—climbed into the saddle of Burch's horse. "Which way, ma'am?" Ramsey asked.

"Hill Street."

They set off up Center Street, turning west at Hill Street. Not far down, just past Sagauche Street, was a small frame house, its exterior painted white with green trim. It was a pretty little house, well suited to Tucker, Ramsey thought. Up close, the paint was peeling and some repairs were needed, but it looked comfortable nonetheless.

"What do I do with Marshal Burch's horse?" Tucker asked as she and Ramsey stopped in front of the small picket fence.

"I'll take him to the livery with Sunshine. If you'll be needin' a horse, I reckon you can lay claim to that pinto later."

"We'll see." The weariness nearly overcame Tucker as she slid down the side of the horse. Ramsey reached over and steadied her. She glanced up and smiled gratefully.

"You'll be all right here?" he asked, concerned.

"Yes," she nodded, with a sigh. "I'm sure some friends will come by to help me. How about you?"

"I'll be fine," he said with a tight smile.

Tucker believed him. He could do anything, she supposed. He

was quite some man. She took a step toward the house, then stopped and turned back. "I really am thankful for all you've done for me, Mr. Ramsey—Kyle. I'll be obliged the rest of my life."

He nodded as he wrapped the reins of Burch's horse around his own saddle horn. "Well, good day, ma'am," he said, turning the mule. He had not shown it, but he was quite happy.

Damn, I ain't ever been this wet, he grumbled to himself as he rode slowly toward Port's Livery. A small carriage with two young, plump women in it passed him. He stopped and turned in the saddle. The carriage stopped in front of Tucker's.

"I reckon she'll be all right, eh, Sunshine," he said, spirits lifting. He edged the mule on.

CHAPTER

⋆ 13 ⋆

After he had dropped the mule and the horse over at the livery stable, he took the shotgun back to Dodge Carver.

"Have much call for it?" Carver asked.

"Nope, but I was some glad I had it with me."

Carver nodded. "You best get off and get some sleep, Kyle."

"Yeah." He walked up Center Street to Scheibel's Restaurant. He ignored the stares that followed him into the place and stayed on him as he sat, ordered, and ate. And eat he did: two steaks so large they overhung the plate, several helpings of boiled potatoes, two bowls of spicy beans, a pan of biscuits coated in butter, three ears of corn, a pitcher of milk, and half a dozen cups of coffee.

"You want some pie?" Mother Scheibel asked, unfazed. She was used to big-eating men.

"What do you have?"

"Cherry cobbler or peach. And brown betty."

"Cherry cobbler sounds fine," Ramsey said. As he waited, he rubbed his hand over his face, trying to drain away some of the weariness. He polished off the cobbler, paid, and walked straight to his room. He had thought of stopping at Webb's Mercantile, but he decided it could wait till morning.

Unstrapping his gunbelt, he dropped it on the floor. He peeled off his still-sopping clothes and dropped them in a heap. Naked, he crawled among the covers. He was asleep before his head was fully down on the pillow.

He felt well rested when he finally awoke. The sun was trying to break through the clouds outside his window, and that helped cheer him. He checked his pocket watch: nine-thirty. He wasn't used to sleeping till such late hours.

He checked his ribs, where the outlaw had winged him. The shallow canal was already scabbing over. It would cause him little trouble.

With distaste, he put on his soiled, damp clothes. He had planned on having breakfast before getting his shave and bath, but he decided against that. Instead, he strolled to Tice Webb's store, where he picked out new pants, two shirts, a hat, and duster. "How much is all that, Tice?" he asked.

"Nothin'," Webb said curtly.

"What?" Ramsey asked, surprised. He thought that perhaps he was not as awake as he had thought.

"I said you don't owe nothin'."

"I ain't of a humor to joke, Tice," he snapped.

"It's no joke, Kyle. Let's just say it's a little payback for all you've done of late against Roberts and his owlhoots."

"I ain't done much."

"Like hell." He paused a moment, whirling his eyes and awaiting the tongue lashing from his wife. To his surprise—and Ramsey's—it never came. Abby Webb's face flushed, but she held her tongue. "You helped me take care of those three in here that one time. Then you killed that one out in the street and wounded one bad enough that like as not he'll die, too, from what I heard. I also heard you took care of several others at their hideout."

"Just one," Ramsey said wearily. "John and Royal got three more." He was tired by all this talk of killing. It was as though some of these people thought it was all a game.

"Don't matter. You're the first one from town who's ever had the gall to go out after those men. So these here things are on the house."

Not wanting to argue anymore, Ramsey nodded. "I'm obliged, Tice. Just put 'em in a box. I ain't goin' far."

Webb hurriedly stuffed the clothes into a box, then put a piece of thick brown paper over it. "Just in case," he said. "I see the sun's tryin' to come out, but I've seen a few raindrops yet this mornin'.''

Ramsey nodded his thanks and left, heading straight for Doc Bedloe's. The medical man was not in the barber shop, so Ramsey climbed the stairs on the side and knocked on the door.

"Come on in," Bedloe's strong voice shouted.

Ramsey did so. Bedloe was sitting at a small, cluttered roll-top desk, eating a plate of eggs and ham. "Ah," he said with a smile, "Mr. Ramsey."

"Where's John?" Ramsey asked, worried.

"Room in back. Have a seat."

Ramsey sat, placing the box on the floor at his feet. "He gonna be all right?"

"I expect so," Bedloe said, shoveling a dripping forkful of eggs into his mouth. "He's one tough son of a bitch."

"That's a fact. But I've seen men gut-shot before. It usually don't bode well for 'em.''

"Fortunately," Bedloe said, not pausing in his eating, "it didn't hit anything major inside. Just missed his heart and several other organs. The worst of it was all the blood he lost. That was what almost killed him. He was out there much longer, we'd be planting him alongside Marshal Burch."

"Can I see him?"

"He's still unconscious. Most likely will be for some time."

Ramsey nodded. "You get the bullet out of him?"

"Sure. Took some doing, but I managed. Good thing Harry was here. I don't think I could've done it by myself."

"I was gonna try gettin' it out while we were out there, but I reckoned it wouldn't be wise."

"That decision *was* wise."

"You gonna be able to give me a shave, Doc?"

"Sure."

"You're not too busy?"

"No. Soon's I finish off this last piece of biscuit here." He spooned on a healthy portion of honey and shoved the biscuit into his mouth. He chewed slowly, looking pleased. "All right, Mr. Ramsey," he said, standing up. "Let's go. I suppose you want a bath, too?"

"Yep," Ramsey said emphatically.

Bedloe nodded. Downstairs, he called his maid and told her to fill a tub. Ramsey gave the woman the box of clothes to take into the back room and then sat in the chair. Twenty minutes later he was soaking in a copper tub full of hot water. He almost fell asleep, so pleasant it was. But finally he scrubbed himself vigorously.

After drying off on thick, rough towels, he dressed in his new clothes, enjoying it immensely. Then he went over to Scheibel's again and filled himself up good on eggs, bacon, and fresh bread. Finished, he looked at his watch: a few minutes before noon. *Reckon I ought to go see the mayor,* he thought.

Without enthusiasm, he strolled up the street, greeting people and looking in windows. Finally he reached Town Hall and entered. He knocked on Mayor Aldridge's open door.

"Come in, Mr. Ramsey," an obviously agitated Aldridge said. "Take a seat." He proffered a chair directly in front of his desk, between Councilmen Antoine Devreaux and Willy Kreuger. It would place Ramsey's back toward the open door.

Ramsey dragged the chair over to a side wall and sat, oblivious to the hard feelings the three officials were beginning to harbor toward him. "That's better," he said with pleasure.

"Quite," Aldridge mumbled. "Cigar, Mr. Ramsey?" he asked aloud.

"Don't mind if I do." He stood up, took the cigar, bit off an end, and then nodded his thanks as Aldridge held a match for him. Ramsey sat back down, puffing in contentment. Maybe life wasn't all bad, he thought.

"Well, Mr. Ramsey," Devreaux said as Aldridge lighted his own cigar, "tell us about your excursion."

"Told you boys all there was yesterday."

"Oh, come, Mr. Ramsey," Aldridge said. "Surely you're too modest. There must be more that you didn't tell."

"Nope." Ramsey blew smoke in the mayor's general direction.

"Are you going to continue to be this uncooperative, Mr. Ramsey?" Kreuger asked.

"I ain't bein' uncooperative," Ramsey said easily, but his tone had chilled minutely. "You boys asked what went on. I told you yesterday. There ain't no more to tell."

"How many outlaws were killed, Mr. Ramsey?" Aldridge asked.

"Three. No, four."

"And how many are still alive?"

"A bunch."

"God damn it, that's not very helpful," Kreuger erupted. "We really must have your cooperation, Mr. Ramsey."

"Any of you fools accuses me of bein' uncooperative one more time and I'll shoot him." His face let them know he was telling the truth. They seemed suitably impressed, so he shrugged and said, "I didn't have a hell of a lot of time for countin' heads while I was there, Mayor. You want, I'll ride back on out there and tell Roberts you was askin', though."

The other three men were stone faced. "Look, Mayor," Ramsey said, not quite contritely, "I didn't even know how many of those bastards there were before all this started. I've heard ten, a dozen, twenty, a hundred. Hell, any of 'em could be right. We got there, and Royal and John laid down a coverin' fire for me. I snuck into this cabin they had and spirited Miss Tucker away. All the while, there was firin' goin' on, and the outlaws was hidin' behind any cover they could find."

He stopped and puffed a few minutes. "I saw four dead. I saw at least half a dozen alive after that. But there might've been two dozen more hidin' out."

Aldridge nodded, accepting the information. "You said yesterday that you didn't think they'd be back soon. Why?"

"The horses, for one thing. But I reckon we've put a dent in their numbers. And figurin' eight, maybe nine—if that one I wounded the other day dies—have been rubbed out in the past couple weeks, they're gonna want to recruit, if they can.

"I also figure they've got at least a couple wounded. I can't say that for certain, but it'd seem likely. If that's true, they'll need time to mend."

"Do you think they'll be back some time, Kyle?" Aldridge asked. "May I call you 'Kyle'?"

"You may." He paused, staring at the burning end of the cigar for some moments. He sighed. "You can bet your ass they'll be back. While I don't know Roberts personally, everything I've heard about the man shows he ain't one to take such a thing lyin' down. He'll be back, yes, sir."

"How long do you think we have, Mr. Ramsey?" Devreaux asked.

"You know as much as I do, Mr. Devreaux. Could be a couple days, could be a couple months. Depends on a lot of things."

"What do you suggest we do?"

"Well, Mayor, if I was you, I'd hire a new marshal, get a posse up, and go out there and finish the job me, Royal, and John started. Then you wouldn't have to be worryin' no more about when they'll come ridin' back through here.''

"Do you think that wise?" Kreuger asked.

"How many times has Roberts and his ilk raided Plentiful already? Three, four times? Five? Ain't a one of them was fun, was it?''

The other three shook their heads.

"You lost several people each time, right?" When he got three nods, he said, "Well, the next time they visit Plentiful is gonna be far worse than anything you've seen from them before.''

Aldridge looked thoughtful, Devreaux worried, and Kreuger like he was about to wet his pants. "What makes you say that?" Aldridge asked.

Ramsey looked at him. *He knows damn well why,* he thought. *He just wants me to spell it out for the other two.* "You really think Roberts is gonna be overcome with joy at havin' his hideout raided? By only three men? And losin' four guns to those? Not to mention that we stole back Miss Tucker, whom he kidnapped special? No, boys, I'd say Mr. Cotton Roberts is going to be powerful agitated when he pays another call on Plentiful." He sat back, smoking down the cigar.

Aldridge watched his two councilmen. Neither had the guts nor the gumption to do anything. And Kreuger probably didn't have the brains to do much else besides. *Well,* he decided, *it's time to put all my cards on the table.*

"I think I like your plan, Mr. Ramsey," he said quietly, almost amused by the startled looks the two councilmen cast in his direction.

"That's good, Mayor. Now all you got to do is find a marshal."

"But we already have one, Mr. Ramsey." He rested his palms flat on the desk and stared levelly at Ramsey. "You."

Aldridge had expected many responses to the announcement but not the burst of laughter that erupted from Ramsey. He accepted and ignored the startled gasps from Kreuger and Devreaux, but Ramsey's amusement was surprising.

"Why does that strike you so humorously, Mr. Ramsey?" Aldridge asked with a straight face.

"Because I ain't no lawman," he chortled.

"Yes, you are, sir," Aldridge said, pointing.

Ramsey looked down in some horror at the damning evidence shining on the left breast of his new red shirt. "Damn," he muttered, all the humor fleeing.

CHAPTER

★ 14 ★

Ramsey reached for the badge to unpin it.

"Before you do that, Mr. Ramsey," Mayor Aldridge said, "you had better know that I do not aim to accept your resignation. You are the marshal of Plentiful now, whether you like it or not." His face was set in determination. The two other town officials sat quietly, dumbfounded.

"Like hell, Mayor," Ramsey said with a sneer. But he dropped his hand, for the moment at least.

Aldridge ran a hand over his face, as if to wipe away the heaviness of his duties. It showed him to be human after all, Ramsey thought. "Mr. Ramsey," Aldridge said wearily, the frustration showing, "you are a legal deputy. Not just for the term of a posse but as long as we want. Or until you get . . ." He paused. "Part of your job is to take over for the marshal when he is incapable of performing his duties. I do not think Marshal Burch is in any position to continue his duties." He cast a dark look at Kreuger, who twittered in humor at the reference.

"You are plumb *loco*, Mayor," Ramsey said heatedly.

"Am I?"

"God damn right. What in hell makes you think you can force

me into this? How are you gonna stop me from ridin' out of here five minutes from now?''

"I can't," Aldridge said simply. "Other than to appeal to your better nature." He almost grinned. "You are, I would figure, a man of your word, Mr. Ramsey. As far as I'm concerned, you gave your word to fulfill all the duties of town marshal for as long as needed when you took that oath.''

Ramsey sat stewing. He *was* a man of his word. All the Ramseys were. They were prideful folk, the Ramseys. And part of that pride stemmed from their willingness to live up to what they said they would do. To back out, especially for no good reason, would leave him feeling less than a man—or less than a Ramsey, which was worse.

"I've done more than my share already," he said without much conviction. "I'm the only one who volunteered to go with Royal and John after that pack of coyotes. All your wonderful citizens, who've lived here since the beginning, refused. Even you have not shown the courage to do what's needed."

Aldridge was cut by the remark, and it showed. Ramsey felt a twinge of pleasure at the mayor's discomfit.

"I have duties that keep me here, Mr. Ramsey," Aldridge said haltingly. "I . . . am . . .''

"Hell, you're young, strong, and, I would think, able.''

"What's that supposed to mean?" he asked, heat flushing his face.

"It means, God damn it," Ramsey said, letting his anger gain the upper hand, "that you got all your parts." He shifted the stump of a left arm, that ended just above where the elbow should have been. It was not an obvious gesture, but Aldridge caught the meaning. "Unless," Ramsey added, stabbing at Aldridge, "you're missing your spine—or somethin' else that makes a man.''

Devreaux gasped, then chuckled. Kreuger stifled a giggle. Aldridge looked pasty, and he could not speak because of the lump of anger that lodged in his throat. Time ticked slowly by as the mayor tried to come up with a retort. "Had I joined the posse after the Roberts gang, there would have been no one left to watch over the town," he finally said lamely.

"Bullshit," Ramsey said without mercy. "You're a coward, just like everybody else in this Godforsaken town. You prefer to sit back on your lazy ass while an old man, an overweight county sheriff—who's stationed himself here just to watch over you fools—and a one-armed drifter try to protect you. Christ, you ought to be ashamed of yourself." Hate, anger, and frustration dripped from every word.

"I been here only a few months is all. I got no ties here, no family, nothing to keep me here. Except this God damn badge," he added, tapping the piece of tin. "And you want me to take over as marshal? Shit!"

Aldridge threw off the shame he felt and asked sharply, trying to turn the tables, "You have something else worthwhile to do with your life, Mr. Ramsey? Or is it your way to run when times get hard? I was given to understand that Texans were a breed apart—tough, strong and independent, not given over to fleeing whenever danger rears its ugly head."

God damn, he's got you there, Kyle, Ramsey thought. He had always been filled with the Ramsey pride, but that had, somehow, faded a little over the years since he'd returned from the Civil War minus an arm and much of his self-esteem. He had faced the tests thrown at him for some time, when he had helped his brother Matt and some others around New Liberty rid the area of the shameful tyranny of Colonel Court Shelton and his son, Gus. But then, when life had turned hard for him in the depression years after the war, he *had* run. He had not called it that at the time. But he knew now that's what it was. He had packed up and left "to find his fortune" in the gold fields of Colorado, but he had just been trying to escape the depression and fear that had become his second nature.

But even that had not worked out. He had panned and found a little gold. He had met Cherokee Lil, a half-black, half-Cherokee prostitute, and set up house with her in a shack along the creek where he panned. But she had been killed, and once again he'd run, unable to face life in the shack without Lil.

He had come to Plentiful. When he had first looked it over, it seemed a town he thought might be a nice place in which to live. But here came trouble dogging his trail again, and he was set to run, to leave it to others, using the excuse of having no ties here.

Ramsey was disgusted with himself. Partly because he saw himself as wanting to run from danger. But there was something else, too. He knew he was being suckered into helping the town by Aldridge. He wanted to help these people, though they were not willing to help themselves. But because he was being trapped into it, he felt a profound sense of displeasure.

Despite his depressing thoughts of having run from adversity much of the past several years, he knew deep down that he was not really that way. He did not run until whatever danger he had faced was taken care of. He would always stay to help people who needed him. It was inborn in him to help those less fortunate or those oppressed. As it was with all the Ramseys.

"Can you guarantee finding enough people for a good posse?" he asked, cursing himself silently.

"I'd like to tell you yes, Mr. Ramsey," Aldridge said, breathing a little easier. He had Ramsey now, he thought, and had deflected the unfavorable comments away from himself. "But I cannot. You have lived here long enough to know the minds of the people of Plentiful."

"You expect me to take care of this by myself?"

Aldridge shrugged. "If you can gather up a posse, all the better," the mayor said smoothly. "If you can't, you can deputize however many men you can find for the job." He held up his hands, palms upward, to signify that he was helpless to do more.

"How about you, Mayor?" Ramsey asked with a smirk. "Care to become a deputy?"

"Afraid not, Mr. Ramsey," he said blandly. "I am the mayor, after all. It would be most unseemly for me to be working for a man I have hired."

Aldridge reached into a drawer of the desk and pulled out a badge. He placed it on the almost empty desktop and then pushed it along in Ramsey's direction with one finger. He sat back, steepling his fingers under his chin, and waited. Finally he said, "Well Mr. . . . er, Marshal Ramsey?"

Why do I get myself into these situations? Ramsey thought, no longer disgusted with himself. Now he was angry at himself. He tried to tell himself he would be a fool for doing this, but it was not working. He reached up and, with some difficulty, unpinned the deputy marshal's badge. He tossed it halfway across the desk.

Aldridge waited, his serene face not betraying the worry he had inside—worry that this one-armed warrior would not accept the position.

Then Ramsey stood up. He reached out and picked up the silver star. He pinned it onto his new shirt.

Aldridge let out a silent sigh of relief. He beamed a broad smile and stood up, holding out his hand. "Welcome aboard, Marshal Ramsey."

Ramsey glanced from Aldridge to Kreuger to Devreaux, then back to Aldridge. "Yeah," he growled, sweeping out of the room and ignoring the mayor's outstretched hand. "God damn fool," he muttered as he stepped outside into the sunshine.

Thinking everyone's eyes were on him, he walked to the marshal's office several doors south of Town Hall. Inside, he took inventory of what was there, checking weapons and ammunition, looking over wanted posters, testing out keys, and more. By mid-afternoon, tired of being cooped up any longer, he went out and wandered through the town, stoically accepting the congratulations of the people he met.

Almost without thinking, he found himself walking up Hill Street and stopping in front of the tidy little white house with the green trim and the white picket fence out front. "You're gonna make a God damn fool of yourself again," he warned himself quietly as he opened the gate to the picket fence and walked toward the porch.

He rapped on the door and stood waiting patiently. He saw the curtains over the window in the door part and a violet eye peer out. He snatched off his hat as Sally Tucker opened the door and smiled brilliantly at him.

"I come to see if you was all right," he said, his voice sounding like his mouth was full of rocks.

"Won't you come in, Mr. Ramsey." She opened the door wider.

"Do you think that's proper?" he asked, looking around.

"I reckon it'll be all right. People will talk anyway. Especially about me after what happened." Her eyes clouded momentarily at the memory, then perked up again.

"All right, Miss Sally."

As he moved in, she saw the silver badge. "Marshal?" she said, a combination of excitement and fear caught up in her voice.

"Yes, ma'am," he said ruefully.

"When?"

"This mornin'. That God damn . . . Oops, pardon, ma'am. Mayor Aldridge talked me into it. But I'll say, I sure as he . . . *heck* don't know why I accepted it."

"You'll do well at it, Mr. Ramsey." She touched the badge with a slim forefinger. "I know you will."

They went into Tucker's small sitting room, comfortably furnished with a divan, several plush sitting chairs, large oval rug, a number of small tables, coal-oil lanterns on the walls, and pictures on one table. Ramsey picked up one photograph in a gilded gold frame. A handsome young man stared back at him.

"Mr. Tucker," Sally said, a soft catch in her voice.

Ramsey nodded and set the photograph back on the table. He sat down when invited by Tucker to do so. "Coffee?" she asked.

"That would be nice, ma'am," Ramsey said. He was ill at ease and beginning to regret having come.

Tucker was not gone long. When she returned, she carried a small silver tray on which sat a tea pot, a mug of hot, black coffee, and empty cup on a saucer, a small pitcher of milk, a bowl of sugar, and two spoons.

Ramsey rested his hat on his knee and poured some sugar into his coffee. He sipped it while Tucker fixed her tea. When she was done, Ramsey asked, "Well, Miss Sally, I did come to find out how you were doin'."

"Personal interest?" she asked with a sweet, disarming smile. "Or part of your job?"

"Both," he admitted, staring at her.

"I'm just fine, Marshal." She almost giggled. "That sounds so . . . strange," she finally said.

"Feels strange, too," he said with a grin. "You sure you're all right?"

"Yes, sir."

"Can you tell me," he said, stopping to clear his throat midway through, "what happened?"

She stared at him a minute, wondering if this were personal or part of the job. She decided that this, too, was both but that he would have to know either way anyway. "Nothing much happened, really," she said in a small voice.

Tucker stopped to sip her tea, then said, "I was in the bank when two men burst in waving their guns around." She looked pensive. "You know," she said in realization, "now that I think of it, they must have been looking specially for me. They came straight for me, ignoring the bank tellers and the other customers. Then they dragged me outside and tossed me on a horse with another man. I was struggling, and the man on the horse—I learned later it was Simon Waddey, who's apparently second in command to Roberts—hit me on the head with something. Roberts and Waddey had words over that later.

"I was stunned from being hit and don't remember much for a long while except for being so uncomfortable on that long ride."

She finished her tea and set her cup down softly. "I was still stunned when we got to their camp, though I was a little more aware of things. They tied me up to that cot," she said with a shudder. "Then they left me alone except to bring me food several times."

"No one bother you?"

"Not really. Roberts came in a few times and talked to me."

"What about?" Ramsey questioned.

"I'd rather not say," Tucker said, her pretty face coloring. "It was nothing that concerns anyone but me. He just told me he . . . how he . . . wanted me . . . and what he was going to . . . to do . . . to me." She looked small and frightened.

"You don't need to say no more about it," Ramsey said soothingly. "But did he ever say anything about what he was going to do, not concernin' you?"

"No," Tucker said, regaining her composure. "Nothing."

Ramsey nodded and set his cup on the table. "Well then, I'll take my leave, Miss Sally." He stood up, clapping on his hat.

Tucker smiled and got up. She went first, and she opened the door and held it for him.

"Well, good day, Miss Sally," Ramsey said.

"Good day, Marshal Ramsey." As he stepped outside, she said, "Mr. Ramsey?"

When he turned, she licked her lips nervously and said, "Yes."

"Yes?" Ramsey repeated, puzzled.

She swallowed, afraid she was making a mistake. "Not so long ago," she said, her voice small and worried, "you asked me to dinner. I never did give you an answer, you'll recall. So I just did."

Ramsey thought for a moment. She had never given him an answer, it was true. Not vocally, anyway. His spirits soared. "It'd be my pleasure, ma'am. When?"

"You may pick me up at seven tonight." She was almost giddy with excitement.

"I'll do so, Miss Sally." He smiled.

CHAPTER

★ 15 ★

"I reckon I'll not be workin' for you no more, Dodge," Ramsey said to the gunsmith. "Leastways not for a spell." They were in the Lone Star Saloon, sitting at a table. Ramsey tried to ignore the other men who began gathering around.

"I understand, Kyle," Carver said. "It's sort of a shame, though. You were a good worker, and I'll miss your abilities at the shop. Still, we need a good marshal. Not that Royal Burch was a bad man, you understand," he added hastily, "but he did have his faults." He knew he was speaking for everyone who had come around the table, but he was still not comfortable in the role of spokesman that had been thrust upon him.

"Only fault he had was the people he worked for," Ramsey said roughly.

"What?" Carver asked, surprised. The crowd of perhaps two dozen men, a goodly portion of them already well oiled with red eye, began to grumble.

"All I've heard for the day I been marshal is how sorry everyone is that poor ol' Marshal Burch bit the dust."

"Well, we are," someone behind Ramsey said.

"That might be so," Ramsey said to the voice, though he was

looking straight at Carver. "Maybe you all are sorry. But if you boys had any gumption, you could have prevented it."

"Like hell!" someone shouted behind Ramsey, and the marshal felt a little unease. He shifted and slid his hand down to free the strap holding the LeMat into its holster.

"How many times did he call for a posse?" Ramsey asked in anger. "And how many of you chicken-hearted bastards offered to go with him after those outlaws? Don't give me no bullshit about bein' sorry Burch is dead and buried."

He let the rumbling die down before he said, "Now I'm callin' for a posse. Me, Burch, and Sheriff Starkey put a dent in Roberts's boys the other day. He's reelin' from that. But he'll be back here sooner or later to extract some revenge. We get a group of men up and go on out there and finish them off, ain't nobody in Plentiful will have to worry about revenge. Now, how about it? Who'll join me?"

As he expected, the men started drifting away, silent and suddenly fearful. But knowing it was going to happen didn't make it any easier for Ramsey to swallow. "How about you, Dodge?" he asked, without hope. Carver, sitting across the small table from him, was the only one left to ask.

Carver squirmed under the harsh gaze of the marshal. "You know I can't do that, Kyle," he whined. "I . . . my wife . . ."

"Chicken-hearted son of a bitch," Ramsey growled, shoving up so hard that the chair crashed to the wooden floor. He stomped out from under the glare of dozens of eyes, trying to regain his temper.

He stopped outside, blinking in the burning sunshine. *You got to stop gettin' so angry over this, Kyle,* he told himself. *You know these people are gonna act this way.*

With a sigh, he headed to Doc Bedloe's office. "How's the sheriff, Doc?" he asked when he entered the barber shop on the first floor.

"Improving. You can't expect too much in so short a time, Mr.—damn, forgot again—Marshal Ramsey."

"Just want to make sure he's gettin' the best care you can give him."

"He is."

"You sure?"

"Yes, God damn it. Now get out of here. I have customers waiting." He looked surly, but that was just the physician's way.

Ramsey grinned. "You've said he'll live, Doc," he said seriously, "and I aim to keep you to that promise."

"Yes, yes, now go on, get."

Ramsey went back out and, in blinking to adjust to the sunshine, almost walked straight into Joshua Cord. "Sorry, Mr. Cord," Ramsey said.

The black looked at him strangely a moment before saying, "My fault, Marshal."

"Like hell. I should've been watchin' where I was going."

Cord stared at him unabashed a moment, then said, "You be an uncommon man, Marshal Ramsey."

"Why do you say that, Mr. Cord?"

"It ain't many white folks act cordial to a man with black skin. 'Specially Southern white folks."

"I got nothin' against people with black skin, Mr. Cord. Never had."

"Most white folks do," Cord said evenly. "You fought in the war, didn't you?"

"Yep."

"I reckon," Cord said, almost grinning, "for the Confederacy?"

"Yep."

"And yet you treat me with mo' respect than nearabout anybody in this town, includin' Yankees. Why's that?"

While Ramsey had thought about the reasons for joining the war on the Southern side, he had never tried to articulate them. This put him on the spot. "Me and my family never had much truck with slavery, Mr. Cord," he said seriously. "Not a one of us could understand why one people should treat another people in such a way just 'cause o' the color of their skin. It just don't make sense.

"But we Texans—and my Scottish ancestors—don't take much to bein' given orders, neither. Not by people and not by governments. Me and my brother Matt joined the Southern cause not 'cause we wanted to keep slavery alive but to keep the North— and its government—from imposin' its will on us. I reckon that's about the best explanation I can give."

The tall, muscular black man gazed deeply into Ramsey's eyes. "I ain't sho' that's the best reason I ever heard of, Marshal. But it beats hell outten most others I heard. And, dumb as it might be, I believe you."

"That's good you do, Mr. Cord," Ramsey said without rancor. "I ain't given much to words and speechifyin'. It's hard for me to tell things that are on my mind, and I was afraid I might not make sense to you."

"You make good sense, Marshal." Cord grinned.

"You mind if I ask you somethin', Mr. Cord?"

"Go on."

"You're a big, strappin' young man. And you don't look like you carry much fear in you. Why didn't you ever join one of the posses Sheriff Starkey or Marshal Burch tried gettin' together to chase after Cotton Roberts?"

Cord laughed, a deep rumbling sound reminiscent of thunder. "Hell, Marshal, that don't be none of my fight. Hell no."

"You don't think they'd accept you because you're black, Mr. Cord?"

"Sho' they'd take me," he laughed. "They'd think it powerful good to have a black man be goin' out to get hisself killed to protect a bunch of white folk."

"I see your point. I don't suppose," Ramsey asked, squinting through the sunlight at Cord, "you'd change your mind and go with me, would you, Mr. Cord?"

"Ain't likely, Marshal. I like you an' all, and you've treated me well, but it still ain't my fight."

"I wish you'd change your mind, Mr. Cord," Ramsey said quietly.

"Soon's the rest of these folks start treatin' me like I'm one of them, rather than *belongin'* to 'em, I might change my thinkin'."

"I reckon," Ramsey said with a sad grin, "that hell'll be colder'n a mountain winter before we see that, eh?"

"I reckon." Cord considered, briefly, helping this unbigoted, one-armed Texan, but he decided against it.

"I understand," Ramsey said. "Well, good day to you, Mr. Cord."

He stepped around Joshua but turned back as Cord said quietly, "I ever do be changin' my mind, Marshal, it'll be because of you."

Ramsey nodded and strolled toward his office. He sat in the dim interior, thankful for its slightly cooler temperatures. He had been marshal officially just over twenty-four hours, since just after noon the day before. But he had accomplished nothing.

Well, something, he thought with a grin. He had made some

headway with Miss Sally Tucker. Their dinner the night before, in Cordelle's Restaurant—a much fancier place than Scheibel's—was one of the finest times he had ever had.

Tucker had worn her fanciest dress. It was red satin and cut alarmingly low over her back and her small but obvious bosom. A locket had dangled from a silver chain around her neck, nestled in her cleavage. A hat and bag had matched her dress. Her hair had been curled in long ringlets, and there'd been a hint of some alluring perfume wafting about her.

Ramsey had been left speechless for several minutes. After that he had been only semiarticulate in telling her how good she looked. She had beamed brightly nonetheless. They had walked slowly down Hill Street toward Center. Self-consciously at first, Tucker had held Ramsey's left bicep, leaving his gun arm free.

He had thought it a little strange too but accepted it. By the time they had arrived at the restaurant, both were no longer shy about it. They had eaten baked chicken, potatoes, and crisp carrots and had dawdled over blueberry pie and coffee.

They had walked silently back to Tucker's house after the dinner. There was nothing that needed to be said; they had just enjoyed each other's company. They had stopped just inside the gate. "I had a wonderful time, Kyle," Tucker had said.

By the glow from Tucker's cheeks and eyes, Ramsey figured she had been telling the truth. He knew he was when he'd said, "I did, too." He had swallowed, then said, "I'd like to do this again."

"So would I."

"Tomorrow?" he had asked hopefully.

"Yes," she had breathed softly. Her lips had been slightly parted, more than by just her little overbite, as if expectantly.

Ramsey was uncertain, but he had thought she wanted him to kiss her. He had bent and done so. She had responded willingly, but only briefly.

"No more, Kyle," she had whispered. She'd been warmed inside, with a feeling she had not known since her husband had died. It was wonderful but at the same time disconcerting.

"Yes, ma'am," he had said. He had stood watching as she turned and headed toward the house. She had lifted up her skirt and petticoats to go up the stairs, and he thought she had lifted them a little higher than was needed. He grinned when he realized she had done it purposefully, to entice him and keep him interested.

But, he thought, sitting in his office, that was about all he had accomplished. Come to think of it, though, he said in his mind, that was a pretty good accomplishment. He smiled.

Still, it did nothing to resolve the situation that hung over the town like a storm cloud. He had talked to everyone he could think of who might be able—and willing—to ride back to Lost Canyon and rid the area of the Cotton Roberts gang. And he had, of course, gotten no acceptances.

Well, he told himself sternly, *you better think of something real soon.*

He leaned back and crossed his ankles upon the desk. There was also the problem Burch had brought up of there being a contact for the gang inside the town. Ramsey had tried making some discrete inquiries around town, but that had gotten him nowhere.

Maybe Burch was wrong, he thought. But he discarded that notion. It made too much sense. But who was it? He wracked his brain. It could be almost anyone, he knew, but it most likely was someone with some stature and importance in Plentiful.

Mayor Aldridge, he wondered. The mayor was pompous and filled with self-importance. But Ramsey did not think him likely. The two other town council members? No, he decided. Devreaux was the owner of the Cloverleaf Saloon. He also owned Miss Prudence's bordello, but people weren't supposed to know that. One of his brothers had been killed in an early raid by the gang, so that probably let him out. And Kreuger was too stupid to have such a secretive role.

He could also rule out Tice Webb and Abel Jackson and a number of others. But that still left him with a list of scores of people who could possibly be the person he sought, including—though not likely—Dodge Carver and the gambler, Alabama.

Ramsey pulled his hat down over his eyes. It was all too much for him to think about anymore. He took a nap.

Darkness was hovering over Plentiful when he awoke and rubbed the tiredness from his face. He lit a coal-oil lantern on the wall, and checked his pocket watch. Six-oh-five. He still had some time yet. He poured some thick coffee from the ever-present pot on the small pot-bellied stove into his mug and sat back down.

He was halfway through the cup of coffee when the answer hit him: If he could find no one here to help him, he would have to go outside for help. And who better to call on than family?

He stood up and walked to the open window. He poured out

the remains of his coffee from his cup. Setting the tin mug on his desk, he went into the back, where a small mirror hung from the wall. It provided a poor reflection, but it would do.

Ramsey slicked down his hair with lime water. As he headed for the door—and his dinner with Sally Tucker—he smiled. Maybe things would work out, he thought.

CHAPTER
⋆ 16 ⋆

Sally Tucker looked stricken. He was leaving her, going away for good. And she could not understand why. She had done all she could do for him, except . . . *No!* she thought, *I can't do that!*

"I'll be back," Ramsey said, almost plaintively. He did not want to hurt Tucker, but he was getting angry that she was not listening to him.

They had gone to Cordelle's again and enjoyed another sumptuous dinner. She was as well dressed as before, with a low-cut dress of wine red, covered with pink lace. It was provocative yet still demure, making him think he had seen more than he really had.

It had kept his mind on the woman and not on the other problems that were plaguing him. But he had made up his mind on what he had to do and he was going to go ahead with it. He could not put it off, so he had decided to tell her on the way home.

He had stalled until they were standing at her fence again. Then he'd said, "I'll be goin' off for a few days, Sally. There's some things need doin'."

That's when the stricken look crossed her face, and he cursed himself silently.

"I'll be back," he told her earnestly. "I'll only be gone a few days."

She was not listening to him—or, if she was, she was not hearing what he had to say. Looking at her pale, delicate face, now looking pained, he thought he knew what was bothering her so much.

"I ain't goin' after Roberts and all his men by myself, Sally," he said reassuringly.

"What?" she mumbled, trying to bring her mind back to the matter at hand.

He repeated himself.

Tucker stood there, shaking her head and trying to figure out what he was talking about. Then it became clear. "Oh, ah," she mumbled, "you think I thought . . ."

"Well, didn't you?" he was confused.

"No."

"But . . ."

"I figure you're smarter than to do something that foolish," she said, touching his cheek.

"Then what . . ."

She sighed, fighting to hold back the flash flood of tears that welled up behind her eyelids. "I know you want to be shed of me," she said, her lower lip beginning to tremble. "And that's all right." It wasn't. Not really. But she couldn't tell that to him. "So if that's what you want, just tell me. I'll understand. You don't have to desert the town just because . . . because . . ." The dam broke, and the tears splashed down her comely cheeks.

"What in hell are you talkin' about?" he asked, exasperated. There was something going on here that he was unaware of, and it frustrated him.

"You," she blubbered, "you . . . you're leaving . . . You don't want . . . want . . . me?" Her shoulders shook with the sobbing.

"Where'd you ever get such a damnfool notion?" he asked, still befuddled.

"Ain't that why you're really leaving town?" she mumbled, pulling a cotton hankie from her purse and dabbing at her eyes.

"Why would I do that?" he said, surprised.

"But . . ."

"I've got business to take care of down in Sagauche is all. I can be down there in a day and a half—maybe a day, if I push Sunshine along some."

"What're you going to do down there?" she asked, suspicious. Her tears had stopped, and she indelicately blew her nose.

"Take care of some business. I told you that."

"What business?"

"I can't tell you," he answered stiffly.

"You got another woman there?" Tucker demanded, anger overriding her sadness.

"No! It's official business. I'm goin' down there as a marshal. But I can't tell you what it is. Like I told you, I won't be gone long. Just a few days."

"You promise?"

"Yes, ma'am. I don't want to be there no longer than I have to."

"A few days is a long time."

"Given the right encouragement, I might move a little faster than I would usually." He smiled.

"Like this?" Tucker asked, wrapping her arms around his midsection and hugging him. She rested her left cheek against his chest.

"I think that'll do," he muttered. He stroked her back.

She pulled back just a bit. "Well, if that's incentive, maybe this will make the encouragement stronger." She reached up and pulled his head down to kiss her. She took the lead this time, her mouth devouring his.

She broke away. Laughing and gasping, she turned and ran toward the stairs. "Hurry back to me, Kyle Ramsey," she said huskily.

Ramsey nodded, unable to speak for the moment.

In the morning, he went through a similar though far less enjoyable routine with Mayor Aldridge. The official thought to argue, but Ramsey finally said, "I got business to take care of down in Sagauche. It's personal business and of no concern to you."

"But you will leave the town unprotected."

Ramsey shrugged. "Name another deputy for a while. I ain't gonna be gone more than a couple days."

"Who?"

"How the hell should I know? Maybe Abel Jackson. Joshua Cord'd make a hell of a deputy, if he could be persuaded to do it."

"A nig . . ." Ramsey's fierce stare cut him off. "I don't think the people in Plentiful would accept a black-skinned man as marshal." Aldridge sniffed.

"Just a suggestion," Ramsey said with a nasty grin. "Anyway, I don't much give a damn. I got business outside of town, and I'm gonna take care of it."

"You're the marshal," Aldridge argued. "You need to find your own deputy." He paused, then added, "Anyone but Cord, of course."

"Maybe I'll just ask Ling Su to take the job," Ramsey said with a grin. The flash of apoplexy on Aldridge's face gave Ramsey a moment's pleasure. "All right," Ramsey said seriously, "I'll ask around some. I find somebody right off, fine. I don't, I'm ridin' out in an hour."

He strode out of Town Hall and to his office. Then he crossed the street to the Lone Star Saloon. "Hey, Abel," he said in feigned jollity, "you busy?"

"Not overly so." The bartender waved a hand around. One lonely customer sat at a table. The women who worked the place were still asleep.

"Good. You are now the deputy marshal of the great town of Plentiful, Colorado Territory." He tossed the deputy marshal's badge on the bar in front of Jackson.

Jackson recoiled in horror. "Like hell!" he snorted.

"My day's already been poorer than meat off a twenty-year-old bull, Abel. I've got business in Sagauche. I'll be back in a couple, three days. I need somebody to watch over the town while I'm gone. And I'm of no humor for nonsense."

"This ain't nonsense, Kyle. I ain't takin' the job, and that's all there is to say about it."

"Yes you are."

"You gonna make me?" Jackson's eyes were amused.

"If need be."

"How?"

"It's within my rights as marshal," Ramsey said with a straight face, "to shut this place down as a public nuisance."

"Shee-it," Jackson said, breaking the word into two syllables. "You can't do that."

"Sure I can."

"Well, you won't."

"Like hell." He looked around. Ada Belle, looking sleepy, wandered in with two of the other girls. She smiled at Ramsey and then waved to him. He waved back. "This place is an affront to the public morals," Ramsey said, turning back to face Jackson. "It leads to public inebriation and the deterioration of the moral fabric of this fine, upstandin' town."

Jackson laughed. "You're lucky you didn't choke on all that gum flappin', Kyle," he said.

"Did sound high and mighty, didn't it?" Ramsey said with a grin. The smile faded. "But I'll do what I said, Abel, and use just that sort of hogwash to defend it in front of Judge Blackthorn, if called on to do so."

"I bet you would, too, God damn it," Jackson said, not at all upset. "All right," he added, picking up the badge. "But you make sure you get your ass back here *pronto*. I ain't lookin' to do this as my life's work, you know."

"Just make sure you don't abuse your authority, Abel," Ramsey said, chuckling. "I don't want you closin' down all the other saloons."

"Hey, that sounds like a hell of an idea to me, Kyle," Jackson said with a laugh.

"Just keep your nose clean while I'm gone." He pushed away from the bar.

"You are comin' back, ain't you?" Jackson asked, his eyebrows raised.

"Yep." He left. Twenty minutes later, he was in front of Tucker's house.

He knocked on the door. She answered, looking worried. "I just wanted to say good-bye, Miss Sally," he said. "And let you know I won't be gone long."

"Still got encouragement to hurry?" she asked. She smiled, but there was a sick feeling in the pit of her stomach.

"Yes, ma'am. But ain't no harm in a bit more encouragin'." He smiled his most charming smile.

She encouraged him again, almost desperately. He smiled again and then walked down the stairs. "Don't you fret none," he called over his shoulder. "I'll be back before you know it."

She waved and closed the door, her heart feeling dread.

Ramsey urged the mule on as fast as he could without harming it. He followed the road out of Plentiful to the north, past the church and the school. The road to Sagauche turned and wound roughly southeastward, following along Sagauche Creek. It was not a well-marked road, but there was little to slow him down except the hilly, rocky terrain.

He didn't stop till well past dark, knowing he had only a few more miles to go to Sagauche. He was in that town early in the morning. First he left Sunshine at the livery stable with orders to the boy working there to make sure the mule had plenty of grain and water and a good currying. Then he stopped in the first restaurant he saw and filled up on a large breakfast, not having eaten more than some jerky and hardtack since breakfast back in Plentiful the day before.

He asked the woman whose husband ran the restaurant where the wire office was. The woman pointed it out, and Ramsey walked unhurriedly there. An older man with a bald head, green eyeshade, and hooked nose greeted him.

"I want to send a wire to Matt Ramsey, in Harrison Corners, Texas."

The wire operator nodded. He licked the end of his pencil and jotted down the name and place. "Message?" he asked.

It took a little while for Ramsey to get it right, but the operator waited patiently, crossing out when necessary, for him to finish. "That all?" he finally asked.

"Reckon so," Ramsey said.

"You want to wait for an answer?" the man asked.

"Nope. And," he added pointedly, "anybody but Matt Ramsey and the operator at the other end hears anything about this wire, I'm gonna come back here and string you up from one of your telegraph poles."

"No need for such threats, mister," the man sniffed, offended. "I'm not given to runnin' around town revealin' messages."

"Didn't figure you were. Just makin' sure."

Ramsey paid him and then walked to the livery stable, where he found that Sunshine had been well cared for. He paid the youth, giving him an extra quarter for himself, and some extra for a small sack of oats. He saddled the mule and rode out of town.

He was about halfway back to Plentiful when he stopped for the night. He pulled into Plentiful just past noon the next day. He was hot, dusty, and tired of being in the saddle, but he stopped at Tucker's house first.

She had been watching for him, and she flew out the door and down the steps before he had stopped. He barely had time to dismount and turn to catch her as she barreled into him, smothering his face with kisses.

He broke away after a few minutes, laughing. "What'll your neighbors think?" he asked. She had always been quite proper, kissing him in public only at night.

"I don't care," she breathed. But she pulled back a little and straightened her dress and hair with short, choppy motions.

"Told you I'd be back quickly."

"I'm glad," she said. "I've been doing a lot of thinking while you were gone . . . about us."

"And?" he asked, rather amused.

"This ain't the place to talk about it, Kyle," she said, suddenly shy.

"All right. I got to get cleaned up and have some lunch. Do a few other things. Shall I call on you for dinner tonight?"

"Yes," she breathed. She blushed.

"See you then," he said. He pecked her on the forehead and swung up into the saddle.

She watched him riding away. When he turned the corner and was out of sight, she turned back to her house, realizing then that she had been holding her breath. She let it out in a *whoosh*. She was frightened but happy at the same time. She smiled.

CHAPTER
⋆ 17 ⋆

When he left Tucker that morning, Ramsey brought his mule down to Port's Livery. Then he went to the Lone Star. "Have any trouble, Abel?" he asked.

"None but the ribbin' I took for wearin' this damn badge from ever' man put his head through the door." He pulled the badge off and dropped it on the bar. "Here, take the damn thing. I never want to see it again."

Ramsey grinned. "Well, since you had such a good time playin' marshal," he said, "I think you owe me a beer."

"Bah," Jackson growled. He got the beer and set it down in front of Ramsey. "Hope you enjoy it," he said in feigned anger, "'cause it'll be the last free anything you get in here."

"Speak for youself, Abel," Ada Belle said, slithering up to Ramsey. "You know, the right man buys a girl a drink, he might just . . . well . . ." She left it hanging.

Ramsey grinned at her. "Get her a drink, Abel." When the bartender had moved off, Ramsey said softly, "I appreciate your offer, Ada Belle. But I reckon it ain't in the cards for you and me. At least not just now."

"Got yourself some snooty 'in-town' woman who don't need

to work for a livin', eh?'' she said, angry and depressed at the same time.

"She ain't so snooty, Ada Belle. She's a nice woman."

"Bull. Ain't no such thing." Ada really had a crusty side to her, and it was showing plainly now. "She'll dump you sure as beer goes flat overnight."

"That'd be a powerful painful thing, Ada Belle," he said honestly. "But I'll live through it, should it happen. If it does," he added, softening his face with a smile and trying to win her over, "you'll be the first one I'll come to for consolin'."

"You ain't gettin' no tender feelin's from this gal, Kyle Ramsey, so don't come 'round lookin' for some when your snow-white and pure little honey throws you over."

Jackson set down Ada's drink. She grabbed it and hurried away angrily.

"What in hell'd you say to her anyway, Kyle?" Jackson asked, bemused.

"None of your business."

"Hell, you went and told her you had your eye on that Sally Tucker, didn't you? God damn fool. You ain't gonna get nowhere with that icy princess. You should've took Ada Belle up on her offer and kept Miss Tucker for showin' around the town."

A blinding flash of anger rippled across Ramsey's eyesight, and he stood stock still until it had passed. "You got a real outhouse for a mouth, Abel, you know that! You ever talk so disrespectful about Miss Tucker—or Ada Belle, either, come to think of it— again and I'll cut your tongue out."

Jackson blanched, believing him. "I didn't mean nothin' by it, Kyle," he stammered. "Shit, I was just joshin'."

"It ain't the kind of joshin' a man should be doin'." He let the anger simmer for a while, as Jackson scuttled off to help another customer. *Come on,* he told himself, *it was only man-to-man banter. And hell, he's probably right about Sally.* He snorted at his own musings and finished off his beer. He picked up the deputy's badge and shoved it into a shirt pocket.

Jackson returned and asked tentatively, "'Nother beer, Mr. Ramsey?''

"Nah, one's enough for now, Abel. Got other things to do." He paused. He wasn't much at making apologies. "I'm obliged for you takin' over for me there while I was gone, Abel," he said lamely.

"No problem, Kyle," Jackson said, relief fluttering over him. "See you later?"

"Maybe later tonight." He headed off. He stopped at Town Hall and poked his head into Aldridge's door to tell the mayor he was back. Then he went to his office, dropped off the extra badge, and made sure everything was as it was supposed to be.

Then it was off to Doc Bedloe's for a shave, bath, and a report on Starkey's condition. "Improvin'," Bedloe said about the latter.

Ramsey stopped at Webb's store and bought new pants and a shirt. This was getting ridiculous, he thought. He hadn't bought so many clothes in God knows how long. *Well,* he told himself firmly, *the ones you're wearing are still plenty serviceable, just dirty.* He vowed to get them to Ling Su's laundry in the morning. And he was thankful for the reward Starkey had given him.

He returned to his room and stripped off his dirty garments, then took a short nap before getting dressed in his new clothes, struggling, as he always did, in pinning up his left sleeve and pulling on his pants. Mostly he no longer thought about the missing arm. But there were times like these, when he was in a hurry or wanted to do something in particular that was hard with an arm missing, that he felt his bowels clot up with disgust and self-pity.

But he managed. He left the boardinghouse and made a circuit of the town, greeting people, checking the doors of businesses that were closed, poking his head in the doors of saloons and bawdyhouses to make sure everything was all right.

Checking his watch, he realized it was time to pick up Tucker. He would have to hurry to make it on time. He did, and the door flew open before he even knocked. Tucker looked stunning, as usual, he thought. She wore a bright yellow satin dress, which exposed no cleavage, but when she turned around, Ramsey whistled. The back was quite low cut.

"Is it all right?" she asked.

"Oh, yes," he said.

She seemed to breathe a little freer knowing that. She flipped a matching yellow wrap around her shoulders, covering up her back. "Ready," she said.

She took the bicep of his left arm, and they strolled away. Ramsey thought she seemed a little anxious, but he could not fathom why.

They sat down to eat, and Ramsey noticed that more than one

set of eyes was turned on them. He figured most of the men were lusting after Tucker and that most of the women were sitting there thinking what a shameless woman she was. Tucker seemed to have relaxed, and she was amused by the stares.

Midway through the meal, a boy of about twelve came running into Cordelle's. He spotted Ramsey and hurried to the table. "My grandpa—Abel Jackson—sent me, Marshal Ramsey," he said breathlessly. "He says there's some trouble over at the Lone Star, and he'd like you to come over quick and set it straight before someone gets hurt."

"What's the trouble?" Ramsey asked, glancing briefly at Tucker in concern.

"Couple of gunslicks got drunk and are harassin' the girls."

"They causin' real trouble or just spoutin' off steam?"

The boy's thin shoulders lifted and fell in a sloppy shrug.

"All right," Ramsey nodded. "I'll follow along directly, boy. You go tell Abel that."

When the boy rushed off, Ramsey said, "Sorry, Sally, but I've got to go. You stay here. Have some pie and coffee. I'll be back before you're done."

Tucker was petrified that something bad would happen to Ramsey. But she knew this was his job and he would have to go. "All right," she whispered. "But please be careful," she added insistently.

"I will." Already his thoughts were on what might lie ahead, and he left brusquely.

Outside, he hurried. He moved quietly along the wall of the Lone Star until he was at the edge of the swinging doors. He peered around, trying to get the lay of what was happening inside.

There were two of them, dressed in dark, dirty clothes. Their faces were mean, hard-bitten, and scarred. One held Jackson's shotgun on the small crowd that was bunched up along the right-hand wall. The bar owner himself lay on the floor, blood seeping from a long gash in his forehead. The boy, looking terrified, cowered behind a chair. Ramsey figured the youngster had gone back into the Lone Star through the back door and then realized the situation had worsened and he could not get out again.

The other gunman had Ada Belle pinned up against the bar and was slobbering all over her in what to him must have seemed to be manly passion. Ada Belle took it stoically. It wasn't the first time she'd been pawed at by a drunken man.

Paddy Sullivan was crumpled in a heap not far from Jackson. Though the bar owner appeared to be breathing, the photographer was lying in a thick puddle of blood. He seemed dead.

"Just throw her skirts up and have at her, Cully," the man with Jackson's shotgun said, laughing raucously.

"I aim to take my time and have some fun here, Honus," the other said, taking a few moments to come up for air before going back to his drooling on Ada Belle's face and neck.

Ramsey took a deep breath as he slid the LeMat out and cocked it. He shoved through the door, taking aim at Honus's head. "You set that scattergun down nice and easy, Honus," he said before the squeaking of the doors could attract any attention.

"Who? What?" Honus started to turn toward the door.

"Stop there, Honus, and set that scattergun down or, by God, if you got any brains at all I'll blow 'em all over the wall. Do it. Now!"

Honus had stopped moving at the sound of Ramsey's voice. He nodded once. He bent over and lay the shotgun on the floor, then straightened.

"Good. Now face the bar. And from where you're standin' lean forward until you're restin' your weight on your arms on the bar."

Honus did as he was told.

Abel Jackson sat up, leaning back against the bar and pulling the bottom of his shirt out to hold up to his bloody forehead. Sullivan groaned and moved some.

Ramsey breathed a sigh of relief, knowing both men were alive. "All right, Cully," he said, swinging that way. "Your turn."

Cully was still half-holding, half-leaning against Ada Belle. He stared with dim eyes toward Ramsey.

"I want you to let Ada Belle go, Cully, and then step up to the bar like your partner there."

Ramsey could see in Cully's eyes that he wanted to just swing Ada Belle in front of him as a shield. Then he could gun down the marshal easily.

"Don't be a God damn fool, Cully," Ramsey said. "Ain't nobody died here yet tonight. There's no reason anyone has to."

"You ain't gonna shoot me. I got this woman in front of me," Cully snarled.

"That's true," Ramsey said reasonably. "But soon's you grab her, I'm gonna backshoot your partner here. And I'll be back outside before you can get off a shot."

"Then I'll kill the woman," Cully said almost gleefully.

"I'll be waitin' right outside the door. Soon's Ada Belle falls, I'll scatter your skull to hell and back."

"Cully, for Christ's sake, let the woman go, God damn it," Honus snapped.

Seconds dragged, and the silence was broken only by Sullivan's groaning and Cully's raspy breathing. Finally the latter grinned, a not very pleasant sight, and stepped back from Ada Belle. He held his hands up and moved arrogantly toward the bar, then leaned on it next to Honus.

Ramsey moved toward them and stood right behind Cully. "Reckon you do have some brains after all, boy," Ramsey said, shoving the LeMat away. He picked up the shotgun and eased down the hammers. "But you do have a problem with your attitude, and I ain't of a mind to worry about you tryin' to pull somethin' on me while I march you off to the calaboose."

"Don't make no account to me," Cully said half-turning, a sneer on his lips.

He got far enough around to see the butt of the shotgun heading in his direction. He could not get out of the way, and the weapon smashed into the cleft between his eyes. Cully made no sound. His eyes just rolled up, and he fell like a poleaxed steer, hitting his head on the bar as he fell.

"I gonna have any trouble with you, Honus?" Ramsey asked quietly.

"No, sir," Honus said emphatically.

"Good. You got any more weapons on you?"

Honus described the three pistols and where they were kept. Ramsey motioned to one of the customers and told him to get the weapons. "Now," he said, "a couple of you boys get Paddy and Abel here over to Doc Bedloe's. A couple other of you cart this bag of shit"—he tapped one of Cully's legs with the toe of his boot—"over to the jail."

It took a few minutes for the work details to sort themselves out, since everybody wanted to help either Sullivan or Jackson over to the doctor's rather than tote a gunslinger to jail. But soon several men shrugged and grabbed Cully.

"Y'all don't need to be none too careful the way you're carryin' him, neither," Ramsey drawled. "All right, Honus, since you're the guest of honor, you lead the way."

Honus lifted his hands up and marched out under the muzzle of Ramsey's LeMat.

At the jail, the men who were carrying Cully threw the gunman into one of the three cells. "Check him over for weapons, boys. And check good."

They did, piling the four pistols they found on Ramsey's desk next to Honus's three pistols, which another man had dropped there when they had all arrived. "Good," Ramsey said. "Now check Honus here. It's not that I don't trust you, Honus—you understand that, eh?"

Honus only nodded. There was no fear on his face, and Ramsey was relieved to see no hate, either. It was just part of life for the gunman. The men found nothing.

"Into the other cell," Ramsey said.

Honus did as he was told, and Ramsey locked the two doors. "Thank you, boys. Next time I see you in the saloon, you can have a free one on me."

The men left happily. Ramsey checked to make sure the cells were locked, then went back to the restaurant. It had all taken only twenty minutes.

Tucker's relief flashed like lightning across her face when she saw him.

"Told you I wouldn't be gone long," he said cheerily.

"Anything bad?"

He described the action quickly, then said, "Are you ready to leave?"

"Yes," she murmured, and a look of worry settled over her again, making Ramsey wonder.

Back at her gate, Ramsey apologized again for having had to leave. He kissed her, reveling in her taste.

He broke the kiss and started to leave, feeling the heat in his loins.

Tucker almost stopped him. She had wanted to bring him into her bed that night—had planned to since morning. It was why she had been so nervous. But now that the time had come, she found she could not. It irritated her. She loved Ramsey, or so she had thought. Now doubts crowded into her mind.

She watched, filled with a mixture of sadness, quiet worry, and guilt as Ramsey walked up Hill Street. She finally turned and headed slowly up the steps to her house.

CHAPTER

★ 18 ★

Ramsey was torn inside. On the one hand, it was the best time of his life. On the other, he grew more nervous with each passing day as the threat of retaliation shrouded the town of Plentiful.

What made him so happy was that he had Sally Tucker; and they enjoyed their evenings together. He would spend his days performing his official duties, often in his office, shielded from most of the day-to-day flotsam of life.

He ate lunch with Tucker every day, either at a restaurant or at her house. Dinner was at her house, and Ramsey found Tucker not only a delightful and interesting companion but also a good cook.

Ramsey found himself hoping more and more that Tucker would allow him into her large four-poster bed of a night. But she did not, and each evening he would leave her at her gate and walk slowly back to Parker's Rooming House, his loins burning. It was the only blot on their relationship, and he was not about to let it ruin things.

Still, the ache in his groin needed relief, and he sometimes gave in to it. On those nights he would walk past the boardinghouse and down to the Lone Star. There he would cool his fiery passions with several cold beers—or with a quick session in a crib with Ada Belle or Sad-Eyed Sally.

Were it not for the trouble he expected to crop up at any time, he would have been happy. Life as the marshal of Plentiful was not all that tedious. There were occasions when he had to calm down some rowdies in one of the saloons or bawdyhouses or haul a petty thief before Judge Amos Blackthorn.

The most interesting thing he had done as marshal was arrest the two drunk gunmen, Cully and Honus, in the Lone Star Saloon. Two days later he hauled them in front of Blackthorn. The judge was a mean-visaged man with bushy, wild eyebrows over deep-set dark eyes behind gold-wire-frame glasses and a bulbous, very large nose that dwarfed the thin, pinched lips below.

The crusty old judge, wanting to get finished and head out for some fishing, sentenced each to two days—already served in the jail—plus a hundred-dollar fine each.

The two paid their money and headed out. As they approached Ramsey, Cully sneered, "Well, Mr. Marshal, seems you made a hell of a fuss for nothin'."

Ramsey stepped into the man's path. "You won't get a warnin' next time, boy," he snarled.

"Neither will you."

"You challengin' me, you dumb son of a bitch?" Ramsey asked, forcing himself to calm down.

Something in Ramsey's eyes served to make Cully lose his arrogance fast. "Now, Marshal," he said, trying to sound smooth, "I never said no such thing."

"Didn't think you had the guts," Ramsey said. He stared deep into Cully's eyes for a moment, then said, "Was I you, Cully, I'd not linger in Plentiful for too long. I might just find you breakin' the law some night when you ain't quite ready, if you take my meanin'."

"I got it." Cully tried to brazen it out, but he was scared.

"That's good." Ramsey stepped out of the way. As Honus passed him, Ramsey said, "The same applies to you, Honus."

"Yes, sir," Honus said meekly before hurrying out behind Cully.

"Better watch your back with them two around, Marshal," Blackthorn said. "Hell, if I'd known they were such idiots, I'd never of let 'em off so easy."

"Should've been able to tell," Ramsey said, quite irritated.

"Reckon so." The judge did not seem at all contrite. "But I figured they were just a couple of boys got likkered up and were spoutin' off some steam."

"Maybe they was," Ramsey said with a sigh. "Maybe they were just tryin' to pull a bluff on me."

"I wouldn't count on that," Blackthorn said.

"I won't." Ramsey strolled out into the sunshine. Cully and Honus were just disappearing into the Cloverleaf Saloon. He marched across the street and leaned against the wall outside of Sullivan's photographic studio, waiting and watching the saloon several doors down on the other side of the street.

As the purplish darkness of sunset crept over Plentiful, Paddy Sullivan came out of his studio. "You still here, Marshal?" he asked.

"Yep." Ramsey yawned. It had been a long afternoon standing there doing nothing. He was hungry, too. "Are you in a rush, Mr. Sullivan?" he asked.

"Why, no, not too much," Sullivan said cautiously. "Some supper with the family. Then maybe a wee stop at the Lone Star. Why?"

"Because you're gonna help me." He did not ask, just stated it flatly. It was the only way to do it, Ramsey thought.

"But Marshal . . ."

"No *buts*, Mr. Sullivan. I've been here most of the day. I got to make water, you know. And I need some supper of my own."

"What do you want me to do?" Sullivan asked, his face pasty.

"Just stand here and keep watch over the Cloverleaf."

"And what'll I be on the lookout for?"

"I reckon you remember them two boys knocked you on the head?"

"Ah, yes. I'll never forget them." He touched the dirty bandage wrapped around his head.

"Good. They're in the Cloverleaf. I want you to stand here in the shadows and watch the door over there. If they come out, you send somebody to fetch me and you follow 'em. At a distance! I don't want you gettin' buffaloed again. But don't let 'em out of your sight, neither. Unless they ride out of town. You got that?"

"Yeah." Sullivan was none too happy about it. "Where'll you be?"

"Miss Tucker's," Ramsey said blandly. "I'll only be gone about an hour." He left hurriedly.

Ramsey was just finishing up his ham and gravy when there was a knock at the door. Sally Tucker went to answer it, and she came back into the small dining room with a boy of about ten.

"Mr. Sullivan said to come get you," the boy said. "Told me you'd give me a quarter if I was to fetch you right off." He held out a grimy mitt expectantly.

"Oh, he did, did he?" Ramsey stood up and grinned. "Reckon you deserve it, boy." He showed the youth a twenty-five-cent piece. Before the boy could grab it, Ramsey asked, "Where was Mr. Sullivan when you last saw him?"

"Center Street. Near Carter's Pharmacy."

"Thanks." He handed the boy the coin. Then he kissed Tucker lightly on the cheek. "I'll be back soon," he said. He went to the door and opened it, and the boy rushed out.

Ramsey walked quickly down Sagauche Street, which paralleled Center. Then he cut through an alley and crossed Center Street to the pharmacy next door to Doc Bedloe's, which was on the corner of Court Street. Sullivan was not around.

The marshal walked slowly south on Center Street, taking in all he could by the light of the lanterns in windows. Finally he spotted Sullivan, who was peering cautiously around the edge of the Swine's Head Saloon.

Ramsey hurried up behind Sullivan. "See something, Mr. Sullivan," he asked.

The photographer jumped, startled. "Begorrah, don't do that, Marshal!" he said, placing a hand over his heart.

"Sorry," Ramsey whispered. "What do you see?"

"Look for yourself," Sullivan said quietly as he moved back.

Ramsey peeked around the corner. Three men were standing in inky shadows down the alley between the saloon and Ling Su's laundry. The three were talking. One scraped a match on the wall and bent over cupped hands to light a cigarette. It was Honus. Ramsey assumed one of the other men was Cully. But he had no idea who the third was. He could not see any faces, and there was no way he would be able to get close enough to see—or hear—anything.

He turned back to Sullivan. "You did well, Paddy," he said. "Next time I see you in the Lone Star, I'll owe you a drink."

Sullivan beamed. "Then I can go now?"

"Yep." He looked back down the alleyway as Sullivan hurried

away. "Damn," Ramsey muttered. Cully and Honus were coming back his way. The third man had disappeared.

Ramsey spun around quickly and walked away, then stepped into a darkened doorway. He waited until he heard the two gunmen come out of the alley and go the other way. Ramsey peeked out and saw Cully and Honus walking swiftly, though a little unsteadily, toward the livery. Ramsey stepped out of the doorway and walked down the street. He stopped under the large overhang at Lopez's Saddlery.

Fifteen minutes later, the two men rode out of the stable and headed down the road southward. As soon as they were out of sight in the gloom, Ramsey ran across to the stable and saddled his mule. He jumped aboard and hurried out, following Cully and Honus.

He tracked them for several miles. The two were taking their time, seemingly in no hurry. Ramsey hung far enough back so they could not see or hear him. There was no other way to go except the road—until they got to the path that cut off westward toward Sentry Pass. And Lost Canyon beyond. Ramsey hesitated a minute before following the two down the path. It could easily be a trap; but he had to know.

He followed cautiously, the mule walking steadily, solidly. Ramsey could hear the murmur of the men's voices not far ahead of him.

Ramsey stopped at Sagauche Creek. The water still swirled under the moonlight where the two gunmen had just crossed. He decided he needed to go no farther. Either Cully and Honus were lost, or they were heading toward Roberts's hideout. He did not think they were lost.

Ramsey felt somewhat vindicated, though he was not happy about it. He had said Cotton Roberts would probably recruit more men, and these two he had been following would fit in nicely with men like Roberts. He wondered how many more men Roberts would hire before he rode down on Plentiful for vengeance.

With a twinge of worry, Ramsey turned his mule homeward. He arrived back in Plentiful well past midnight. He was tired and sweaty and, though he hated to admit it, he missed Tucker more than was comfortable. He unsaddled the mule at the livery and made sure the animal had feed and water. Then he slowly plodded up the street to his boardinghouse.

It was difficult for him to get to sleep. He had wanted to go to

Tucker's and pound on the door till she awoke, just to let her know he was back. But that would only cause trouble, he reasoned. Still, it did not make relaxing easier, knowing she would be worried about him.

Finally the long day, the tension, and the time in the saddle got the better of him, and he felt the web of sleep closing in on him.

It was bright with morning sun when he awoke. He stretched and felt a bit odd inside. Then he realized he was nervous, worried that Tucker would be angry at him.

She was. He went to her house straight off and was greeted by a stare that was icier than a mountain valley in winter. He tried over and over to explain to her that he had been exhausted and that he was trying to preserve her reputation as much as possible.

But Tucker was not buying it. At least not for a long time. Finally he got angry and slammed down his palm hard on the table. "I have tried," he said roughly, "to do what I thought was best. To do right by you as I saw it. I don't know what kind of injudicious thoughts you got in your mind, woman, but unless they take into account what I told you—which is the truth—well then, it's all nonsense."

He grabbed his hat and slapped it on. "I'll be seein' to some breakfast now, ma'am, if you're of a mind not to object to it too awful much. Good bye."

Ramsey thought Tucker would stop him, but she didn't. He stopped by the house again just past noon, not for lunch, really, but to give—or make—one last try for reconciliation.

Tucker's face, when she opened the door, was puffy and blotchy from crying. He came in, feeling guilty. But he did not know what to say. They sat silently in the parlor for a long time.

Finally Ramsey could not stand it any longer. "There's no need for all this hatefulness," he said softly. "Maybe I did do wrong by not comin' by here last night. But that ain't the way I saw it. I figured if I came by here so late at night like that, people'd be bound to talk. I'd not want to put you in that fix, Sally."

"You could've at least come by and told me you was all right," she said, her voice a mixture of anger and worry. "I stayed up half the night waitin' for you. Do you know what kind of demons I conjured up about you last night? I thought you were dead somewhere and people were afraid to come tell me. Or worse— I thought you'd ridden off and left me for some reason." She was crying again.

"I'd never do no such thing!" Ramsey said, surprised that she would even think it.

"Well, I *know* that," Tucker said, blotting away the tears with a crumpled hankie. "But your mind does funny things to you sometimes...." She couldn't figure out where else to go with that thought, so she let it drop.

"That's a fact." He smiled at her, hoping to break Tucker's icy countenance.

It seemed to work, as Tucker's lips cracked and some light sprang back into her tear-dulled eyes.

Tucker stood up, walked the few steps between them, and perched on Ramsey's lap. She kissed him long and hard, wondering where she was heading.

Mayor Aldridge had stopped by several times since Tucker had returned to Plentiful after her ordeal at the hands of the outlaws. He always did so when Ramsey was not around—like when Ramsey had gone off to Sagauche. And he seemed quite interested in her.

The mayor *was* quite handsome, Tucker had thought more than once. And he was settled here. He was not a drifter like Kyle Ramsey. He was here to stay, and he made good money. She would never want for anything if she were to latch onto Mayor Marlin Aldridge.

She was confused as she broke off the kiss with Ramsey and rested her head on the man's broad chest. She sighed. *It will all work out for the best,* she told herself firmly.

CHAPTER
★ 19 ★

Several days after Honus and Cully had left town, Ramsey watched as a man rode into town alone. He had the same look about him as the other two—that of a professional gunslick. He was of medium height, with cold, cruel eyes and thin, bloodless lips. He was dressed all in black, relieved only by the startling white of the twin ivory-handled Colts girding his waist.

Ramsey was annoyed. He was angry at Roberts in general and growing more so because the outlaw seemed to be using Plentiful as a recruiting station for new men. It added credence to his suspicions—aroused by the late Marshal Burch—that Roberts had someone in town helping him on the sly. After Ramsey had seen Cully and Honus talking with someone in a dark alley and then riding out on the trail for Lost Canyon, it had only made Ramsey more certain that there was an insider for the gang in Plentiful.

Spitting into the dirt, Ramsey unhooked the strap across the hammer of the LeMat. He walked unhurriedly down the street as the gunman stopped and dismounted in front of the Cloverleaf Saloon. The man was tying his horse to the hitching rail as Ramsey strolled up.

"Afternoon," Ramsey said, touching the brim of his hat.

"Afternoon, Marshal," the man said. The words were mild, but the hard, tight cast to the face belied their mildness.

Ramsey was unafraid. There was a good chance that this wandering gunfighter was far faster on the draw than Ramsey. But at this range, Ramsey's LeMat—set to use the barrel of buckshot—would shred the man before he could get any kind of aim at Ramsey at all.

"Stoppin' in town long?" Ramsey asked politely.

The man threw his hands into the air, as if to say "I don't know."

"What's your name?"

"Whiskey Bill Thorne," the man said, as if the very words were enough to strike fear into the heart of anyone who heard them.

"Well, Mr. Thorne," Ramsey said, unfazed, "I like a quiet town."

"So do I."

"That's good, though I'd never of thought it, judgin' by the hardware you're carryin'."

"A man's got to be careful when he rides alone these days," Thorne said levelly.

Ramsey nodded, unconvinced. "I suggest you leave them Colts in their holsters while you're in my town, Mr. Thorne."

"We'll see," Thorne said coolly. "Now," he added, tipping his black Stetson a fraction, "if you don't mind, Marshal, I'd like to cut the trail dust from my throat."

"Have at it," Ramsey said. "Just pay heed to my words, though."

Thorne did not answer. He just stepped around Ramsey, who turned, following the gunman with his eyes. Thorne shoved his way into the saloon.

Things were quiet all the rest of that day, as well as that night and the next morning. Then Adolph Bock, who ran the feed and grain store, burst into Ramsey's office. His fat face was flushed and he puffed for air. "Der is trouble near mein business!" he gasped. "Dat gunman vhat came into town yesterday . . ."

Ramsey didn't wait to hear anymore. He slapped his hat on and ran out the door. He moved quickly down the street. The gunman was no longer near Bock's feed store. Ramsey could see the gunfighter down past South Street, but he could not tell from where he was what was going on. The streets at the south end of town were nearly deserted, as townsfolk cowered behind their doors.

Ramsey scooted down the alley between his office and Scheibel's Restaurant. He skidded around the corner onto Garita Street and headed south until he came to South Street. There he swung back west, toward Center Street.

He slowed as he closed in on the workshop section of Plentiful, sliding up along the wall of Lopez's Saddlery. He peered around the corner.

Whiskey Bill Thorne was standing just outside the door of what once had been Sam Port's wagon shop before he had moved it next to his brother's livery across the way. The gunman's left arm was around the neck of a black girl of about fourteen. He held her tightly against him, while his hand rested on the girl's plain cotton shift. He cupped one of the girl's budding breasts.

He had a Colt pistol in his other hand, and he had fired two shots that Ramsey had heard. The pistol was cocked and aimed at Joshua Cord, who stood in a crouch, enraged. He looked to Ramsey like a caged animal, wanting to attack but knowing it was futile.

"What's the matter, nigger boy?" Thorne taunted Cord. "Somethin' botherin' y'all?" He laughed cruelly. "Well, I told y'all what I'd pay for this here little bitch, and that's all I'm gonna pay. Y'all will have to wait for the next man to come along to get more for her. But if y'all insist on aggravatin' me, boy, y'all ain't gonna get nothin' but shot."

Cord said nothing, but the veins throbbed angrily in his neck and temples. He looked about ready to charge.

Thorne fired the pistol, and the bullet kicked up dirt between Cord's black work boots. "Don't y'all even think of comin' after me, boy," Thorne snarled, his words dripping with hate. "I aim to taste me this little black gal here. I don't mind killin' you first, though, if you're of a mind to die." He sneered and squeezed the girl's breast.

The girl's ebony face was frightened, but she had no tears. She stood as still as she could, bravely facing her danger, though she was scared and disgusted. This white man holding her in such a vile way smelled of sweat, cheap whiskey, and tobacco.

Ramsey crept out, heading toward Thorne. The outlaw had his back turned almost fully toward Ramsey. The marshal took out the LeMat and cocked it. Then he was almost atop Thorne. He pressed the muzzle of his pistol to the back of the outlaw's head.

"Y'all so much as cut wind and the back of your head'll be gone before you're finished," Ramsey rasped. He felt an anger of indignation he had not felt in a long time.

"Who're you?" Thorne asked in a gargling whisper.

"Marshal Ramsey. You know what a LeMat is?"

"Yep."

"Then you know what the buckshot'll do to you if I was to pull the trigger right now?"

"Yep," Thorne whispered. He thought he might urinate in his pants.

"Good," Ramsey said almost reasonably, proud that he was able to keep his rage under control. "Then we understand each other. Now, I am gonna give you a list of things to do. It's a short list. When I've finished, I'll tell you to begin. You will do them in the order I tell you, and the way I tell you, or there won't be enough left of your head to fill a shot glass. Understood?"

"Yep." Thorne felt his knees trembling a little.

"All right. First I want you to very slowly raise that pistol skyward and then ease the hammer down. Then you will let the girl go. When she is out of the way, you will bend straight over and place the Colt on the ground. Then you'll place your other Colt next to it and carefully step away from both of 'em. Got it?"

"Yep." Thorne was worried. He figured for sure he was going to die, and he did not want that. No, not one little bit.

"Good. You may commence."

Thorne's right hand moved as if it were fighting through a snowbank. When the pistol was pointing straight up, he eased the hammer down, praying that the sweat on his hand would not let the hammer slip. Then it was finished.

"You done good so far, boy. Keep a-goin'."

Thorne peeled his hand off the girl's breast, then unlatched his elbow so the arm came away from Effie Cord's throat. The girl raced toward her father, who smothered her up in his arms, mumbling to her.

"I didn't think you had it in you to remember all this, Thorne," Ramsey said sarcastically. "Now let's finish it off proper."

Thorne's shirt was soaked with sweat as he bent over carefully and set the Colt pistol on the ground. He gave momentary thought to keeping the gun in hand and diving. He might have a chance that way. Then he realized he would be blown apart. With a sigh, he eased out the other Colt, once again thinking of using it. A whirl, a quick flick of the thumb, and . . .

No, he realized, that, too, would be foolish. He decided he had no choice but to trust the marshal.

It dawned on him that surrendering would not be so bad. He'd get carted off to jail and then be brought before a judge. What judge in his right mind would give him a hard time for trying to sport a little with some black gal? That's all they were good for anyway. Everyone knew that. Yes, things would work out.

He straightened up carefully and then stepped away from the pistols.

"A little farther," Ramsey said. When Thorne did as he was told, Ramsey moved up. In order to pick up Thorne's pistols, he would have to put his LeMat away. He did not want to do that, so he kicked them out toward the street. Everyone who had come out to watch stayed away from the guns.

"Mr. Cord," Ramsey said almost cheerily. "I do expect you might have a hankerin' to pay your respects to Mr. Thorne here. I get that right?"

Cord stared at Ramsey for a moment, wondering if the marshal were trying to taunt him. He realized Ramsey was serious. Cord grinned widely, straightening. "Well, Marshal Ramsey, I expect I could find the time fo' such a thing."

The big black man took his arms from around his daughter and whispered something to her. Then he strolled toward Thorne. The outlaw looked at Ramsey with real fright in his eyes. "What in hell's goin' on heah, Marshal?" he asked, his voice quavering.

"Eh?" Ramsey questioned, his face a mask of naïveté.

All the cockiness had left Thorne some minutes back. He was scared. He glanced at Cord, then licked his lips. "Y'all ain't gonna let these heah nigra have—"

Cord's huge fist smashing into Thorne's mouth stopped him in midsentence.

Ramsey watched in interest as Cord set about pummeling Thorne with crushing blows, slamming the outlaw around. Whenever he could gain a moment's respite, Thorne scuttled away from the hammering fists. But Cord was relentless.

The crowd had grown, but the people were silent. They did not know who to cheer for, exactly. They certainly did not want to cheer on a bloodthirsty outlaw who had almost certainly come through here on his way to join the Cotton Roberts gang. But still, they could not champion a black man, a former slave.

However, there was enough interest, and *oohs* and *aahs* erupted with each shattering punch. Several men tried taking bets, but since there was no evidence of any contest, there were no takers.

"All right, Josh," Ramsey finally called.

"I ain't stoppin' now, God damn it, fo' you or nobody," Cord growled.

"I'd hate like hell to have to shoot you after all this, Josh," Ramsey said calmly. "Now let him be. You've done enough damage to him."

Cord punched Thorne once more before stepping back. His great chest rose and fell heavily. He moved slowly toward Effie.

Ramsey was amazed that Thorne was still standing. The outlaw's face was a bloody mask, his nose shattered and his lips mashed flat. He had spit out several teeth. He weaved, and his breath rasped in and out harshly.

"Let's go, Thorne," Ramsey said.

Thorne lurched ahead a step, then another. He seemed to lose his footing, and he staggered half a dozen steps to the side, while the crowd chuckled and tittered. He righted himself and tried again but once more tottered off to his left. Finally he fell.

Ramsey held back the grin. Thorne had fallen half a foot from his pistols. Ramsey stayed nonchalant, waiting.

Thorne suddenly moved fast, rolling onto his back and jerking up one of the pistols. He swung it toward Ramsey, thumbing back the hammer at the same time.

Ramsey fired coolly. Several people screamed as the blast of buckshot tore away Thorne's face and much of his head. Thorne's dead fingers jerked and the pistol fired, boring a hole into the dirt inches from Thorne's foot.

"All right, everybody go on home," Ramsey roared, suddenly weary and disgusted with himself. He could have easily prevented this, yet he had lured the man to his own death. It did not set well with him. Ramsey soothed his conscience by telling himself that the man most likely was a killer and that he had treated both Joshua and Effie Cord with the utmost disdain. "Go on!" he roared. "Get!"

As people started drifting off, Ramsey walked toward Vessig's sawmill. "I want one of your wagons, Emil," Ramsey said.

"And vhat for?"

"What in hell do you think for?" Ramsey snapped, anger at himself and everyone else in the town boiling over.

"Ya, I vill bring," Vessig said, taken aback.

As Ramsey walked back toward the body to wait, Cord and his daughter came by. "Thanks, Marshal," Cord grumbled. He hated to be beholden to anyone anymore.

"You're welcome," Ramsey answered simply. He had not done it to make Cord obliged to him. He had done it for two reasons: It was his job, and he would not permit such treatment of anyone.

He picked up Thorne's pistols one at a time and shoved them in his belt as the Cords walked off. A few minutes later, Ramsey heard the clanking of Vessig's wagon.

CHAPTER

★ 20 ★

Ramsey was working inside his office when two tough-looking men rode into Plentiful from the north. Ramsey stepped outside and leaned back against the wall, watching the two closely.

The older one was tall, lean, and hard. Broad shoulders stretched the cotton shirt near to bursting across his back. He had dark eyes, a square, solid jaw, and a thick crop of black hair under a well-worn Stetson. He wore blue denim pants and boots that had seen plenty of work. On his right hip rode a no-nonsense .44-caliber Colt. The man had a general air of danger and deadliness about him.

The horse he rode added to the effect. It was a small, jet-black stallion. From the looks of him, the horse had once roamed wild on the plains of Texas or some such place.

The other man was little more than a boy. Ramsey would have said sixteen, if he had been asked. He was fair of face and hair; lanky youthfulness still clung to his spare frame. His peach-fuzzed face was open, but there was an overall look of determination about the young man. The Colt he wore at his hip looked like it had been used before, too, though perhaps not as much as the Winchester rifle in the saddle scabbard.

Like the older man, this one wore pants of blue denim. They

were worn but still plenty serviceable. And he wore a long-sleeved cotton shirt with a flowery pattern in green woven though the white background.

"Those two boys look like trouble," Mike O'Halloran said.

O'Halloran, apparently, was not the only one who thought the newcomers might be trouble. Quite a number of people who were in the vicinity stopped whatever they were doing to stare fearfully at the two mounted men.

"Could be," Ramsey said, looking at the editor of the *Plentiful Bugle*. The man was young, and he had large, owlish eyes behind thick glasses. He wore a white shirt, the sleeves stained with ink, and a long apron that was coated with more ink. He wiped his hands on a piece of rag.

"I'd keep a close watch on them two, was I you, Marshal," O'Halloran said.

"I intend to," Ramsey said. He was a little irritated, but he did not want to get angry at O'Halloran. The journalist thought it his job to snoop, to pry, and to offer sage—and not so sage— advice, whether anyone asked for it or not. "But I'd recommend that you stay away from them. They look like a couple real hard- cases to me—men not prone to bein' questioned by some nosy newspaperman."

"I have to do my job, Marshal," O'Halloran said seriously, blinking his big eyes solemnly. "Just like you have to do yours. Our jobs are not always easy."

"Just go careful, Mike."

"I will." The newsman shuffled off back to his office two doors down.

The two men had stopped in front of the Lone Star Saloon and tied off their horses. Smacking trail dust from their hats, they entered the saloon, the young one grabbing his Winchester from the saddle scabbard. The young man carried the rifle, Ramsey noted, like he knew how to use it.

Ramsey pushed away from the wall, headed toward the Lone Star.

Silence settled over the saloon like a preacher's words over his congregation. The customers were afraid after what had happened the last time two gunmen had entered the place.

Abel Jackson was not about to be overpowered again. As the two men walked up to the bar, Jackson pulled out his double-barreled shotgun. Keeping his right hand on it, he set it on the bar. "What'll it be, boys?" he asked harshly.

"Mighty inhospitable greeting, mister," the darker man said evenly, a glint of hardness in his eyes.

Jackson shrugged. "I ain't a very hospitable man."

"Even to a couple fellow Texans?" the big man asked, smiling slightly and trying to put the bartender at ease. "Hell, we stopped here 'cause of the name of the place."

"Don't mean a hill of beans to me, boys, whether you're from Texas or some God damn Yankee state. Now, you boys want a drink, you best let me know now. You don't, I'd be mighty obliged if you was to leave my saloon."

"Sure is cold in here, Buck, don't you think?" the older man said, turning toward his companion.

"Like the Dakota Territory in January, Matt," the younger answered. It didn't mean much that he had never been closer to the Dakota Territory than he was now.

Jackson was not swayed toward friendliness. "Like I said, gents, either order something or go foul someone else's saloon."

"Two beers," Matt said tightly, hovering between anger and amusement.

Jackson lifted the shotgun and strolled down the bar. He set the weapon down and drew two beers from a tap. Then he picked up the scattergun in his right hand and the two mugs in his left. Setting the mugs down in front of Matt, he snarled, "That'll be ten cents, mister."

Matt silently handed him a coin, then lifted his mug in a sardonic salute to the bar owner. He took a sip.

Ramsey stood just outside the doors, off to the side and out of the way, watching. He stayed there for more than an hour. But the two newcomers stood quietly sipping their drinks. So Ramsey finally went about his business.

With some slight trepidation—since Sally Tucker had not fully gotten over her anger—he headed for Tucker's house. When he entered the neat home, Tucker had a supper of pork chops, potatoes and gravy, peas, and biscuits ready.

"That was a fine supper, Sally," Ramsey said, trying to cut through the curtain of polite aloofness Tucker wore. It annoyed him. She was pleasant enough and showed no anger toward him, but she remained far away from him nevertheless.

"Thank you," she answered, with strained civility.

"Maybe," Ramsey said, not really wanting to say this but feeling that he must, "I ought not to be comin' 'round here no more, Sally." His mouth was dry, and there was a dull, dead feeling in his stomach.

Tucker looked startled, then caught herself. "Maybe," she said slowly, "that would be best." It was said so very softly he almost did not hear her.

"If that's what you want . . ." he said, standing and picking up his hat. The ache in his stomach had spread, and he felt numb inside.

"I didn't say that's what I *want*," Tucker retorted obstinately.

She didn't really want that. But neither did she want to see quite so much of Ramsey as she had been. She had come to realize that she did not love Kyle Ramsey, though she liked him more than a little. Not that she loved Mayor Aldridge either, but she thought more often these days that it might be nice to invite the town official to supper of an evening.

"Well, is it?" Ramsey asked, his annoyance growing along with the numb feeling. Too late he concluded that he loved Sally Tucker. His stomach was soured by what was happening.

"I don't know," Tucker said, her calm exterior beginning to crack. "I . . ." She didn't know what she wanted to say. She looked down at the table and played with a corner of the tablecloth.

"I reckon," Ramsey said harshly, irritation overriding his sadness, "that you best make up your mind." He was tired of the game playing.

"I don't want you to stop coming by," Tucker said, raising her head to stare at him. Her eyes were wide and sorrowful.

Ramsey tried not to look at those beautiful violet orbs. "But not all the time, is that it?" he asked, feeling like he had just been punched in the gut.

"Yes," she whispered, dropping her gaze again.

"Good-bye, Miss Sally," Ramsey said with as much dignity as he could conjure up. He stepped around her and headed stiffly toward the door. Then he was outside, torn between anger and a stomach-wrenching sense of loss.

The vexatious thoughts that plagued Ramsey made sleeping difficult that night. He pondered over and over what had gone wrong. Things had seemed so fine between himself and Tucker; then, over the past several days, it had gone, like a rug yanked out from underneath them. After Cherokee Lil and now this, his sense of loss was nearly devastating.

Through sheer exhaustion, he finally managed to sleep. But when he awoke he felt little refreshed. As soon as he opened his eyes, his brain started in again, worrying over the problem like a dog working on a bone. "Hell, God damn it," he growled as he stalked angrily off toward Scheibel's for breakfast.

For the next several days he went about his business. It kept him busy enough to lessen the time his mind spent on annoying him with thoughts of Tucker and their new separateness.

Once again, as the time increased since the last raid by the outlaws, the more comfortable the citizens of Plentiful became. It was as if they had forgotten the past. And that meant that life returned to normal, which in turn meant that Ramsey was kept busy with his regular duties as marshal.

The day after he'd said farewell to Tucker, he caught a petty thief stealing some beans, cloth, and apples from Webb's store. Then he had a heart-to-heart chat with Alabama, warning the gambler—again—that he would run him out of town the next time he got a complaint about the cardsharp's nimble-fingered dealing.

There was, of course, the usual assortment of drunks to deal with. It usually meant he arrested them, more often than not without too much tussling, then carted them off to the jail where they could sleep it off. Unless they gave him a lot of trouble, Ramsey was prone to releasing them with a warning the next morning.

And he dealt with the usual number of arguments, fistfights, dog bites, petty complaints, an occasional shooting, folks racing their horses or carriages up Center Street, and so on.

None of this was difficult, but it managed to keep Ramsey occupied. Especially since all the while Ramsey tried to keep a watch on the two new gunmen, Matt and Buck. But both conducted themselves in a mostly gentlemanly manner, not threatening anyone. That might have been because most of the people were scared to death of the hard-eyed, quiet gunslicks.

They did, however, try to go out of their way to meet townspeople, even introducing themselves to Mayor Aldridge and the two town council members, Antoine Devreaux and Willy Kreuger.

Abel Jackson even informed Ramsey of that first evening.

"I know, Abel," Ramsey said. "I been wondering what they're

up to. But they ain't doin' anything wrong, so there's not a hell of a lot I can do about it.''

"Reckon not. Just wanted you to know is all. I don't trust them two boys, even if they are Texans.''

Ramsey smiled crookedly.

After a few days, Ramsey began to put the two out of his mind, paying them hardly any attention.

Five days after Matt and Buck had arrived, the newsman, Mike O'Halloran, came into Ramsey's office.

"What's up, Mike?'' Ramsey asked, shoving the papers away from him. This was what he hated the most—paperwork. He was glad for the reprieve.

"I reckon you've been keeping an eye on those two gunmen rode into town a few days ago.''

"Yep. So?''

"They're riding out.''

Ramsey looked interested. "Which way?''

"South.''

Ramsey almost smiled. "How long ago?''

"Just now. A few minutes at most. Thought you'd like to know straight off.''

"Thanks, Mike.'' Ramsey clapped on his hat and left the office, walking rapidly toward the livery. Fifteen minutes later he was riding Sunshine out of town southward, following the trail of the two gunmen.

He caught up with them about two miles outside of Plentiful. It was not hard, since they were sitting in the shade of some aspens, waiting for him.

"Thought you'd never get here, Kyle,'' Matt said, smiling. He stuck out his hand.

"That'll never do, Matt,'' Kyle said, stepping up and throwing his arm around the dark-haired man. They hugged briefly, and after stepping back they whooped for joy.

"And you, Bucky, how are you, boy?''

The younger man grinned wide. "Fine, big brother. Just fine.'' He hugged Kyle, too.

"How was your trip?'' Kyle asked as all three sat down.

"About what you'd expect,'' Matt answered. "Long, hot, and give me a sore ass.'' He grinned.

"You're just gettin' old, Matt, is all.''

"Hell!" Matt snorted. He turned and said, "Buck, fetch up that pint bottle from my saddlebags."

Buck nodded and got the bottle. Kyle asked, "How's Amos? And his family?"

"Doin' well." Matt answered. "He's usin' the old place, as well as his own now. You knew that, didn't you?"

"No, I hadn't," Kyle said. "But it's fittin'. He's the oldest and ought to have the family place."

"Well, he says it ain't right that only he has it. He says any time any of us wants our share, it'll be there. But I think he actually likes it this way."

Kyle shrugged. He had no use for farming. Never had. Neither had Matt nor Bucky. They were cut from a different cloth than Amos and Luke, who was a couple of years older than Bucky.

"Anyway, he's got both places producin' real well. Cotton still, mostly, with some corn. He's got some truck crops, too, of course. And a couple head of cattle plus a number of hogs for butcherin'. Their four young'uns are sproutin' like weeds, and Rose Margaret's due to drop another'un soon."

"No!" Kyle sounded surprised but wasn't really.

"Yep. And Amos is even thinkin' of runnin' for some office. Ain't sure which one he wants, though."

That did surprise Kyle. He shook his head at the oddness of such a thing. He took a sip from the bottle that came around. "That appears strange," he muttered.

Matt grinned. "Not half as strange as you sittin' here with a silver star on your chest."

"Bah," Kyle snapped. He took another sip and passed the bottle on. "How about Luke?" he asked.

"Doin' nearabout as well. He was splittin' his time between runnin' horses up on the Trinity and helpin' Amos. Married himself a girl from over to Jack County a while back."

"Two years ago this summer," Buck interjected.

Matt nodded. "That sounds about right. Anyway, he found out, like the rest of us did, that runnin' horses ain't no way to make a livin' no more. So he took up property next to Amos. The two of 'em help each other out. Got maybe a dozen hands between 'em, too."

Kyle was surprised again, though he guessed he shouldn't have been. The world changed, and people had to keep up with it. "Didn't Luke ask for his share of Paw's place?" he asked.

"Nope. Amos offered, but he turned it down, sayin' Amos deserved it, being the oldest and all." He shrugged. "He's doin' all right, though." He smiled. "Had his first child a couple months back. A boy. Called him Samuel."

Kyle smiled. It seemed fitting that the first-born son after their father had passed on would be named after him.

They all sat quietly, listening to the hum of the insects, the chirping of a sparrow, the squawk of a jay, the wind ruffling through the leaves of the aspens.

They thought back to the old place in Fannin County, each seeing different things there: Matt a fine home, with the possibility of good crops and perhaps a family with Kate Silcox; Kyle seeing it as a prison, a place that would have bored him to death over the years had he stayed; Bucky remembering with fondness not so many years ago when he and his brothers and friends had regularly spent time in the creek.

The three thought of their father and mother, both dead now several years. They were saddened by the memories but bolstered by them, too. Samuel and Alice Ramsey had been of good strong stock, determined Scots who could face adversity without breaking. They had passed that trait on to their sons.

CHAPTER

⋆ 21 ⋆

"Well," Matt finally said, not wanting to dwell on such sad thoughts for too long, "it seems you're about up to your ass in manure this time, Kyle. What in hell's goin' on?"

Before Kyle answered he finished off the last of the red eye and tossed the empty bottle aside. "It's like I told you in the wire," he said with a sigh.

"You never said a hell of a lot in that wire."

Kyle explained about the Cotton Roberts gang and its raids on the town. He added plenty of details he had not mentioned in the wire calling on his brothers for help.

When he was finished, Matt said, "Sounds like a bunch of boys who deserve to be strung up. Or gunned down."

"They ain't the most neighborly of folks," Kyle agreed.

"So you want us to go in there and do somethin' about them?"

"Nope. I just want you to become part of the gang. Next time they ride into Plentiful, they'll be in for some surprise with you ridin' with 'em."

"If you know where their hideout is, why didn't you just go in after them with a posse?"

"Hell," Kyle snapped, "there ain't a man in town got the balls to face Roberts's men. 'Cept maybe Marshal Burch—and he's dead—and Sheriff Starkey, who's still laid up with a bad wound he got when we went in there last time."

"So that's why you wanted us to ride into town without people knowin' we was related, eh?" Bucky said. "Play actin' like we wanted to join the outlaws."

"Not really. The real reason is that I suspected someone in town was supplyin' the outlaws with information. I wasn't sure at the time I sent you that wire, though I'd heard of it."

"Well, it worked," Bucky said with a grin.

"Figured. Who is it?"

"Willy Kreuger," Matt said quietly.

"He's too God damn stupid," Kyle snorted.

Matt looked at his brother with eyebrows raised.

"Hell, he's as dumb as a fencepost. Everybody in Plentiful could tell you that."

"Didn't strike me or Buck that way."

Kyle sat in thought for a moment, then took in a big breath of air, which he let out with a violent explosion. "That son of a bitch's been play actin' all this time! God damn!" He fumed silently for a few moments.

"Play actin'?" Bucky asked.

"Yep. Plays like a God damn fool all the time. That's how he gets elected. Everybody in Plentiful thinks he's an idiot. They figure he's too stupid to cause any trouble, so they vote for him." He stared out through the dappled shadows cast by the aspens. "God damn. God damn!" Kyle muttered. "I'm gonna shoot that lyin' bastard soon's I get back to Plentiful."

Matt almost chuckled, but he looked at his brother with concern. "You all right, Kyle?" he asked.

"Yep. Why?"

"Just ain't like you to go on like this."

"I'm just madder'n a bee-stung bull is all," Kyle allowed. "Damn, I hate to think how that bastard must be sittin' back there in town, laughin' at what a fool he's made of me. Well, he ain't gonna be laughin' much longer."

"We got more important things to think on first," Matt said sharply. "Mr. Kreuger can wait a spell."

"Like hell." Kyle was fighting to control his rage at the thought of being duped.

"Now, you listen to me, big brother"—actually Matt was a bit bigger, but not by much; however, Kyle was older by about a year and so was forever to be Matt's big brother. "This Roberts don't sound like a man to let such ill treatment—as he's bound to see it—go unpunished."

"That's a fact."

"Yeah, well, if that's true, he'll be ridin' back for Plentiful soon, I'd say. It's been, what, more than two weeks since you wired me and Buck?"

"Near three, I reckon."

"Well, you think he's gonna spend the rest of the summer sittin' around on his ass somewhere, especially when you know where his hideout is?"

"Reckon not."

"You know damned well not. So we take care of Roberts and his cohorts. Then we can deal with Mr. Bald-Faced Liar Kreuger at our leisure."

Kyle did not want to admit it, but his brother was right. He just hated being taken for a fool and not being able to deal with the situation straight off. He sighed, letting some of the anger settle down into his belly, where it would not affect his mind. "All right," he muttered.

Matt looked at Bucky and grinned, then back to Kyle. He was amazed—as he always was when he saw them together—by how alike Kyle and Bucky looked. They had taken after their sandy-haired father for the most part. Matt and the other two brothers, Amos and Luke, had taken more after their mother.

Then Matt frowned. Something more was eating at Kyle. He knew Kyle too well to have his brother hide something from him. "You got somethin' else stuck in your craw, brother?" he asked bluntly.

"Nope," Kyle said without conviction.

"Like hell." Matt growled. "Let it out, boy. Me and Buck are here to help you. We can't do as good a job if you won't tell us all."

"It ain't got nothin' to do with the matter at hand."

"It does if it's affectin' you, Kyle," Bucky said. He was no longer the boy Kyle remembered. Bucky was nearly as tall as he was, and though he had plenty of filling out to do, he was not a boy. He was a man. And as a Ramsey brother, he took his rightful place in speaking up when he saw the need. "We're family. Ramseys, by God. The only ones who really give a damn about you. We ain't about to turn our backs if somethin' bad's latched onto you."

Kyle plucked a blade of grass and fiddled with it a moment before sticking it in his teeth. Chewing on the blade of grass, he told, as emotionlessly as he could, of Sally Tucker and how he and she had grown apart.

When he was finished, neither brother said anything. They nodded solemnly in understanding.

"Love's a strange business, Kyle," Matt said. "We all know that. Sounds to me, though, like this Miss Tucker ain't gave up on you altogether. I reckon you ought to try'n see to gettin' her back—once this business with Roberts is done and over with. That's got to come first."

"Bah," Kyle snorted.

"Don't give me that nonsense," Matt said with a good-natured jab on Kyle's arm. "You need a woman. A good woman. One like . . ." He stopped, the grin frozen on his face.

"It's all right," Kyle said.

"She was a hell of a woman, Lil was, Kyle."

"I know. I'm powerful sorry she's gone. There's times I think she's still around. I can see her and smell her and . . ." he trailed off lamely. "Aw, hell!"

Matt nodded. "Now you know what I been goin' through for all this time since Kate . . ." he said softly.

"Yep."

They fell silent, the two older brothers thinking of their lost loves, the younger one knowing better than to open his mouth.

Finally Kyle asked, "You boys all set on what to do?"

"Yep," Matt answered, breaking out from the sorrowful memories that had flooded his brain. "Kreuger told us how to get to Roberts's hideout."

"He still holed up in Lost Canyon?"

"That's what Kreuger called it."

"You two don't have to do this, you know," Kyle said. He figured there'd be no talking his brothers out of this adventure, but something inside forced him to give them the opportunity of turning it down.

"You hear somethin', Buck?" Matt asked, grinning widely.

"I thought I did," the young man said, also smiling and getting into the game. "But I can't quite place it."

"Hard to put your finger on," Matt admitted gleefully. "Kind of reminds you, though, of what the bunkhouse sounds like after Manuel's served up a batch of his special beans to the boys.''

"Yeah, Matt, that's it!" Bucky said with a laugh. "We can all thank the good Lord, though," he added, casting his eyes momentarily heavenward, "that it don't carry the same odor."

Matt tried to add to the statement, but the gusts of laughter spewing from him prevented it.

Kyle sat still, trying to keep the stony look on his face. But he could not hold it for very long. In seconds he had joined his two brothers in their guffaws.

"So I take it," Kyle finally managed some time later after gaining back his wind and seriousness, "that you boys ain't gonna back out."

"When has a Ramsey ever backed out of such a thing?" Bucky demanded.

They all quieted again, and Kyle said, "Well, I reckon there's not much more to say, is there?"

"Nope," Matt answered for himself and Buck.

"I'll get out somehow and warn you when things are gonna break," Bucky said with determination.

"You do so only if you can do it safely," Kyle said roughly. "I don't want you gettin' your ass killed. I'll find out soon enough when they're comin'. I'll allow as how it'll help to know before-hand, but we'll make do whatever."

"Sure," Matt said soothingly, though still grinning.

"I'm serious, damnit!" Kyle growled. He cut off the anger. "You boys know where to find me, should one of you get through?"

His two brothers shook their heads in the negative.

"Daytime, I'm usually at the office. But I don't reckon you'll come prancin' through durin' daylight. I got room six at Parker's Rooming House, on Center Street, halfway between Butler and Hill Streets. If I ain't there, I'll probably be in the Lone Star."

Matt and Bucky nodded. Matt grinned and said, "You ain't gonna be courtin'?"

Kyle tried to smile but failed. "Not for a spell." He paused, then did manage a grin. "Course, there's always Ada Belle." When his brothers looked blank, Kyle said, "She's one of the girls who works the Lone Star."

Matt and Bucky grinned and winked. But Kyle grew solemn.

"There is something I'd like you boys to do, though, while you're with those owlhoots—if you can."

"Anything," Buck said with fierce determination.

"It was almost three days before me, Marshal Burch, and Sheriff Starkey got Sally out of Roberts's hideout. Sally told me that in all that time she was there, no one in the gang touched her. I'm curious as hell whether she was tellin' true."

"You suspect something?" Matt asked.

Kyle shrugged. "I just want to know if she was fouled by those bastards." His tone let his brothers know that if Sally had been ravished by the gang, he would have another, more personal, score to settle with Roberts.

"Word has it that Roberts was sweet on Sally and stole her off to have for his own. But if that's true, then why in hell didn't he do nothin' to her? It don't make sense."

"Maybe he's a gentleman deep down," Matt said, sarcasm lacing through his words.

"Shit," Kyle muttered.

"We'll find out," Bucky said cockily.

"Just don't get in a jam for it," Kyle said harshly. "I don't want Roberts nor none of his men suspectin' *anything*. I want you boys in good with them when the time comes to plant those sons a bitches."

"Don't you worry none about us, Kyle," Matt said. There was no hint of a question in his voice. "If there's information to be had, by the good Lord, we'll get it. And we'll do so without none of them being the wiser. Right, Buck?"

"Right." There was a hard glint in the youth's eyes. Kyle was saddened by it. He knew Matt was, too, but there was little either older brother could do about it now. The die was cast, and young James Buchanan Ramsey was the man he was.

CHAPTER
★ 22 ★

There was nothing more to say, so the three Ramsey brothers shook hands, offered good-natured hugs, and then rode off, Kyle northward the several miles to Plentiful, Matt and Bucky southward on the arduous trail toward Lost Canyon.

Kyle unsaddled the mule in town and walked toward his office. He was tired—of life, of all these troubles. He waved briefly at Dodge Carver as he passed the gunsmith's shop. He had not seen the burly shop owner much of late, though he could not say he was sorry about that. He had hated working in that small shop. It was stifling hot in there most days, and the odor of gun oil and powder and metal filings, as well as Carver's sweaty body, filled the shack.

Kyle waved, nodded, or doffed his hat to the many people who went about their business along the wide main street of Plentiful. The smug, unconcerned attitude of most of the people angered him somewhat, though he managed to keep himself tightly reined. They seemed to think either that Roberts posed no more danger, or that, if he did, Kyle would handle it.

He stopped at Doc Bedloe's. The physician was shaving someone when Kyle entered. "Looking for another shave, Kyle?" Bedloe asked.

"No, sir," Ramsey said with a tight smile. "Just wanted to check on John. I've been busy of late and ain't had much of a chance to look in on him."

"I sent him home a couple days ago," Bedloe said, straightening.

"You did?" Ramsey asked, surprised.

"Hell yes."

"Then he's comin' along well?" Ramsey asked hopefully.

"He'll be fine, I expect. It'll take a spell, though."

"Think I could stop by and pay my respects to him?"

"Don't see why not. Unless he'd rather you didn't. It's up to him now. It's all out of my hands." Bedloe grinned, though, and said he knew that the county sheriff would like to have Ramsey visit.

"Thanks, Doc." Ramsey said. "I reckon I can drift by for a few moments. Well, good day to you." He left and bought a pint of whiskey. Then he headed toward John Starkey's house, on the east side of town, on Garita Street, which ran parallel to Center, a block east of it.

There was no fence out front, and the house itself had seen better days. It was a plank house but looked unpainted. Ramsey saw as he approached that it had been painted brown at one time, but the paint had long before faded, cracked and peeled away until it consisted of a few lonely flakes here and there. Ramsey rapped on the door, afraid he might knock it in by accident.

"Who's there?" a voice called from inside.

Ramsey recognized it as Starkey's. It was missing the booming resonance of old, but there was no mistaking it. "Kyle Ramsey," the marshal said loudly.

"Come on in," Starkey said. "But step easy, since I got my Colt aimed at you."

Ramsey went in carefully and stood just inside the door.

"Damn, it's good to see you, Kyle," Starkey said.

Ramsey's eyes adjusted to the dark interior, and he smiled when he saw the sheriff sitting at the rickety table. The lawman was just slipping his Army Colt into its holster. Ramsey moved into the room.

The place was a mess. Clothes and blankets were strewn about. The few dishes, pots, pans, and cups that Starkey possessed were dirty and lay around. Dirt was everywhere. Two faded photographs sat on a small table by a dilapidated sitting chair along one wall.

Tack and other gear stood in haphazard piles. A mangy red-bon
hound gnawed on a bone in the far corner. The animal growle
at Ramsey until Starkey snapped, "Shut up, Cooter."

Ramsey pulled the pint of whiskey from a pocket and set it o
the table. Then he sat in the other chair at the table, facing Starkey
He hoped it would hold him. But he figured that if it could hol
the sheriff's bulky body it could hold him. "How you feelin'
John?" he asked.

"Fit," Starkey said curtly.

That was a lie. He had lost considerable weight, and his ski
hung on him like a worn suit, drooping at jowls, neck, and, from
what Ramsey could see, waist. His face in the light of the lanter
was pasty looking. Still, his eyes sparkled and his hands looke
strong.

"Like hell," Ramsey with a chuckle.

"All right, I fibbed some," Starkey said, grinning. He coughed
then said, "Truth tellin', I ain't so bad. I figured when I got hi
that I'd bought the farm for sure. I been shot before, but Christ
not that bad."

"I thought you'd be pushin' up daisies too. You looked prett
poorly there for a spell."

Starkey grinned again. "I don't remember much after gettin
hit. I remember it hurt like hellfire, but I kept on a-ridin', holdin
Royal's body on his horse. We got through that grove of aspen
there, and I met you. Then . . ." He was angry at not being abl
to remember.

"Wasn't much to remember. Me'n Sally bandaged you up bes
we could. Got you back on your horse and rode like hell fo
Plentiful."

"Reckon you made it, then."

Ramsey nodded.

"Royal?"

"He was dead damn near soon's he got shot, I reckon. He wa
growin' cold when you caught up with us. But I managed to ge
him back here. Black's Mortuary did him up well, and we had
hell of a service for him. Reverend Worcester preached up a righ
powerful sermon for his send-off."

"Sorry I missed it," Starkey said sadly. "I considered Roya
Burch one of the best of men, even if he was a God damn Yankee."
He coughed again, then wheezed a bit in catching his breath. Ther

he asked, "What's goin' on with Roberts and his band of bastards?"

Ramsey shrugged. "Ain't seen hide nor hair of any of 'em since we called on 'em."

"You don't think he's rode off and left us, do you?" Starkey questioned, squinting at Ramsey as if to say he hoped Kyle were not that foolish.

"Hell no. I expect him to repay our call sooner or later. I'd have expected him already, but thinkin' on it, I reckon we did him more damage than we thought at first."

"Settin' there lickin' his wounds, you think?"

Ramsey nodded. "Yep, and tryin' to replace some of the men we planted for him."

"You think so?" Starkey asked as he stood up to get two dirty cups.

"I know so. There've been gunslicks I ain't ever seen or heard of ridin' into Plentiful almost regular the last week or so. I arrested two of 'em for bein' drunk and raisin' hell. Judge Blackthorn let 'em off with a warnin'. Next thing I know, they was headin' for Roberts's hideout."

"You follow 'em?" Starkey asked, sitting down and plunking the cups on the table between them, then pouring some whiskey into each.

Ramsey nodded and sipped from his cup. "Far enough to know they couldn't be goin' noplace else. Soon after that, one boy rode into town by himself. Took to throwin' his weight around. Reckon he was tryin' to prove to everyone that he was worth joinin' the gang. He finally got out of hand."

"What happened to him?" Starkey asked, interested.

"He's payin' his respects to Beelzebub."

"Good," Starkey nodded firmly.

"Two others come in a couple days ago," Ramsey added blandly. "They acted fine in town. Just had the look about 'em. Just this mornin' they rode out of town."

"You followed them too, eh?" Starkey didn't really need an answer. "And there's no doubt they're headin' for Lost Canyon?"

"Nope."

"This is mighty worrisome, Kyle," Starkey said. "You're all alone. I know—and you know—you ain't gonna get anyone from town to back your play they come ridin' through again."

Ramsey shrugged.

"You got a plan?"

"Nope. I'll wait to see what happens. Deal with it then."

"That's foolish, boy. Powerful foolish."

Ramsey shrugged. "Not much else can be done."

"You try callin' for help from my deputy down in Sagauche? Or callin' on the federal marshals?"

"Nope. Your deputy's got his own work to take care of. And you know them federal marshals ain't gonna give a damn."

"Yeah. Christ!" Starkey exploded, slamming a fist on the table in anger. He rose and stalked about the room. "Christ, if only I was better!"

"Well you ain't. So sit down and rest yourself. The more agitated you get, the longer it's gonna take for you to heal up proper."

"Bah," Starkey snarled. But he sat down anyway.

"I got business to tend to," Ramsey said, draining off the red eye in his cup. "You take care of yourself now, you hear?"

"Yeah. Look, you need help, you come get me. You catch wind of Roberts headin' for Plentiful, you come and fetch me. I ain't full better, but I can still help some."

Ramsey nodded. He had no intention of doing any such thing, but he would not tell the sheriff that. "Sure, John." He walked out, leaving the half-full bottle of whiskey on the table. He spent the rest of his day on routine business.

Five nights later, he was strolling up the street toward the Lone Star when someone hissed at him from an alley.

"Buck?" he whispered, slowing.

"Yep."

Kyle stopped naturally and gazed at the street. There were few people about, and none were paying him any attention. He stepped back into the alley. It was pitch black a few feet in, and he could barely see his brother's face even when they stood nearly nose to nose.

"You got information, Buck?" Kyle asked. He was worried that something might have happened to Matt.

"The gang's on its way. They'll be here come mornin'."

"Damn," Kyle whispered. But he felt some relief: At least the waiting would be over. "You and Matt all right?"

"Sure. The gang left late today and made a camp about halfway here. Soon's everyone was asleep, I walked my horse out of camp and headed here fast as I could.''

"You have any trouble?''

"No. Thought I was gonna there for a few minutes, trying to sneak out past some of those bastards in the camp. But I made it.''

Kyle nodded, even though his brother could barely see it. "You and Matt ready for what needs doin'?" he asked.

"Yes, sir. You?''

"I reckon. Don't much like it, though.''

"None of us likes all this killin', Kyle,'' Bucky said with an insistent tone to his voice. "I ain't never faced the war like you and Matt, but I've faced gunfire and all.''

"You don't have to tell me that, little brother. I'll never forget what you did for Lil back at the shack.'' He sighed. "Matt wanted to protect you from this kind of life, Buck. You know that, don't you?''

"Yes, sir.'' Bucky drew himself up to his full height. "But he couldn't. I ain't so sure I would've wanted him to anyway. Maybe one time, a couple years ago, but . . .'' He rubbed his nose. "But it's too late for all that thinkin' now anyway.''

"Yes,'' Kyle said sadly. "But me and Matt are still happy you never went off to the war.''

"Why?'' Bucky asked, startled. "If I'd of been old enough—''

"Nobody's ever old enough for war like that, boy, and don't you doubt my words. There's too many horrible things to be seen there.''

"But it's necessary times.''

"At times, yes. Trouble is, Buck, war has a way of makin' a man think life ain't so precious in God's eyes or his own. Some folks like Roberts and his men just took to the slaughter in the war, and now they can't get it out of their blood no more. A man's life don't mean shit to people like that. And,'' he added, suppressing a shudder, "it can happen to damn near anyone without him knowin' it till it's too late.''

"Kyle, I ain't as old as you or Matt,'' Bucky said with deep solemnness. "And I ain't seen so much of the world as you two. But if what you said is true, then just about any man was in that war—on either side—would've become a murderin' savage like Roberts. But most didn't. And you know why?''

"No, why?" Kyle asked, rather in bemusement. He thought it a hoot that his baby brother was going to explain the world's workings to him.

"Because of family," Bucky said heatedly. He knew what Kyle was thinking of all this. He could see it in the pale glow of the face so near his own, lighted a little by the blazing moon.

"What?" Kyle asked, stunned.

"Because of family. You and Matt never became killers. Not in the same way as Roberts. You've killed before, but you get no pleasure from it. You just do what needs doin'. And the reason you didn't turn out bad like Roberts is because of family. You had Maw and Paw to go home to and us younger ones to look after for a spell. Amos was there to lend support. And sister Anna Louise. There was a heap of love in that house. Family love. We might've had our differences of a time, and us boys got a little rambunctious now and again. But we never did nothin' in anger against each other."

Kyle stood perfectly still for some moments, staring at the ghostly image of his brother's face glowing in the light of the full moon. "You've grown, Buck," he finally said. "In body—and in mind. You've got a heap of wisdom. A lot more than most folks much older than you."

He paused. "I think you're tellin' the truth, too. I reckon havin' you and Matt and the others has kept me from goin' *loco* and crossin' over to be like Roberts. Even if we're miles apart, I know I can count on y'all. It's a powerful comfortin' feelin'."

Bucky beamed proudly.

"All right now, boy," Kyle said gruffly. "You best get your ass back to that camp before someone realizes you're missin'. And try to get some sleep. You'll need all your wits about you tomorrow."

CHAPTER

★ 23 ★

After his brief meeting with Buck, Kyle went to the Lone Star to
ponder what was to come. He ordered a beer.

"You all right?" Abel Jackson asked as he set the mug down
in front of Ramsey.

"Yep." Now that he thought about it, Ramsey was feeling
quite good. All the waiting would be over soon. With that knowledge planted inside him, much of the tenseness that had sat on
his shoulders like an ill-fitting jacket had fled.

"You look different, Kyle," Jackson said. "You sure you're
not ailin' or somethin'?"

Ramsey grinned. "I'm doin' just fine."

Ada Belle sidled up and said dully, "Buy a girl a drink, Kyle?"
She liked Ramsey—a lot—and was some put out that he no longer
paid her much attention. But she thought she had to keep trying.

"Sure," Ramsey said with a warm smile.

Hope rose anew in Ada Belle's heart. "You're not gonna tell
me to go away?" she asked, surprised.

"Nope." The luster of Ramsey's good feelings was dimmed
minutely by the thought of his past treatment of Ada Belle. But
he would not let that ruin the night for him. "Should I?"

"You've done so more than once of late, you know," Ada

155

Belle said, a touch of bitterness coating her words. "You've been so wrapped up in Miss Prim," she added, wrinkling her nose, "that you ain't had much time for the likes of a slattern like me." She was torn between anger at his treatment of her and self-pity.

Ramsey could think of nothing to say, so he said nothing.

Ada Belle's drink arrived and she sipped at it, trying to mute the raging of her conflicting feelings.

Ramsey swallowed a mouthful of beer. He looked at Ada Belle. With a bit of shock, he realized for the first time that she was more than just a painted strumpet or the bitter harridan that most people thought she was. No, she was a woman, he realized, with all a woman's wants and needs and desires.

She was nowhere near as beautiful as Sally Tucker, but a certain comeliness lurked behind the hard face and the layers of paint. Her aquiline features would, Ramsey thought, be rather fine and attractive without the mask of paint and the facade she had built up to protect herself. Ada Belle was a little shorter than Tucker, rather fuller of bosom and a bit thicker of waist. Her lips under the garish red were bitten and chewed down, as were her fingernails. Her eyes were tired. Or maybe just haunted, Ramsey thought.

He felt a pang of pity for her. He thought it was too bad she had been forced by circumstance into this hard life. It had left her a hard and bitter woman, with a bleak future. She seemed far older than her years.

Then he realized that other people had been forced into lives not of their own choosing. He was one. The loss of his arm had changed him inside, in ways he still did not fully understand. But he knew that he often did things—helped where he should have rode on, faced danger when he should not have—just to prove, to himself if no one else, that he was still a man.

Matt and Bucky, too, had been forced by the cards life dealt them to do things they would have preferred not doing. Both had been forged in the fires of gunsmoke hell, changing them forever, making them what they had become. Kyle could not change that. And he could not change Ada Belle's life path either.

"You got the time—and the inclination—to spend a few hours with a broke-down, one-armed marshal?" he asked suddenly, forcing the morbid thoughts back and down. He waited anxiously, realizing that he cared what her answer would be.

Ada Belle stared up at him for a moment, still fighting the angry

onflict inside her. Then she smiled hesitatingly. "I sure do," she
aid, suddenly feeling shy.

"Good," Ramsey nodded, relieved. "Abel, gimme a bottle of
our best forty-rod to take along with me," he ordered. When it
vas delivered, he grabbed it. "Shall we go, my lady?" Ramsey
sked gallantly.

Ada Belle latched a small hand onto the stub of Ramsey's left
rm. She headed for the rear of the saloon and the door to the
ribs out back. He headed toward the front door. They jerked each
ther to a stop and they looked at each other, she with a question
n her eyes, he with amused surprise.

"I aim," he said after clearing his throat, "to have you around
or the night, Ada Belle. If you're so willin'. And I ain't gonna
pend all that time in no cramped crib."

"Your room?" she asked, her breath catching in her throat
nomentarily.

"Yes, ma'am." He smiled.

She returned it with warmth, a lightheaded feeling coming over
er.

When Kyle arose it was still dark. He stumbled around a bit,
getting dressed and cursing silently at each noise. He did not want
o wake Ada Belle, who slept quietly under the colorful quilt.

Moonlight filtered into the room, touching Ada Belle's face.
t—and the relaxation that came with sleep—made her face look
ofter, younger, and more attractive.

He felt almost guilty, feeling as if he had used Ada Belle. He
could not tell her that he was afraid this might be his last night
live. He harbored no illusions. Matt and Buck might be his aces
n the hole, but the rest of his hand was mighty slim. The three,
even though they would have surprise on their side, would still
be well outnumbered. Ramsey did not like his chances, but there
was no way he could back out now.

He angrily shoved the guilt away as he leaned over and brushed
Ada Belle's smooth, paint-free face with his lips. She murmured
in her sleep. He smiled. He did not—probably could not—love
Ada Belle. But she was a good woman nonetheless and one with
whom he might want to spend more time. Providing he was still
alive by noon.

He slipped out of the room and walked quietly down the stairs.
He stood outside on the sidewalk, savoring the fine, clear, cool

morning. It was not yet dawn, and the taste of dew was in the air. He thought it a shame that such a fine day would soon be marred by bloodshed and death.

He lightly fingered the badge on his chest, wondering if he had made a mistake in pinning on the cheap piece of metal. But it was too late for such thinking now. Roberts and all his men would be here before much longer—and Matt and Bucky would be with them.

Glancing back up toward his window, Ramsey smiled. Like Ada Belle upstairs, Plentiful was peaceful now, the quiet broken only by an occasional dog barking or a cock crowing. He heard the flapping of a shutter somewhere.

Ramsey headed down past South Street and turned right toward the creek. There a squalid shack stood off all alone. Ramsey strode up to it and hammered on the door.

There was a scrabbling noise, and he thought he heard a pistol being cocked. A woman hushed a child. Then a deep, rumbling voice asked, "Who is it?"

"Marshal Ramsey."

"What you want?" There was no fear in that growl of a voice, but no anger either.

"I need your help, Mr. Cord. Let's get your ass out here."

Joshua Cord opened the door and stood there wearing just his ragged-bottom cotton pants. "You orderin' me to do somethin'?" Cord asked, a hint of anger in his voice now.

"Don't get on your high horse with me, Mr. Cord," Ramsey said evenly. "You know I ain't the kind to do such a thing."

"I know," Cord grumbled in apology. "But can't it wait?"

"Mr. Cord," Ramsey said civilly, though his tone was touched with urgency, "some time today—probably real soon—Cotton Roberts and his horde of murderin' bastards are gonna come ridin' down on Plentiful. I got to do what I can to stop 'em."

"Anybody else know about this?"

"Nope."

"I told you once befo', Marshal, this ain't my fight."

"I ain't askin' you to fight, Josh. I need some help settin' up barricades."

"Why should I do that?" He was growing angry. Did the marshal think that he could just order him around because he was black? He knew that was not the truth, but still it all rankled him.

"I can't do it by myself," Ramsey said coolly. He lifted his stump out to the side a bit, calling attention to the deficiency.

"Can't you find nobody else to hep you?"

"Maybe. But I ain't asked nobody else."

"You think you kin jis' come to the only nigra in town and order him around? That it? Don't want to put out none of the white folks?"

"You know better than to spout such booshwah at me, Mr. Cord." He paused, then said angrily, "You ever think that maybe you're the only one in town I can trust?"

"Shee-it," Cord growled.

Ramsey shrugged. "You owe me," he said simply.

"What?"

"By the Lord, Joshua, he be right." Suddenly a woman was standing next to Cord. She was tall and slim, sleek looking, with finely chiseled features and a long, thin nose. Her skin was even darker than Joshua's. She wore a simple cotton shift that did little to conceal her well-developed body, and a kerchief was tied around her short kinky hair.

"How do, Marshal," she said, her smile bright in her beautiful dark face.

"Miz Cord," Ramsey said, tipping his hat.

"You know he be right, Joshua," Charlotte Cord added, stroking Cord's muscular arm. "It weren't fo' Marshal Ramsey, Effie'd be raped and maybe dead by now. He wants hep, you best hep him." She showed no deference for Joshua's size or his place as her husband.

Cord nodded slowly. "I reckon I—we—owe you, Marshal," he acknowledged. "Bein' woke from sleep like I was, well . . ." He shrugged. "Reckon I wasn't thinkin' none too good."

"Wasn't thinkin' at all," Charlotte said. But the affection that was evident in her voice took the sting out of the words. "You want some coffee, Marshal?" she asked. "Maybe some breakfast? I got some eggs from the chickens and a spot of ham. Reckon I could scare up enough fo' all us."

"No, ma'am," Ramsey said. "But thanks anyway." He knew the Cords were barely able to feed themselves. They certainly did not need an extra mouth at the breakfast table.

"Charlotte ast you to breakfast, Marshal," Cord said in that rumbling bass voice. "She'll be powerful put out you didn't take her up on it."

Ramsey could see on Charlotte's face that her husband was right. She was proud of her home, as dilapidated as it was, and of her abilities as a cook. She would be insulted. "All right then, ma'am," he said. "But I warn you, I'm a light eater most mornin's." He figured he would somehow pay them back later—if he lived to do so.

"That's a lie," Charlotte said with a laugh. It was a clear, crystalline sound. "You'll eat yo' fill. I know you be worried we ain't got enough fo' ourselves. But Joshua"—she stroked her husband's arm lovingly—"be a good provider. He and the good Lord will see that all's well fo' us and that we make do."

"Yes, ma'am," Ramsey said, ashamed.

In minutes he and Joshua were sipping at mugs of coffee as the smell of baking biscuits and sizzling ham and eggs filled the small room. In the lanternlight, Ramsey saw that the room was neat and tidy. Only the outside was poor looking. Three children—fourteen-year-old Effie, ten-year-old young Joshua, and seven-year-old Marcus—sat quietly, looking with a mixture of curiosity and fear at the one-armed white man.

Breakfast was on the table soon enough, and the two men dug in hungrily. Ramsey forgot his pledge to eat lightly and shoveled it in. He had not realized how hungry he had been. Charlotte did not seem to mind.

"What's yo' plan, Marshal?" Joshua asked as they ate.

"I aim to blockade both ends of Center Street as best I can, then sit and wait."

"Ain't much of a plan."

Ramsey shrugged. "Ain't much else I can do."

Joshua grunted. He was annoyed. Part of it was that he saw Ramsey as a brave—or maybe just stupid—man, defending Plentiful with his life when no one else in town would back him. And he was annoyed at himself, too. He liked Ramsey, and he felt the heavy responsibility of being in debt to the marshal. But still he could not find it in himself to join Ramsey in facing the outlaws, mostly because that would mean he was protecting a bunch of white folk who wouldn't give him the time of day.

"What yo aim to use fo' this blockade, Marshal?"

"Call me 'Kyle.' I reckon I'll commandeer as many wagons as I can find. Whatever else comes to hand."

Joshua nodded. He shoved back his empty plate and stood up. Charlotte handed him a simple brown cotton shirt. As he put it on, he said, "We'd best git, Kyle, you want to be ready when those boys come a-callin'."

Ramsey shoved the last of a biscuit dripping with egg into his mouth. "Good breakfast, Miz Cord," he mumbled with his mouth full.

"Thank you, Marshal. Now go on, git, the two of you."

CHAPTER

★ 24 ★

"Where to first?" Cord asked as the two men hurried outside.

"The livery. Borrow a couple horses. And George's brother has a couple old wagons out back."

They entered the quiet, dark stable. Ramsey got Sunshine and another mule, while Cord grabbed two strong-looking horses.

Dawn was brightening the sky to the east, pushing the men. There were, indeed, several wagons out back in the corral that served both Port brothers. They hooked up two quickly, not being too careful about it since they were not going far. They brought them north up Center Street to just past the center of town, a little south of Butler Street and in front of Town Hall. There the two turned them sideways, taking more time than they should have to maneuver them into place one behind the other across the street.

They hurried back to the livery. George Port was waiting there for them, arms akimbo, anger splashed across his ruddy face. "What in hell you two doin'?" he asked in a nasty tone.

"Official business," Ramsey snapped.

"Come on, Marshal," Port wheedled. "What's goin' on? I'm layin' in bed and someone pounds on my door tellin' me some nigger's takin' horses and wagons from my livery. I come down here and find you helpin' him."

"Usin' such a tone—and makin' such references about my iend here—are powerful good ways to get planted over in yon emetery, George," Ramsey snarled, shoving past the man. "Now et out of the God damn way before I shoot you right where you re."

"I'll talk to Mayor Aldridge about this," Port whined.

"You do that, George," Ramsey hissed. "Now move!" He oved past Port.

Ramsey and Cord hooked up two more old wagons out back, arted them north just past Court Street, and maneuvered them to position. The blockades were not more than fifty or sixty ards apart in the center of town. Once completed, however, they ould prevent anyone from gaining easy access to the area. There ere no cross streets here that could be used for sneaking in. There ere some alleys, but Ramsey could do nothing about them now.

"These ain't gonna stop that gang, Kyle," Cord said as they nished.

"Reckon not. But I reckon it'll slow 'em down some, though."

"You ought to be able to git somethin' else to put across the ad and across the sidewalks, too, so they can't ride on up that ay."

"Got any ideas?"

"There be one hell of a pile of timber out behind Vessig's awmill."

Ramsey started to grin.

"And Bock just got in a load of hay. Bunch of bales'd do jis' ne fo' blockin' off the sidewalk."

"Come on then." Ramsey hurried toward Vessig's. With nough light now, most of the tradesmen had arrived at their shops. hey stood around and watched Ramsey's labors with some in- erest.

Ramsey strode straight up to Vessig and said without prelimi- ary, "Listen to me, Emil, and listen good. In my official capacity s marshal, I am comandeerin' all your timber."

Vessig started to argue, but Ramsey cut him off. "Not now, mil. Just listen and then do what I tell you. You—and any of our workers that're around—will help Josh load all the timber ou can get your hands on into a couple of your wagons. Then ou will go with him and unload it where and how he tells you. is orders are my orders. Understood?"

"But vhat—"

"Good, you do understand," Ramsey snapped, shutting o' Vessig's complaints. "You give Joshua any shit and I will hol you while Josh beats the livin' hell out of you. Then I'll lock yo up in the town jail and let you sit there until you're' dead."

Without waiting for further argument, Ramsey jumped ont Sunshine's bare back and galloped toward Bock's seed, grain, an hay warehouse, on the northwest corner of Center and Cou streets. He went through the same basic speech with Adolph Bock not letting the heavyset German get a word in.

When the hay had been loaded onto several wagons, he wei down Court Street to Sagauche Street, north to Butler, and the back around to the northernmost barricade on Center. He ha Bock's men stack the bales on the sidewalk and then under th wagons. As they finished, Cord, Vessig, and several sawmi workers arrived from the north side with a wagonload of log: which they stacked in front of the wagons as well as on top c them.

"Purty damn good, eh?" Cord said with a grin.

"Not bad. Come on, Adolph, let's get the other end." The went back the way they had come, followed by Cord and Vessig' men.

Since the south was the direction from which Ramsey expecte Roberts's men to arrive, he took more care with stacking the hay When it was done, there was a solid barrier that would provid ample cover. It also would stop the outlaws, since they could nc go around it or jump over it.

"Thanks, Josh," Ramsey said, wiping sweat from his brov with the sleeve pinned up over his stump. "Just one more thing I'd be obliged if you was to take Sunshine and the other animal back to George's."

Cord nodded. He took the animals and walked away. Ramse turned to head for his office, just as Mayor Aldridge, Antoin Devreaux, and Willy Kreuger arrived.

"What in hell is the meaning of all this?" Aldridge demanded waving his arms at the barricades.

"Roberts is on his way, Mayor," Ramsey said curtly.

"How do you know that?" Aldridge was clearly agitated.

Ramsey stared at Aldridge but watched Kreuger out of the corne of his eye. "I got sources that tell me so." He noted with som satisfaction that Kreuger looked a bit startled, though he covere it quickly and well.

"I should have been told about this. I—"

"I ain't got time for chattin', Mayor," Ramsey snapped, out
patience. "Unless you want to pick up a rifle and help me face
se boys, get the hell out of my way and let me tend to my
siness. I'll argue proprieties with you later. If I'm still alive."

Aldridge choked back his retort. He was a smart man, and he
ew Ramsey was right. "Very well," he sniffed, turning to
ve, his two minions in his wake.

Word was spreading through town and people scurried about
eir business, afraid to be on the streets. Several were angered
en they rode into town and found the barricades. Of course
ey quickly calmed their anger and rode off again when they
ard why the barricades were there.

Ramsey marched to his office and loaded a shotgun. He stuck
veral extra shells in his shirt pocket. As he was setting the gun
wn, Ada Belle burst into the office. She tried several times to
y something, but no words came out, only foolish sounds. She
t down in his chair. Her unpainted face was attractive despite
e worried lines creasing it.

"Go home, Ada Belle," Ramsey said softly.

"I want to stay with you," she gasped.

"It ain't gonna be pretty," he said evenly. "And I don't reckon
ll come out of it alive."

Ada Belle whimpered, but she did not move.

Ramsey shrugged and picked up a Henry rifle. From his desk
took a box of metal cartridges and started feeding them into
e tubular magazine. He set the rifle back into the rack. He felt
ore comfortable facing a crowd with the shotgun. If there was
me and opportunity, he would try to get back here and grab the
fle.

He picked up the scattergun. With a glance at Ada Belle's
orried face, he stepped outside and rested the shotgun against
e wall. Then he leaned against the same plank wall, waiting.

A few minutes later, Sally Tucker walked up. She was flushed
om her speedy walk, but she seemed hesitant to speak.

"Mornin', Miss Sally," Ramsey said evenly. But his heart
rched at the sight of her.

"Hello, Kyle." She seemed unusually reserved. She touched
s arm. It sent a shock through her, and she jerked her hand back.
"I heard Roberts is coming," she muttered.

"Yep."

"Are you planning to face the gang all alone?"

He waved his arm in the air, as if to say it was nothing.

"Run, Kyle!" she said urgently. Her eyes pleaded with him. "Run! Now! Just take off. No one will blame you."

"It's too late for that now, Sally."

She was weeping. But he said harshly, "You don't need carry on so. You'll not miss me long." He paused, then added bitterly, "I reckon I'm halfway out of your mind—and your heart—already."

"But why?" she panted, sobbing.

"It's gone too far to back out now, Sally." He looked up the street. "I didn't want this damn badge to begin with. But I got stuck with it, and I took an oath to do my best to protect Plentiful. All I'm doin' is my job."

"But . . . I . . . you . . ."

"Sally," Ramsey said sadly, "this ain't the time or the place. If I live through this, which don't seem likely, we'll get together somewhere if you want and we can talk this out."

He could hear a rumbling noise in the distance, coming from the south. It was a familiar sound by now. Urgently, he said, "Go home, Sally. Now!"

She looked up, frightened. Her eyes widened, and her mouth formed an almost perfect oval. She hesitated, touching his cheek a moment. Then she spun and ran.

Ramsey took one deep breath. Then he took the shotgun and walked slowly toward the southern barricade. People had stopped and were listening. Most realized what it was and began to scatter. By the time the dust could be seen half a mile or so off, Ramsey was the only one on the street.

But not for long. A moment later Sheriff John Starkey strolled out from the alley next to the marshal's office, the mangy, flea-bitten hound plodding alongside the shuffling lawman. Starkey was winded when he caught up to Kyle, but he caught his breath quickly. "Mornin', Kyle," he said cheerfully.

"What in hell are you doin' here, John?" Ramsey asked, surprised to see the lawman.

"Come to help."

"I don't need no help."

"Like hell."

"You should be back in your shack, mendin'."

"I been layin' on my ass for a month. That's plenty of time to mend."

Ramsey looked at the sheriff. The man's back was still straight, though his flesh sagged where he had lost much of his weight. Still, the eyes sparkled, and there was plenty of color in his face. He also looked mighty determined.

"This ain't necessary, you know, John," Ramsey said softly.

"Yeah, it is." Starkey spit tobacco juice into the dust. "You was the only one offered to help me and Royal take out after these bastards. We should've finished the job then, but we had the woman to worry after. But I owe this here to you, for your help. And I owe it to Royal, and by Christ, I owe it to myself. A man's got to stand up for what's right sometimes, even if it does mean gettin' his ass shot off in the doin'." He grinned, casting aside the gloom.

Ramsey nodded once curtly. "Here." He handed Starkey the shotgun. "Might be some more effective than your Colt for what we'll be commencin' to do here soon," Ramsey said.

Starkey nodded.

The cloud of dust was getting nearer as Ramsey and Starkey stopped at the barricade. Suddenly Joshua Cord's large frame loomed over the mountain of wagon, hay, and wood. He jumped down next to the two lawmen.

Ramsey looked at him in surprise. The broad shoulders rose and fell in a shrug, and a grin split the dusky face. "You ain't got to live with Charlotte when she's got her mind fixed on somethin' I ain't doin'," he said.

"Don't stay here just 'cause your woman made you come out here, Joshua," Ramsey said without humor.

The black eyes flashed threateningly. "I ain't here 'cause of Charlotte," he growled. "I's here 'cause you risked yo' ass fo' my daughter. Haulin' some logs and hay ain't much of a payback fo' such a thing."

Ramsey knew he would not be able to change Cord's mind. Besides, he was glad for the help. "There's a couple Henry repeaters in the office. The one on the left is loaded and ready to go. Box of shells is on the desk. Fetch it and then climb up on— or inside, if you'd rather—a building somewhere so's you can shoot down on those bastards when the time comes."

"I'd ruther stay here and face 'em down with you and Sheriff Starkey." Cord felt his manhood had been impugned.

"You ain't no good with that old pistol of yours, Josh," Ramsey said reasonably. "Which means you ain't gonna do no good here. I know damn well you can use that Henry. And you'll be a help of a lot more help up high with a good line of sight."

Cord growled an oath.

"Just one thing! Ain't nobody here knows this but me—and now you two. I got two brothers who'll be ridin' in with Roberts. They're on our side, and I don't want neither of you shootin' them." He explained in a few words about their plan and then described Matt and Bucky.

"Oh," he added, almost as an afterthought, "if either of you see Willy Kreuger poke his head out somewhere and he's got a gun in hand, drop him."

The others were puzzled, but there was no time for questions.

"Now go," Ramsey said urgently to Cord, who raced up the street toward Ramsey's office.

The dust cloud was thick now and the rumble of hooves was loud. Ramsey loosened the LeMat in its holster. Seconds later the horde pounded into town.

CHAPTER

★ 25 ★

The pack of mounted gunmen thundered up Center Street, screeching out fearsome cries. This was all rote to them now—rush into town with a screaming roar, once there fire off their guns to scare hell out of the citizens, rob the bank, kill a few people to discourage pursuit, and ride out again.

They never expected a solid barricade across the middle of the main street, and a few of them had trouble reining in their horses before the animals slammed into the barrier. They all made it, but it took some moments before they could calm their dancing horses.

In that short span, Kyle Ramsey had climbed up onto one of the wagons and balanced himself on the teetering pile of lumber and straw. "Y'all've come plenty far enough," Ramsey roared. "Drop your pieces and surrender peaceable."

Cotton Roberts led the laughter. "You must be the new marshal," he said after the laughter had subsided. "The one," he chuckled, "that took over after we did in that old fart Royal Burch." There was a hard gleam in his eyes. "You've caused me no end of trouble of late, Reb. What's your name, boy?"

"Kyle Ramsey."

"Well, *Marshal* Ramsey," Roberts sneered, "I'd suggest you

get your ass down from that wagon and take a hike somewhere if you know what's good for you.''

Ramsey watched with his peripheral vision as Starkey made his way down the barricade to his right. "The good citizens of Plentiful," Ramsey started, hoping he did not choke on the words. "have had their fill with your rampagin', Roberts. And I'm here to make sure it's put to a stop.''

"Hell," Roberts laughed, and most of the other men joined in, "what're you gonna do to stop me—us?'' He shook his head in amazement. "God damn, you got sand in you though, boy. I'll say that for you. Standin' here all by yourself. And with only one arm, too.'' Again his head shook in amazement. He was glad, though, that Ramsey was standing his ground. This new marshal had been nothing but trouble, and Roberts would be happy to put a few slugs into him right off.

"Don't be so certain I'm alone," Ramsey said, praying that Starkey was set and that Cord had made his way to where he could be of use.

Roberts laughed some more. "Where's your help then?'' he asked with a chuckle. He made an exaggerated sweep of the area with his eyes.

But a few of the outlaws nervously cast looks up at windows and rooftops, suddenly becoming aware that this might be an ambush.

"It's here," Ramsey said levelly.

"You boys scared?'' Roberts called over his shoulder. "Does this one-armed marshal standin' here all by his lonesome put the fear of God into you boys?''

There was a grumbling of negatives as the outlaws, not having seen any enemies other than Ramsey, relaxed.

"Now, Marshal," Roberts said in oily tones, "why don't you just get on down from there and let us go about our business.''

"I reckon I *am* your business, Roberts.'' The sun bore down on Ramsey's back, and he could feel sweat seeping down his sides and from under his hat.

Roberts seemed more than a little irritated. "I'd not go so far as to say that, Marshal. I reckon that if you was to get down from there and leave us go about our business in peace, I'd be obliged to let you ride on out of town later in one piece.''

"Didn't your mama ever teach you that lyin' wasn't right?'' Ramsey asked with a sneer. He felt a twinge of pleasure as Roberts jerked with annoyance. "Now, I know and you know and all your men here know that I was the one came into your hideout and snatched back Miss Tucker right out from under your noses."

Ramsey smiled as an angry grumble sped through the grouped men. He was also smiling at the minute nod Matt had made in his direction. Matt and Bucky were at the back of the pack of outlaws, seemingly part of them but aware of all that was going on.

"Now," Ramsey continued, "I'm gonna give you clods just one more warnin'. Drop your weapons and surrender."

"Or what?" Roberts said disdainfully.

"Or your asses'll wind up in a pine box over to Black's Mortuary," Ramsey said simply. He was anxious to have this done with. He would prefer to end it without bloodshed, but he thought the chances of that were about nonexistent. And if there was to be gunplay, he wanted to get it finished quickly.

"Son of a bitch!" Roberts roared as he went for his pistol.

Everyone else seemed to move at the same time. Ramsey ripped out the LeMat and let fly with the barrel of buckshot. He had once heard someone describe the LeMat as a good gun for crowd control. "First you level 'em with the buckshot, then you pick off the survivors with the revolver," the man had said as they had sat around a camp during a lull after one of the battles of the Civil War. Ramsey was about to find out how true that was.

He noticed that the buckshot had sprayed both Roberts and the man next to him—Simon Waddey, Roberts's second in command. Both were still alive but staggered, and Roberts had dropped his pistol.

As Ramsey jumped down behind the protection of logs and hay, he snapped the small lever on the LeMat's hammer. He aimed and began firing the revolver. Three shots smashed into Roberts's chest, punching him back off his horse. He was dead before he hit the ground.

From his right, Ramsey heard the sputtering roar of Starkey's ten-gauge scattergun. He saw Waddey fall, his chest a morass of blood and torn flesh. Ramsey was aware that another outlaw was down on his right. He glanced over that way and saw Starkey standing on a bale of hay, resting the shotgun across other bales.

Ramsey fired again, seeing that two more outlaws were down. He nodded with satisfaction as two of his bullets plowed into Cully's chest. He grinned as the breeze pushed the fog of powder smoke away for a moment, and he saw Matt and Bucky, still on their horses, firing away.

The two Ramsey brothers had been prepared before the gunbattle began. As Matt watched Kyle trade barbs with the outlaw leader, he had turned to his younger brother. "Don't make a big show of it, Buck, but haul your piece out." Matt had eased his Colt out, and Bucky had done the same. The younger Ramsey would have wished he could use the Winchester. He was a lot more proficient with it than he was with the Colt, but it would have been nearly useless, he figured, in such close quarters.

The two had sat, Colts cocked. "You aim to backshoot somebody?" Bucky had asked, not liking the possibility at all.

"Yep." Matt had been tense, as he always was while waiting for the action to start. He was not fond of the idea of backshooting someone either, but there were—not counting him and Bucky—thirteen outlaws against just the three brothers. There was no way for him or Bucky to have known about Starkey and Cord.

"I ain't sure I like that idea, Matt."

"Times like this a man's got to do what's needed," Matt had said ruthlessly. "We don't take a couple of these boys out right off, Kyle's gonna be dead faster'n hell."

Bucky had nodded assent.

"Ready now," Matt had said urgently. "You take Owl Peters first; try for Gomez next if you can. I'll take out Pyle and Calero."

Bucky had nodded, nervous. He had done this before, several times, but it never seemed to get easy for him, like it had become with Matt and Kyle. He wished he was more like his two older brothers. But he knew that he would do what was necessary.

Bucky had been a bit slower than Matt in realizing the fight was commencing. By the time he had aimed at Peters's squat wide back and pulled the trigger—after a moment's hesitation and reluctance to do this—Matt had gunned down both Manuel Calero and Wayne Pyle.

Matt fired evenly now, noticing Bucky's hesitation. Then he noted with relief that Bucky had done what he was supposed to. As Bucky turned his pistol toward Jorge Gomez, Matt quickly reloaded. He too had been hesitant the first time he'd had to shoot someone in the back, long ago during the war. It had never gotten to be easy—knowledge that probably would have surprised

Bucky—for him, but he could do it without stalling when the situation called for it.

Bucky fired three times at Gomez before hitting him once. The Mexican was bobbing on his horse, excited and nervous at the same time. He arched his back as the slug plowed into it, and he started to turn to see who had shot him. Bucky fired again, putting the bullet through Gomez's neck, just above the adam's apple. Gomez choked and then spit some blood before slowly falling off the side of his horse.

Bucky thought he might be sick, but he forced himself not to think about it. Praying all the while that he would not be shot, he reloaded his pistol as quickly as he could. When he was finished, he could barely see. A pall of dust had been stirred up by hooves, and it mingled with the gunsmoke hung over the battle. "Matt?" he yelled, frightened but trying to hold it back.

"I'm here, Buck," Matt roared from off to the side a bit. "You all right?"

"Yep," Bucky shouted, relief flooding through him. He felt like he had to urinate. He clenched his groin muscles and fired carefully at a figure seen dimly in the swirling cloud.

Matt heard the gutteral roar of a shotgun, and he was nervous about that. He did not know where it came from, and he did not like shotgun blasts being fired indiscriminately. Then he heard the snap of a repeating rifle. "Move back, Buck!" he bellowed.

He backed his horse until he was free of the cloud. It felt good to be able to breathe air again instead of dirt. Bucky rode out of the fog, looking pasty with fright, though he had it under control.

"What's wrong, Matt?" he asked, fear prickling his innards.

"Couple of guns firin' I don't know about." He pointed one way. "Shotgun firin' over there." He pointed again. "Repeatin' rifle—probably a Henry—from up there somewhere."

"Lord! You think Kyle's all right?"

"I heard his LeMat just a bit ago."

"We gonna try'n find the feller with the rifle?"

Matt sat with his head cocked for a moment. In the midst of the cloud, he dimly saw a man cartwheel off his horse to his left. He grinned. "Nope. I don't know who the hell he is, but he's on our side." He glanced at his brother. "You all right, boy?"

The youth nodded, biting his lip.

"You ready for another run at these bastards?"

"Yes, sir," Bucky said, firming up.

Matt let go a ripping Rebel yell and kicked his horse.

Just after he had seen his two brothers, Kyle fired four mor
times. He wasn't sure, but he thought he hit two men at least onc
each. It was hard to tell anything now with the thick haze.

Ramsey scrunched up under the cover of the logs and worke
as quickly as he could to reload the LeMat. It was tough goin;
in the heat, the tenseness of battle, and the cloying clouds of dus
and smoke that dried his throat. He worked steadily, used to th
routine by now, even if he was slowed by his disability.

As he worked, he could hear the regular snap of the Henr
repeater fired by Joshua Cord from somewhere above. Ramse
was not sure whether Cord was on a roof or just firing from
someone's second-floor window. It didn't much matter now.

Up on the roof of Town Hall, Cord had delayed firing at first
He was confused. How odd, he had thought, that he was her
backing up a Confederate officer, defending a town full of whit
people who would barely talk to him. He wrestled with it becaus
he felt heavily the debt he owed Kyle Ramsey for having save
his daughter from Whiskey Bill Thorne.

Then he decided. Kyle might have fought for the South in th
war, but the war was long over, and Kyle Ramsey had show
time and again through his words and actions that Cord was jus
another man—not a *black* man, just a man—to Ramsey.

He grinned. Besides, this would help even the score some fo
a heap of past injustices Cord had suffered. He snapped the leve
down and then back up. He aimed and fired, feeling a jolt o
satisfaction when he knocked an outlaw off his horse with his firs
shot.

Within seconds his vision was blurred by the rising column o
dust and smoke, and it was hard for him to find anything to aim
at. He fired almost indiscriminately, making sure he kept his line
of fire away from where he knew Kyle, Starkey, and Ramsey's
two brothers were.

The amount of lead slamming into the timber protecting Kyle
had diminished to almost nothing. Horses still whinnied or snorted,
and an occasional shot was heard. Then the gunfire stopped.

"Matt! Buck! You boys out there?"

"Yep!" the two brothers chorused.

"You all right?"

"Fine," Matt answered for them both.

"John?"

"Here and fine, Kyle," the sheriff shouted.

"Josh?"

"All's well, Marshal."

With a deep breath, Kyle peeked up over the logs. The veil of dust and smoke was beginning to drift away. The ground in front of the barricade was littered with figures, most not moving. Ramsey took a close look and made sure that all the outlaws were accounted for.

He stood up carefully, his LeMat ready. Easing his way over the timber, he jumped down off the wagon onto the ground. He walked cautiously toward the first prone figure.

"I got you covered," Cord called down.

Ramsey waved his thanks and slipped the LeMat away. He looked to his right, and Starkey nodded. The sheriff was on the same side of the barricade now, leaning back against the wall of hay, cradling the shotgun at the ready.

Matt and Bucky rode up and dismounted near Kyle. They tied their horses to the wagon. The three men wound their way through the battlefield. This was nothing new to Kyle and Matt, but Bucky was having something of a hard time with it.

"You'll be fine, little brother," Kyle said softly.

Bucky only nodded.

Ten of the thirteen were dead. The other three—including Honus—were wounded, though not severely. As the three Ramseys marched the three outlaws toward the barricade, people began to filter out of their homes or businesses to stare in awed silence.

"Some of you people best get over here and start haulin' these bodies down to Black's Mortuary. You tell old man Black that he's to give 'em the cheapest coffins he's got—if he's of a mind to. If he ain't, he can wrap each body in a blanket and roll it in a hole up in boot hill. Tell him to send the bill to Mayor Aldridge."

The mayor, standing nearby, flinched, but he said nothing.

"Some of you others start cleaning up these barricades. Whoever lent us materials to use can have 'em back."

Doc Bedloe hurried up. "Can I help?" he asked, looking over the gory scene with a practiced eye.

"Just with these three," Kyle said, waving his LeMat at the prisoners. "It weren't for some poor shootin' on somebody's part,'' he added with a grin, ''we wouldn't have need of your services at all.''

''You want me to fix 'em here?''

''Nope. We're takin' 'em down to the jail. You can have at 'em there.''

CHAPTER
⋆ 26 ⋆

After the battle, Kyle, Matt, Bucky, Sheriff Starkey, and Josh Cord marched the three surviving members of the gang down to the marshal's office. Ada Belle was still there, sitting in Kyle's chair. Her face was blotchy, and anyone who saw her knew she had been crying uncontrollably.

Ada Belle gasped and her eyes got as big as platters when Kyle walked into the room unscathed. She jumped up, ready to rush into his embrace—until she saw Matt and Buck. She froze, her face an odd mask of relief, love, and despair. "You're alive," she finally managed to stutter.

"Yep." Kyle nodded. He and the others crowded the outlaws into the room. "Look, Ada Belle," Kyle said, a bit frustrated and still tense after all the fighting, "I got business to tend to for a while."

"But I . . ."

"Not now," Kyle insisted, his face and neck burning. He knew damn well his brothers and the two other men were hiding sniggers. "I'll come by and see you later. But right now I got things to see to. Doc Bedloe's on his way over for these three fools, and there's yet some unfinished business."

Ada Belle stood there a moment, not sure whether to be shocked, disappointed, angry, or all three. Tears welled up in her large, stunned eyes, and her lower lip quivered. Suddenly she bolted for the door.

"Shit," Kyle muttered, shoving one of the prisoners through the doorway into one of the cells in back. "Get your ass in there," he growled.

When the three were safely locked up, the lawmen went back into the office area.

"Well," Cord said with an exaggerated yawn, knowing Matt and Bucky wanted to question Kyle about Ada Belle, "reckon I'd best be gettin' back home to my family." He set the Henry rifle back into the wall rack.

"Guess I'll be movin' on too," Starkey said. He grimaced. "This old boy ain't as spry as he used to be. This mornin's little set-to seems to have set me to achin' again," he admitted. He laid the shotgun on the desk.

He and Cord headed for the door together. "I'm obliged to you both," Kyle said, meaning it. "I'd of been pushin' up flowers now if it wasn't for you two."

The two smiled at him. "Just payin' back dues long owed," Starkey said. He and Cord walked out. Through the window, Kyle could see them stop right outside the door. Cord bent a bit and whispered something to Starkey. The sheriff nodded. A moment later, the muscular Cord had an arm under Starkey's armpits and was helping the sheriff walk away.

"Was she the filly?" Matt asked blandly.

"Who? Ada Belle?" Kyle said, not amused. He shook his head. "Naw. She's just a gal who works the cribs back of the Lone Star."

Bucky's eyes widened. "You mean she's a . . ."

"Yep," Kyle growled. "And she's a nice person besides."

"You courtin' her?" Matt asked, unconcerned.

"Nope."

"Maybe you ought to. Women that good lookin' are mighty hard to come by in these parts."

"Bah," Kyle growled.

Doc Bedloe entered, followed by his assistant, Harry Laird. "Well," Bedloe bellowed cheerfully, "where's my patients?"

"In back. Where the hell do you think?" Kyle snarled.

"My, my, we're touchy, ain't we?" He winked at Matt and

Bucky, both of whom grinned at him. "Well, come on, Harry," he said, "let's go see what the damage is."

"Want someone to cover you, Doc?" Matt asked.

"Those three likely to cause trouble?"

"Expect not," Matt said, rubbing his right palm across his chin. "They don't look to be too bad wounded, but I think the fight's gone out of 'em."

"We'll be all right then," Bedloe said. It wasn't the first time he had worked on hard or dangerous men.

Just after the two medical men had gone toward the cells, the front door of the office opened. Sally Tucker stepped in hesitatingly. "Kyle?" she asked quietly.

"Sally," Kyle said, his voice catching.

She looked at Matt and Buck. "I see you're busy, Kyle," she said softly. "I'll come back later."

"It's all right, Sally." He pointed. "These are my brothers, Matt and Buck."

Each doffed his hat when his name was mentioned.

"Hello," Tucker mumbled. "Well, I just wanted to make sure you were all right, Kyle," she said after a moment's hesitation. "Stop by later. There's some things I want to talk over."

Kyle nodded, feeling an ache in his gut.

When Tucker was gone, Matt stepped up and put a big hand on one of Kyle's shoulders. "But that's the one, eh, brother?"

Kyle nodded, not sure how his voice would sound if he tried to speak.

"She's a pretty one, all right," Matt said.

"I'll say!" Bucky added fervently.

"But I do believe you got yourself a problem here, Kyle," Matt said. He smiled to ease the pain he knew his brother must be feeling inside.

Kyle shrugged.

"What problem?" Buck asked.

Matt hesitated, then Kyle said softly, "Might's well tell him, Matt. He deserves to know."

"Know what?" Buck was interested, and he felt ashamed that he could not see what was going on right in front of him.

"Kyle here's got himself a hankerin' somethin' bad for yon Miss Sally."

"That's understandable." He grinned. "I would too, had I seen her first."

"Trouble is," Matt said sadly, "Miss Sally don't feel near the same for Kyle."

"Why?" Buck burst out.

"Who in hell knows, Buck? It's that way with men and women sometimes."

"Well, he can win her over," Buck said stubbornly. He usually believed his brothers could do anything they set their minds to.

"Maybe." Matt strolled over to look out the window. Already the town was calming down, though the people still celebrated the end of the Roberts gang. He turned back to face his younger brother. "But," he added with an impish grin, "old Kyle didn't stop there. No, sir."

"Huh?"

"Miss Ada Belle feels about Kyle the way he feels about Miss Sally. Trouble is, he feels about Ada Belle that way Miss Sally feels about him."

"Life sure ain't easy sometimes, is it?" Buck said, shaking his head slowly.

"Bah," Kyle growled.

"No, it ain't, Buck," Matt said, no longer grinning. "And since he's a Ramsey, he'll have to be settin' things to right." It was not a threat—just an acknowledgment of the way Ramsey men did things.

Kyle did not answer him. He was saved from answering when Bedloe and Laird returned. Laird dropped the keys to the cells on Kyle's desk. "They'll be fine and fit for the hangin'," Bedloe said almost gleefully.

"Thanks, Doc," Kyle said. "Send your bill to Mayor Aldridge."

"Hell, this one's on me." Bedloe chuckled. He asked, more seriously, "You boys all right? Nobody hurt?"

"We're fine." Kyle sighed. Fatigue sat on his shoulders like a second skin. "But you might want to go on over to Sheriff Starkey's place and see to him. He might've set himself to painin' again with all his adventuresomeness this mornin'."

"I'll do so." Bedloe stared at Kyle a few moments before asking, "You sure there ain't somethin' painin' *you*?"

"Nothin' you can fix, Doc," Kyle said, trying to smile but failing.

Bedloe shrugged. "Then I'll take my leave." He started for the door. With his hand on the latch, he faced into the room and

d, "I thank you boys for what you did. Everybody else in
vn's mighty grateful, too."

"Just doin' my job, Doc," Kyle said, wanting the old man out
his office.

Bedloe nodded and left.

"Before you open up and start on me again about this other
siness, Matt," Kyle said, "I'm tellin' you I don't want to hear
So let it rest." He paused, feeling a bit better that he had gotten
t off his chest. "You boys hungry?" he asked.

"Hell, yes!" Bucky said, brightening.

"Then I reckon we ought to go get somethin' to eat."

Matt grabbed his arm. "What about Kreuger, Kyle?" he de-
nded.

"Kreuger ain't goin' nowhere. Even if he did, it'd be easy
ough to track him down. But I want that bastard to sweat some.
: knows God damn well I know about him now, and he'll be
se to pissin' his trousers by the time we pay him a visit."

"Serves him right," Buck grumbled. Then he grinned. "Now
's go fill up on some grub."

They ate well—and free, so happy were the citizens of Plentiful
the work done that morning by the three Ramseys.

"Folks here seem nice," Buck said when they were walking
ck to the marshal's office after their meal.

"Shit!" Kyle snorted. "If I could've found two people in this
vn besides Josh and John that had any gumption at all, none of
s would have happened. And you boys'd still be down there in
xas relaxin'."

"Relaxin'!" Buck said sharply, insulted. "Why I'll have you
ow that me and Matt and the others all work our tail feathers
f regular down there. You think such work's easy? Ranchin'
d farmin'? They ain't easy at all. Not when we're tryin' to catch
d break horses still and . . . What the hell's the matter with you
o?" he demanded indignantly.

Matt and Kyle were laughing in great gusting waves.

"Well, what's so funny?" Buck was enraged at being laughed

"You should've heard yourself, Buck," Matt finally managed
say around guffaws.

"Well, God damn it, we do work hard."

"Christ, Buck, think!" Matt chortled. "Me'n Kyle were doin'
that and more before you were born."

Buck clapped his mouth shut, chopping off his retort. *How could you have been so stupid?* he thought. *Standin' there jab-berin' like an idiot!* His neck and ears burned with embarrassment.

"We all act the fool at times, Buck," Matt said consoling, throwing an arm around the youth's shoulders.

Buck shoved Matt's arm off, but he felt much better. And he knew Matt knew it.

Back in the office, Kyle said, "You boys want to join me in arrestin' Mr. Willy Kreuger?"

Matt looked at him as if to say "Wild horses couldn't keep me away."

Kyle nodded. "Raise your right arms," he ordered. Reluctantly the brothers did so. Kyle swore them in as deputy marshals for the town of Plentiful. He tossed each a badge.

Buck's eyes were huge with wonder. "Lookit this, Matt!" he said excitedly, holding out the badge.

"I see it," Matt growled, though he was pleased too. "Just put the damn thing on."

The three left and walked the few doors to Town Hall, where they entered Aldridge's office.

"Welcome, boys," Aldridge said, rising and hurrying over to shake each man's hand. "Glad you came by. We"—he waved his hand at Judge Blackthorn, Kreuger, and Devreaux—"have wanted to thank you on behalf of the town for your efforts this morning." He fairly beamed.

"You're welcome," Kyle said, his face stony.

"Something wrong?" Aldridge asked, alarmed.

"Unfinished business from this mornin'," Kyle snarled.

"What?" Aldridge asked, looking truly surprised. "The gang is done for. You three and—"

"It ain't done yet," Kyle snapped, cutting the mayor off. "Ain't it, Kreuger?"

Kreuger looked defiant, his eyes radiating heat.

"What the hell are you talking about, Marshal?" Aldridge asked, puzzled. "You're not making sense."

"You might want to ask Councilman Kreuger here if I'm making sense," Kyle snapped.

"Willy?" Aldridge questioned, turning to face Kreuger. "Do you have any idea of what they're talking about?"

"None," Kreuger said curtly. He was sweating, not entirely because of the oppressive, muggy heat.

Aldridge looked at Kyle, questions still abounding in his eyes.

"Perhaps," Kyle said angrily, "Mr. Kreuger would like to explain just what he got out of recruitin' men for the Roberts gang?"

"What!" Aldridge asked, startled. He turned again. "Willy?"

"They're lying," Kreuger snarled. He had dropped the stupid look and retiring demeanor.

"The game's up," Kyle said. "You can explain yourself at your trial. Now, you got two choices. One, you can come along peaceable. Or two, you can resist and cheat the hangman."

The judge and Devreaux looked from one man to the other but stayed silent. Kreuger stared with hate-frosted eyes at the three lawmen. Then he seemed to sag back in the plush chair. He almost groaned, and his right hand went to his heart. His left came up with a bandanna and mopped the sweat from his brow. "My heart," he whispered. "I'm not a well man."

"Bullshit," Kyle snarled. "Now get your fat ass up out of that chair."

Kreuger moved—and very quickly. He pulled his hand away from his heart, and in it was a pistol he had always worn in a shoulder holster under his coat. But before he could get the hammer pulled back, he found himself staring down the muzzles of a LeMat and two Colts. "Make your choice," Matt said menacingly.

Kreuger choked back a sob. Moving very slowly, he carefully reached his right arm out and set the pistol on the edge of Aldridge's desk. His face was white as new snow.

Five days later, Matt and Buck were on their horses, ready to leave Plentiful.

Two days before that, Judge Blackthorn had convened a court in the Lone Star Saloon. A jury of twelve was duly sworn in and settled in chairs to one side. The rest of the town either crowded into the saloon or stood just outside, relying on others to relay information to them. All the bodies inside made the saloon uncomfortably hot.

The trial for the three men wounded in the fight did not take long. Their lawyer did what little he could, but the townsfolk were in no mood for mercy. In less than an hour, all three were found guilty and sentenced to hang.

Then it was Kreuger's turn. His lawyer made impassioned pleas and called character witnesses. Then Matt took the stand and related how Kreuger had hired him and Buck to join the Roberts gang. He also testified that two other newcomers to the gang—Honus and Cully—had told him that they also were recruited by Kreuger.

The lawyer could poke no holes in Matt's story.

Minutes later, James Buchanan Ramsey told the same story.

Then it was Kyle's turn. He told of—and displayed—the loot and incriminating notes and such he had found in Kreuger's house after he had arrested the councilman.

With that, the jury found Kreuger guilty, and Blackthorn sentenced him to hang along with the three others.

"Why don't you come on back to Texas with us?" Buck asked. "It's where you belong."

"I got unfinished business here, Buck," Kyle said with a smile.

"What business?" Bucky asked. "The gang's done away with, unless you're fixin' to wait around for the hangin'."

"I am. But there's other things."

"Like what?" Buck demanded.

Kyle tapped the star on his chest.

"That's easy enough fixed," Matt said softly.

Kyle grinned ruefully, sadly. "Well, there's still that matter of Sally and Ada Belle. I got to set things straight, Buck," he said quietly. "I don't know exactly yet how I'm gonna do that. But I care for Miss Sally too much not to try; and I owe it to Ada Belle to try, too."

"Might be some hard livin' here, you know," Matt said matter-of-factly.

"Hell, when did a Ramsey ever give a damn about hard livin'?" Kyle said with a grin.

Matt's face split in a wide handsome smile. He whooped, then shouted, "Come on, Buck."

And then the two were gone, racing their ponies and kicking up the dust.

A special offer for people who enjoy reading the best Westerns published today. If you enjoyed this book, subscribe now and get ...

TWO FREE WESTERNS!
A $5.90 VALUE—NO OBLIGATION

If you enjoyed this book and would like to read more of the very best Westerns being published today, you'll want to subscribe to True Value's Western Home Subscription Service. If you enjoyed the book you just read and want more of the most exciting, adventurous, action packed Westerns, subscribe now.

TWO FREE BOOKS

When you subscribe, we'll send you your first month's shipment of the newest and best 6 Westerns for you to preview. With your first shipment, two of these books will be yours as our introductory gift to you absolutely FREE, regardless of what you decide to do.

Special Subscriber Savings

As a True Value subscriber all regular monthly selections will be billed at the low subscriber price of just $2.45 each. That's at least a savings of $3.00 each month below the publishers price. There is never any shipping, handling or other hidden charges. What's more there is no minimum number of books you must buy, you may return any selection for full credit and you can cancel your subscription at any time. A TRUE VALUE!

∼ Mail the coupon below ∼

To start your subscription and receive 2 FREE WESTERNS, fill out the coupon below and mail it today. We'll send you your first shipment which includes 2 FREE BOOKS as soon as we receive it.

Mail To: True Value Home Subscription Services, Inc.
P.O. Box 5235
120 Brighton Road
Clifton, New Jersey 07015-5235

10350

YES! I want to start receiving the very best Westerns being published today. Send me my first shipment of 6 Westerns for me to preview FREE for 10 days. If I decide to keep them, I'll pay for just 4 of the books at the low subscriber price of $2.45 each; a total of $9.80 (a $17.70 value). Then each month I'll receive the 6 newest and best Westerns to preview Free for 10 days. If I'm not satisfied I may return them within 10 days and owe nothing. Otherwise I'll be billed at the special low subscriber rate of $2.45 each; a total of $14.70 (at least a $17.70 value) and save $3.00 off the publishers price. There are never any shipping, handling or other hidden charges. I understand I am under no obligation to purchase any number of books and I can cancel my subscription at any time, no questions asked. In any case the 2 FREE books are mine to keep.

Name _____

Address _____ Apt. # _____

City _____ State _____ Zip _____

Telephone # _____

Signature _____
                    (if under 18 parent or guardian must sign)

Terms and prices subject to change. Orders subject to acceptance by True Value Home Subscription Services, Inc.